GOTHIC
HIGH-TECH

GOTHIC HIGH-TECH

Stories by
Bruce
Sterling

Subterranean Press 2011

First Edition

ISBN
978-1-59606-404-1

Subterranean Press
PO Box 190106
Burton, MI 48519

www.subterraneanpress.com

TABLE OF CONTENTS

PART I:

Favela
Chic

I SAW THE BEST MINDS OF MY GENERATION DESTROYED BY GOOGLE

———————— ||•

Los Angeles, 2026

Ted got busted because we do graffiti. Losing Ted was a big setback, as Ted was the only guy in our gang who knew how to steal aerosol spraycans. As potent instruments of teenage social networking, aerosol spraycans have "high abuse potential." So spraycans are among the many things us teenagers can't buy, like, for instance, handguns, birth control, alcohol, cigarettes, and music with curse words.

I tried hard to buy us another spraycan. I'm a street poet, so really, I tried. I walked up to the mall-store register, disguised in my dad's business jacket, with cash in hand. They're really CHEAP, aerosol spray cans. Beautiful colors of paint, just screaming to get sprayed someplace public where everybody has to see what's on our minds. The store wouldn't sell me the can. The e-commerce system simply would not allow that transaction. The screen just went gray and stayed gray.

That creepy "differential permissioning" sure saves a lot of trouble for grownups. Increasing chunks of the world are just…magically off limits. It's a weird new regime where every mall and every school and every bus and train and jet is tagged and tracked and ambient and pervasive and ubiquitous and geolocative…. Jesus, I love those words…where was I?

Right. We teenagers have to live in "controlled spaces." Radio-frequency ID tags, real-time locative systems, global positioning systems, smart doorways, security videocams.... They "protect" us kids, from imaginary Satanic drug dealer terrorist mafia predators. We're "secured". We're juvenile delinquents with machine nannies on our backs, on our pockets, in our purses, on our shoes. There's no way to turn them off. The Internet was designed without an off-switch.

So my pal Ted, who stupidly loved to tag his own name on the walls, got sent to reform school, where the security is insanely great. Me, I had a much higher grade-point average than Ted, but with no handy Ted to steal spraycans, the words of the prophet have vanished from the subway walls.

So much for my campaign to cover the town with graffiti street-stencils of my favorite teen pop-stars: George Orwell and Aldous Huxley.

And Shakespeare. I used to hate Shakespeare, because the teachers would park us in front of the webcam terminals, turn on the Shakespeare lessons, and leave the building. But then, somehow, they showed us "Macbeth," a play which actually MEANS something to us. Grownups don't understand that (or they wouldn't be teaching it) but "Macbeth" is the *true, authentic story of my generation.* This is Macbeth's world, and us teenagers just live in it.

Dig this: those "Weird Sisters," who mysteriously know everything? They can foretell anything, instantly, like Google? Plus, the witches make it all sound really great—only, in real life, it totally sucks? Well, those "Three Weird Sisters" are the "Internet of Things," they're "Ubiquitous Computation," they're "Ambient Findability." The truth is written all over the page (or the screen—my school can't afford to give us any "pages"). Just read that awesome part where they're boiling pseudocode in their witch-cauldron! They talk exactly like web designers!

Macbeth stumbles around seeing ghosts and virtual-reality daggers. That sure makes sense. Every day of my life, I see people with cellphones yelling eerie gibberish in public. The world of Macbeth is totally haunted and paranoid! You can't get one minute's privacy, even inside your own bed!

So, I did my class report about Macbeth, and every kid in my English class instantly agreed with me. I'm not the most popular guy in school, but they started CHEERING me. And Debbie, this wacky Goth chick in my class who identifies with Lady Macbeth.... After my class report, Debbie sleep-walked out of the classroom and pretended to hang herself! Of course the teen-suicide subroutines in the school jumped onto Debbie immediately. Debbie broke the software rules, so Debbie is toast, just like Ted.

•‖————————‖•

My Dad—he's still alive, apparently—he sent me email from China and said that I ought to "recruit" Debbie into my "social group dynamics of online identity production." My Dad always talks like that. I haven't seen Dad face to face in six years. Look: I am a 17 year old male, okay? I don't want to send Debbie any hotlinks and video! I want to take Debbie out! Maybe we could take our clothes off! But there isn't any "out" for me and Debbie. There isn't any "off," either.

Okay, I admit it: Debbie is insane. The fact that Debbie really likes me, that just proves it. Debbie ACCEPTS this sick state of reality. She EMBRACES it. We are doomed.

Imagine that Debbie and me somehow go out together. We want to network with our peer-group, teenager-wise. I need to figure out what's hip and with-it and rebellious, and Debbie needs to know what the other cyber-Goth chicks are wearing. Is that okay? No!

It's not that we can't do it: it's that all our social relations have been reified with a clunky intensity. They're digitized! And the networking hardware and software that pervasively surrounds us is built and owned by evil, old, rich, corporate people! Social-networking systems aren't teenagers! These machines are METHODICALLY KILLING OUR SOULS! If you don't count wall-graffiti (good old spray paint), we have no means to spontaneously express ourselves. We can't "find ourselves"—the market's already found us and filled us with map-pins.

At our local mall, events-management sub-engines emit floods of locative data. So if Debbie and me sneak in there, looking for some private place to get horizontal, all the vidcams swivel our way. Then a rent-a-cop shows up. What next? Should we go to Lovers' Lane? There aren't any! They eliminated all those! They were tracked down with satellites and abolished with GoogleMaps.

Okay, sure: I know I sound pretty depressed. Us teenage poets depress easily. You know what they tell me whenever I rant like this? "Get a hobby." Play imaginary fantasy computer games! That is allowed

11

me! Wow, thanks! When she nursed me as a baby, my Mom dropped me right on my head to play Wonder-World of Witchcraft. I sure know where *that* story goes. If "religion is the opiate of the people," then immersive multiplayer 3D virtual worlds are hardcore Afghani heroin. My Mom will never make it back into the labor force: because Mom's way too busy building herself up to 146th-level SuperMasonic Tolkien-Fantasy Ultra-Elf Queen! Like that helps! Look, I can show you Mom's gaming environment, right on the screen here. My Mom's a Welfare Elf Queen <CR> <system crash> <hard reboot>

Debbie: why do you access me, when you know that makes things hard for me? Why do you IM, and tag, and link to me? Why do you telephone? And why, why, why do you write me silly notes on paper? I am so sick of you, Debbie.... Why, why do you hack me? It is just to see the things that you know I am writing about you...

Debbie, you believe in us. You think we are the future.

I am so miserably happy, just now.

KIOSK

I.

The fabrikator was ugly, noisy, a fire hazard, and it smelled. Borislav got it for the kids in the neighborhood.

One snowy morning, in his work gloves, long coat, and fur hat, he loudly power-sawed through the wall of his kiosk. He duct-taped and stapled the fabrikator into place.

The neighborhood kids caught on instantly. His new venture was a big hit.

The fabrikator made little plastic toys from 3-D computer models. After a week, the fab's dirt-cheap toys literally turned into dirt. The fabbed toys just crumbled away, into a waxy, non-toxic substance that the smaller kids tended to chew.

Borislav had naturally figured that the brief lifetime of these toys might discourage the kids from buying them. This just wasn't so. This wasn't a bug: this was a feature. Every day after school, an eager gang of kids clustered around Borislav's green kiosk. They slapped down their tinny pocket change with mittened hands. Then they exulted, quarreled and sometimes even punched each other over the shining fab-cards.

The happy kid would stick the fab-card (adorned with some glossily fraudulent pic of the toy) into the fabrikator's slot. After a hot, deeply exciting moment of hissing, spraying and stinking, the fab would burp up a freshly-minted dinosaur, baby-doll or toy fireman.

Foot-traffic always brought foot-traffic. The grownups slowed as they crunched the snowy street. They cast an eye at the many temptations ranked behind Borislav's windows. Then they would impulse-buy. A football scarf, maybe. A pack of tissues for a sneezy nose.

Once again he was ahead of the game: the only kiosk in town with a fabrikator.

The fabrikator spoke to him as a veteran street-merchant. Yes, it definitely *meant something* that those rowdy kids were so eager to buy toys that fell apart and turned to dirt. Any kiosk was all about high-volume repeat business. The stick of gum. The candy bar. The cheap, last-minute bottle-of-booze. The glittery souvenir keychain that tourists would never use for any purpose whatsoever. These objects were the very stuff of a kiosk's life.

Those colored plastic cards with the 3-D models…. The cards had potential. The older kids were already collecting the cards: not the toys that the cards made, but the cards themselves.

And now, this very day, from where he sat in his usual street-cockpit behind his walls of angled glass, Borislav had taken the next logical step. He offered the kids ultra-glossy, overpriced, collector cards that could not and would not make toys. And of course—there was definitely logic here—the kids were going nuts for that business model. He had sold a hundred of them.

Kids, by the nature of kids, weren't burdened with a lot of cash. Taking their money was not his real goal. What the kids brought to his kiosk was what kids had to give him—futurity. Their little churn of street energy—that was the symptom of something bigger, just over the horizon. He didn't have a word for that yet, but he could feel it, in the way he felt a coming thunderstorm inside his aching leg.

Futurity might bring a man money. Money never saved a man with no future.

II.

Dr. Grootjans had a jaw like a horse, a round blue pillbox of a hat, and a stiff winter coat that could likely stop gunfire. She carried a big European shopping-wand.

Ace was acting as her official street-guide, an unusual situation, since Ace was the local gangster. "Madame," Ace told her, "this is the finest kiosk in the city. Boots here is our philosopher of kiosks. Boots has a fabrikator! He even has a water fountain!"

Dr. Grootjans carefully photographed the water fountain's copper pipe, plastic splash basin, and disposable paper pop-out cups. "Did my guide just call you 'Boots?'" she said. "Boots as in footgear?"

"Everybody calls me that."

Dr. Grootjans patted her translation earpiece, looking pleased. "This water-fountain is the exhaust from your fuel cell."

Borislav rubbed his mustache. "When I first built my kiosk here, the people had no running water."

Dr. Grootjans waved her digital wand over his selections of panty-hose. She photographed the rusty bolts that fixed his kiosk to the broken pavement. She took particular interest in his kiosk's peaked roof. People often met their friends and lovers at Borislav's kiosk, because his towering satellite dish was so easy to spot. With its painted plywood base and showy fringes of snipped copper, the dish looked fit for a minaret.

"Please try on this pretty necklace, madame! Made by a fine artist, she lives right up the street. Very famous. Artistic. Valuable. Regional. Handmade!"

"Thank you, I will. Your shop is a fine example of the local small-to-micro regional enterprise. I must make extensive acquisitions for full study by the Parliamentary committee."

Borislav swiftly handed over a sheet of flimsy. Ace peeled off a gaping plastic bag and commenced to fill it with candy bars, placemats, hand-knitted socks, peasant dolls in vests and angular headdresses, and religious-war press-on tattoos. "He has such variety, madame! Such unusual goods!"

Borislav leaned forward through his cash window, so as to keep Dr. Grootjans engaged as Ace crammed her bags. "Madame, I don't care to boast about my modest local wares.... Because whatever I sell is due to the people! You see, dear doctor-madame, every object desired by these colorful local people has a folk-tale to tell us...."

Dr Grootjan's pillbox hat rose as she lifted her brows. "A folk-tale, did you say?"

"Yes, it's the people's poetry of commerce! Certain products appear... the products flow through my kiosk.... I present them pleasingly, as best I can.... Then, the people buy them, or they just don't buy!"

Dr. Grootjans expertly flapped open a third shopping-bag. "An itemized catalog of all your goods would be of great interest to my study committee."

Borislav put his hat on.

Dr. Grootjans bored in. "I need the *complete, digital* inventory of your merchandise. The working file of the full contents of your store. Your commercial records from the past five years will be useful in spotting local consumer trends."

Borislav gazed around his thickly packed shelving. "You mean you want a list of everything I sell in here? Who would ever find the time?"

"It's simple! You must have heard of the European Unified Electronic Product Coding System." Dr. Grootjans tucked the shopping-wand into her canvas purse, which bore an imperial logo of thirty-five golden stars in a widening spiral. "I have a smart-ink brochure here which displays in your local language. Yes, here it is: 'A Partial Introduction to EU-EPCS Regulatory Adoption Procedures.'"

Borislav refused her busily flashing inkware. "Oh yes, word gets around about that electric barcoding nonsense! Those fancy radio-ID stickers of yours. Yes, yes, I'm sure those things are just fine for rich foreign people with shopping-wands!"

"Sir, if you sensibly deployed this electronic tracking system, you could keep complete, real-time records of all your merchandise. Then you would know exactly what's selling, and not. You could fully optimize your product flow, reduce waste, maximize your profit, and benefit the environment through reduced consumption."

Borislav stared at her. "You've given this speech before, haven't you?"

"Of course I have! It's a critical policy issue! The modern Internet-of-Things authenticates goods, reduces spoilage, and expedites secure cross-border shipping!"

"Listen, madame doctor: your fancy bookkeeping won't help me if I don't know the soul of the people! I have a little kiosk! I never compete with those big, faceless mall stores! If you want that sort of thing, go shop in your five-star hotel!"

Dr. Grootjans lowered her sturdy purse and her sharp face softened into lines of piety. "I don't mean to violate your quaint local value system.... Of course we fully respect your cultural differences.... Although there will be many tangible benefits when your regime fully harmonizes with European procedures."

"'My regime,' is it? Ha!" Borislav thumped the hollow floor of his kiosk with his cane. "This stupid regime crashed all their government computers! Along with crashing our currency, I might add! Those crooks couldn't run that fancy system of yours in a thousand years!"

"A comprehensive debate on this issue would be fascinating!" Dr. Grootjans waited expectantly, but, to her disappointment, no such debate followed. "Time presses," she told him at last. "May I raise the subject of a complete acquisition?"

Borislav shrugged. "I never argue with a lady or a paying customer. Just tell me what you want."

Dr Grootjans sketched the air with her starry wand. "This portable shelter would fit onto an embassy truck."

"Are you telling me that you want to *buy my entire kiosk?*"

"I'm advancing that option now, yes."

"What a scandal! Sell you my kiosk? The people would never forgive me!"

"Kiosks are just temporary structures. I can see your business is improving. Why not open a permanent retail store? Start over in a new, more stable condition. Then you'd see how simple and easy regulatory adoption can be!"

Ace swung a heavily laden shopping bag from hand to hand. "Madame, be reasonable! This street just can't be the same without this kiosk!"

"You do have severe difficulties with inventory management. So, I will put a down-payment on the contents of your store. Then," she turned to Ace, "I will hire you as the inventory consultant. We will need every object named, priced and catalogued. As soon as possible. Please."

Borislav lived with his mother on the ground floor of a local apartment building. This saved him trouble with his bad leg. When he limped through the door, his mother was doing her nails at the kitchen table, with her hair in curlers and her feet in a sizzling foot-bath.

Borislav sniffed at the stew, then set his cane aside and sat in a plastic chair. "Mama dear, heaven knows we've seen our share of bad times."

"You're late tonight, poor boy! What ails you?"

"Mama, I just sold my entire stock! Everything in the kiosk! All sold, at one great swoop! For hard currency, too!" Borislav reached into the pocket of his long coat. "This is the best business day I've ever had!"

"Really?"

"Yes! It's fantastic! Ace really came through for me—he brought his useful European idiot, and she bought the whole works! Look, I've saved just one special item, just for you."

She raised her glasses on a neck-chain. "Are these new fabbing cards?"

"No, Mama. These fine souvenir playing cards feature all the stars from your favorite Mexican soap operas. These are the originals, still in their wrapper! That's authentic cellophane!"

His mother blew on her wet scarlet nails, not daring to touch her prize. "Cellophane! Your father would be so proud!"

"You're going to use those cards very soon, Mama. Your Saint's-Day is coming up. We're going to have a big bridge party for all your girl-friends. The boys at the Three Cats are going to cater it! You won't have to lift one pretty finger!"

Her mascara'ed eyes grew wide. "Can we afford that?"

"I've already arranged it! I talked to Mirko who runs the Three Cats, and I hired Mirko's weird gay brother-in-law to decorate that empty flat upstairs. You know—that flat nobody wants to rent, where that mob guy shot himself. When your old girls see how we've done that place up, word will get around. We'll have new tenants in no time!"

"You're really fixing the haunted flat, son?"

Borislav changed his winter boots for his wooly house slippers. "That's right, Mama. That haunted flat is gonna be a nice little earner."

"It's got a ghost in it."

"Not any more, it doesn't. From now on, we're gonna call that place… what was that French word he used?—we'll call it the 'atelier'!"

"The 'atelier!' Really! My heart's all a-flutter!"

Borislav poured his mother a stiff shot of her favorite digestive.

"Mama, maybe this news seems sudden, but I've been expecting this. Business has been looking up. Real life is changing, for the real people in this world. The people like us!" Borislav poured himself a brimming cup of flavored yogurt. "Those fancy foreigners, they don't even understand what the people are doing here today!"

"I don't understand all this men's political talk."

"Well, I can see it on their faces. I know what the people want. The people… They want a new life."

She rose from her chair, shaking a little. "I'll heat up your stew. It's getting so late."

Kiosk

"Listen to me, Mama. Don't be afraid of what I say. I promise you something. You're going to die on silk sheets. That's what this means. That's what I'm telling you. There's gonna be a handsome priest at your bedside, and the oil and the holy water, just like you always wanted. A big granite headstone for you, Mama, with big golden letters."

As he ate his stew, she began to weep with joy.

•⊩————⊩•

After supper, Borislav ignored his mother's usual nagging about his lack of a wife. He limped down to the local sports bar for some serious drinking. Borislav didn't drink much any more, because the kiosk scanned him whenever he sat inside it. It used a cheap superconductive loop, woven through the fiberboard walls. The loop's magnetism flowed through his body, revealing his bones and tissues on his laptop screen. Then the scanner compared the state of his body to its records of past days, and it coughed up a medical report.

This machine was a cheap, pirated copy of some hospital's fancy medical scanner. There had been some trouble in spreading that technology, but with the collapse of public health systems, people had to take some matters into their own hands. Borislav's health report was not cheery. He had plaque in major arteries. He had some seed-pearl kidney-stones. His teeth needed attention. Worst of all, his right leg had been wrecked by a land-mine. The shinbone had healed with the passing years, but it had healed badly. The foot below his old wound had bad circulation.

Age was gripping his body, visible right there on the screen. Though he could witness himself growing old, there wasn't much he could do about that.

Except, that is, for his drinking. Borislav had been fueled by booze his entire adult life, but the alcohol's damage was visibly spreading through his organs. Lying to himself about that obvious fact simply made him feel like a fool. So, nowadays, he drank a liter of yogurt a day, chased with eco-correct paper cartons of multivitamin fruit juices, European-approved, licensed, and fully patented. He did that grumpily and he resented it deeply, but could see on the screen that it was improving his health.

So, no more limping, pitching and staggering, poetically numbed, down the midnight streets. Except for special occasions, that is. Occasions like this one.

Borislav had a thoughtful look around the dimly lit haunt of the old Homeland Sports Bar. So many familiar faces lurking in here—his daily customers, most of them. The men were bundled up for winter. Their faces were rugged and lined. Shaving and bathing were not big priorities for them. They were also drunk.

But the men wore new, delicately tinted glasses. They had nice haircuts. Some had capped their teeth. The people were prospering.

Ace sat at his favorite table, wearing a white cashmere scarf, a tailored jacket and a dandified beret. Five years earlier, Ace would have had his butt royally kicked for showing up at the Homeland Sports Bar dressed like an Italian. But the times were changing at the Homeland.

Bracing himself with his cane, Borislav settled into a torn chair beneath a gaudy flat-screen display, where the Polish football team were making fools of the Dutch.

"So, Ace, you got it delivered?"

Ace nodded. "Over at the embassy, they are weighing, tagging and analyzing every single thing you sell."

"That old broad's not as stupid as she acts, you know."

"I know that. But when she saw that cheese-grater that can chop glass. The floor wax that was also a dessert!" Ace half-choked on the local cognac. "And the skull adjuster! God in heaven!"

Borislav scowled. "That skull adjuster is a great product! It'll chase a hangover away—" Borislav snapped his fingers loudly— "just like that!"

The waitress hurried over. She was a foreign girl who barely spoke the language, but there were a lot of such girls in town lately. Borislav pointed at Ace's drink. "One of those, missie, and keep 'em coming."

"That skull squeezer of yours is a torture device. It's weird, it's nutty. It's not even made by human beings."

"So what? So it needs a better name and a nicer label. 'The Craniette,' some nice brand-name. Manufacture it in pink. Emboss some flowers on it."

"Women will never squeeze their skulls with that crazy thing."

"Oh yes they will. Not old women from old Europe, no. But some will. Because I've seen them do it. I sold ten of those! The people want it!"

"You're always going on about 'what the people want.'"

"Well, that's it! That's our regional competitive advantage! The people who live here, they have a very special relationship to the market economy." Borislav's drink arrived. He downed his shot.

"The people here," he said, "they're used to seeing markets wreck their lives and turn everything upside down. That's why we're finally the ones setting the hot new trends in today's world, while the Europeans are trying to catch up with us! These people here, they *love* the new commercial products with no human origin!"

"Dr. Grootjans stared at that thing like it had come from Mars."

"Ace, the free market always makes sense—once you get to know how it works. You must have heard of the 'invisible hand of the market.'"

Ace downed his cognac and looked skeptical.

"The invisible hand—that's what gives us products like the skull-squeezer. That's *easy* to understand."

"No it isn't. Why would the invisible hand squeeze people's heads?"

"Because it's a search engine! It's mining the market data for new opportunities. The bigger the market, the more it tries to break in by automatically generating new products. And that headache-pill market, that's one of the world's biggest markets!"

Ace scratched under his armpit holster. "How big is that market, the world market for headaches?"

"It's huge! Every convenience store sells painkillers. Little packets of two and three pills, with big price markups. What are those pills all about? The needs and wants of the people!"

"Miserable people?"

"Exactly! People who hate their jobs, bitter people who hate their wives and husbands. The market for misery is always huge." Borislav knocked back another drink. "I'm talking too much tonight."

"Boots, I need you to talk to me. I just made more money for less work than I have in a long time. Now I'm even on salary inside a foreign embassy. This situation's getting serious. I need to know the philosophy—how an invisible hand makes real things. I gotta figure that out before the Europeans do."

"It's a market search engine for an Internet-of-Things."

Ace lifted and splayed his fingers. "Look, tell me something I can get my hands on. You know. Something that a man can steal."

"Say you type two words at random: any two words. Type those two words into an Internet search engine. What happens?"

Ace twirled his shot-glass. "Well, a search engine always hits on something, that's for sure. Something stupid, maybe, but always something."

"That's right. Now imagine you put two *products* into a search engine for things. So let's say it tries to sort and mix together…a parachute and a pair of shoes. What do you get from that kind of search?"

Ace thought it over. "I get it. You get a shoe that blows up a plane."

Borislav shook his head. "No, no. See, that is your problem right there. You're in the racket, you're a fixer. So you just don't think commercially."

"How can I out-think a machine like that?"

"You're doing it right now, Ace. Search engines have no ideas, no philosophy. They never think at all. Only people think and create ideas. Search engines are just programmed to search through what people want. Then they just mix, and match, and spit up some results. Endless results. Those results don't matter, though, unless the people want them. And here, the people want them!"

The waitress brought a bottle, peppered sauerkraut and a leathery loaf of bread. Ace watched her hips sway as she left. "Well, as for me, I could go for some of *that*. Those Iraqi chicks have got it going on."

Borislav leaned on his elbows and ripped up a mouthful of bread. He poured another shot, downed it, then fell silent as the booze stole up on him in a rush. He was suddenly done with talk.

Talk wasn't life. He'd seen real life. He knew it well. He'd first seen real life as a young boy, when he saw a whole population turned inside out. Refugees, the unemployed, the dispossessed, people starting over with pencils in a tin cup, scraping a living out of suitcases. Then people moving into stalls and kiosks. "Transition," that's what they named that kind of life. As if it were all going somewhere in particular.

The world changed a lot in a Transition. Life changed. But the people never transitioned into any rich nation's notion of normal life. In the next big "transition," the 21st-century one, the people lost everything they had gained.

When Borislav crutched back, maimed, from the outbreak of shooting-and-looting, he threw a mat on the sidewalk. He sold people boots. The people needed his boots, even indoors, because there was no more fuel in the pipelines and the people were freezing.

Kiosk

Come summer, he got hold of a car. Whenever there was diesel or bio-fuel around, he sold goods straight from its trunk. He made some street connections. He got himself a booth on the sidewalk.

Even in the rich countries, the lights were out and roads were still. The sky was empty of jets. It was a hard Transition. Civilization was wounded.

Then a contagion swept the world. Economic depression was bad, but a plague was a true Horseman of the Apocalypse. Plague thundered through a city. Plague made a city a place of thawing ooze, spontaneous fires, awesome deadly silences.

Borislav moved from his booth into the freezing wreck of a warehouse, where the survivors sorted and sold the effects of the dead. Another awful winter. They burned furniture to stay warm. When they coughed, people stared in terror at their handkerchiefs. Food shortages, too, this time: the dizzy edge of famine. Crazy times.

He had nothing left of that former life but his pictures. During the mayhem, he took thousands of photographs. That was something to mark the day, to point a lens, to squeeze a button, when there was nothing else to do, except to hustle, or sit and grieve, or jump from a bridge. He still had all those pictures, every last one of them. Everyday photographs of extraordinary times. His own extraordinary self: he was young, gaunt, wounded, hungry, burning-eyed.

As long as a man could recognize his own society, then he could shape himself to fit its circumstances. He might be a decent man, dependable, a man of his word. But when the society itself was untenable, when it just could not be sustained—then 'normality' cracked like a cheap plaster mask. Beneath the mask of civilization was another face: the face of a cannibal child.

Only hope mattered then: the will to carry on through another day, another night, with the living strength of one's own heartbeat, without any regard for abstract notions of success or failure. In real life, to live was the only "real."

In the absence of routine, in the vivid presence of risk and suffering, the soul grew. Objects changed their primal nature. Their value grew as keen as tears, as keen as kisses. Hot water was a miracle. Electric light meant instant celebration. A pair of boots was the simple, immediate reason that your feet had not frozen and turned black. A man who had toilet paper, insulation, candles: he was the people's hero.

When you handed a woman a tube of lipstick, her pinched and pallid face lit up all over. She could smear that scarlet on her lips, and when she walked down the darkened street it was as if she were shouting aloud, as if she were singing.

When the plague burned out—it was a flu, and it was a killer, but it was not so deadly as the numb despair it inspired—then a profiteer's fortune beckoned to those tough enough to knock heads and give orders. Borislav made no such fortune. He knew very well how such fortunes were made, but he couldn't give the orders. He had taken orders himself, once. Those were orders he should never have obeyed.

Like a stalled train, civilization slowly rattled back into motion, with its usual burden of claptrap. The life he had now, in the civilized moving train, it was a parody of that past life. That burning, immediate life. He had even been in love then.

Today, he lived inside his kiosk. It was a pretty nice kiosk, today. Only a fool could fail to make a living in good times. He took care, he improvised, so he made a profit. He was slowly buying-up some flats in an old apartment building, an ugly, unloved place, but sturdy and well-located. When old age stole over him, when he was too weak to hustle in the market any more, then he would live on the rents.

A football team scored on the big flat screen. The regulars cheered and banged their flimsy tables. Borislav raised his heavy head, and the bar's walls reeled as he came to himself. He was such a cheap drunk now; he would really have to watch that.

•H———H•

Morning was painful. Borislav's mother tiptoed in with muesli, yogurt, and coffee. Borislav put his bad foot into his mother's plastic footbath—that treatment often seemed to help him—and he paged through a crumbling yellow block of antique newspapers. The old arts district had always been a bookish place, and these often showed up in attics. Borislav never read the ancient "news" in the newspapers, which, during any local regime, consisted mostly of official lies. Instead, he searched for the strange things that the people had once desired.

Three huge, universal, dead phenomena haunted these flaking pages: petroleum cars, cinema, and cigarettes. The cars heavily dragged along their hundreds of objects and services: fuels, pistons, mufflers, makers of sparks. The cigarettes had garish paper packages, with lighters, humidors, and special trays just for their ashes. As for the movie stars, they were driving the cars and smoking the cigarettes.

The very oldest newspapers were downright phantasmagoric.

All the newspapers, with their inky, frozen graphics, seemed to scream at him across their gulf of decades. The dead things harangued, they flattered, they shamed, they jostled each other on the paper pages. They bled margin-space, they wept ink.

These things were strange, and yet, they had been desired. At first with a sense of daring, and then with a growing boldness, Borislav chose certain dead items to be digitally copied and revived. He re-released them into the contemporary flow of goods. For instance, by changing its materials and proportions, he'd managed to transform a Soviet-era desk telephone into a lightweight plastic rain-hat. No one had ever guessed the origin of his experiments. Unlike the machine-generated new products—always slotted with such unhuman coolness into market niches—these revived goods stank of raw humanity. Raw purpose. Raw desire.

Once, there had been no Internet. And no Internet-of-Things, either, for that could only follow. There had only been the people. People wanting things, trying to make other people want their things. Capitalism, socialism, communism, those mattered little enough. Those were all period arrangements in a time that had no Internet.

The day's quiet study restored Borislav's good spirits. Next morning, his mother re-commenced her laments about her lack of a daughter-in-law. Borislav left for work.

He found his kiosk pitifully stripped and empty, with a CLOSED sign in its damp-spotted window. A raw hole loomed in the wall where the fabrikator had been torn free. This sudden loss of all his trade-goods gave him a lofty thrill of panic.

Borislav savored that for a moment, then put the fear behind him. The neighborhood still surrounded his kiosk. The people would nourish it. He had picked an excellent location, during the darkest days. Once he'd sold them dirty bags of potatoes here, they'd clamored for wilted carrots. This life was easy now. This life was like a good joke.

He limped through the biometric door and turned on the lights.

Now, standing inside, he felt the kiosk's true nature. A kiosk was a conduit. It was a temporary stall in the endless flow of goods.

His kiosk was fiberboard and glue: recycled materials, green and modern. It had air filters, insulated windows, a rugged little fuel cell, efficient lights, a heater grill in the floor. It had password-protected intrusion alarms. It had a medical scanner in the walls. It had smart-ink wallpaper with peppy graphics.

They had taken away his custom-shaped chair, and his music player, loaded with a fantastic mashed-up mulch of the complete pop hits of the 20th century. He would have to replace those. That wouldn't take him long.

He knelt on the bare floor, and taped a thick sheet of salvaged cardboard over the wintry hole in his wall. A loud rap came at his window. It was Fleka the Gypsy, one of his suppliers.

Borislav rose and stepped outside, reflexively locking his door, since this was Fleka. Fleka was the least dependable of his suppliers, because Fleka had no sense of time. Fleka could make, fetch, or filch most anything, but if you dared to depend on his word, Fleka would suddenly remember the wedding of some gypsy cousin, and vanish.

"I heard about your good luck, Boots," grinned Fleka. "Is the maestro in need of new stock?"

Borislav rapped the empty window with his cane. "It's as you see."

Fleka slid to the trunk of his rusty car and opened it.

"Whatever that is," said Borislav at once, "it's much too big."

"Give me one minute from your precious schedule, maestro," said Fleka. "You, my kind old friend, with your lovely kiosk so empty, I didn't bring you any goods. I brought you a factory! So improved! So new!"

"That thing's not new, whatever it is."

"See, it's a fabrikator! Just like the last fabrikator I got for you, only this one is bigger, fancy and much better! I got it from my cousin."

"I wasn't born yesterday, Fleka."

Fleka hustled under his back seat and brought out a sample. It was a rotund doll of the American actress, Marilyn Monroe. The doll was still unpainted. It was glossily black.

Marilyn Monroe, the ultimate retail movie-star, was always recognizable, due to her waved coif, her lip-mole, and her torpedo-like bust. The passage of a century had scarcely damaged her shelf-appeal. The woman had become an immortal cartoon, like Betty Boop.

Kiosk

Flecka popped a hidden seam under Marilyn's jutting bust. Inside the black Marilyn doll was a smaller Marilyn doll, also jet-black, but wearing less clothing. Then came a smaller, more risqué little Marilyn, and then a smaller one yet, and finally a crudely-modelled little Marilyn, shiny black, nude, and the size of Borislav's thumb.

"Nice celebrity branding," Borislav admitted. "So what's this material?" It seemed to be black china.

"It's not wax, like that other fabrikator. This is carbon. Little straws of carbon. It came with the machine."

Borislav ran his thumbnail across the grain of the material. The black Marilyn doll was fabricated in ridges, like the grooves in an ancient gramophone record. Fabs were always like that: they jet-sprayed their things by piling up thin layers, they stacked them up like pancakes. "'Little straws of carbon.' I never heard of that."

"I'm telling you what my cousin told me. 'Little nano tubes, little nano carbon.' That's what he said." Fleka grabbed the round Marilyn doll like a football goalie, and raised both his hands overhead. Then, with all his wiry strength, he smacked the black doll against the rust-eaten roof of his car. Chips flew.

"You've ruined her!"

"That was my car breaking," Fleka pointed out. "I made this doll this morning, out of old plans and scans from the Net. Then I gave it to my nephew, a nice big boy. I told him to break the doll. He broke a crowbar on this doll."

Borislav took the black doll again, checked the seams and detailing, and rapped it with his cane. "You sell these dolls to anyone else, Fleka?"

"Not yet."

"I could move a few of these. How much you asking?"

Fleka spread his hands. "I can make more. But I don't know how to make the little straws of carbon. There's a tutorial inside the machine. But it's in Polish. I hate tutorials."

Borislav examined the fabrikator. The machine looked simple enough: it was a basic black shell, a big black hopper, a black rotating plate, a black spraying nozzle, and the black gearing of a 3-D axis. "Why is this thing so black?"

"It's nice and shiny, isn't it? The machine itself is made of little straws of carbon."

"Your cousin got you this thing? Where's the brand name? Where's the serial number?"

"I swear he didn't steal it! This fabrikator is a copy, see. It's a pirate copy of another fabrikator in Warsaw. But nobody knows it's a copy. Or if they do know, the cops won't be looking for any copies around this town, that's for sure."

Borislav's doubts overflowed into sarcasm. "You're saying it's a fabrikator that copies fabrikators? It's a fabbing fab fabber, that's what you're telling me, Fleka?"

A shrill wail of shock and alarm came from the front of the kiosk. Borislav hurried to see.

A teenage girl, in a cheap red coat and yellow winter boots, was sobbing into her cellphone. She was Jovanica, one of his best customers.

"What's the matter?" he said.

"Oh! It's you!" Jovanica snapped her phone shut and raised a skinny hand to her lips. "Are you still alive, Mr. Boots?"

"Why wouldn't I be alive?"

"Well, what happened to you? Who robbed your store?"

"I'm not robbed. Everything has been sold, that's all."

Jovanica's young face screwed up in doubt, rage, frustration and grief. "Then *where are my hair toys?*"

"What?"

"Where are my favorite barrettes? My hair clips! My scrunchies and headbands and beautiful pins! There was a whole tree of them, right here! I picked new toys from that tree every day! I finally had it giving me just what I wanted!"

"Oh. That." Borislav had sold the whirling rack of hair toys, along with its entire freight of goods.

"Your rack sold the best hair toys in town! So super and cool! What happened to it? And what happened to your store? It's broken! There's nothing left!"

"That's true, 'Neetsa. You had a very special relationship with that interactive rack, but...well..." Borislav groped for excuses, and, with a leap of genius, he found one. "I'll tell you a secret. You're growing up now, that's what."

"I want my hair toys! Go get my rack right now!"

"Hair toys are for the 9-to-15 age bracket. You're growing out of that market niche. You should be thinking seriously about earrings."

Jovanica's hands flew to her earlobes. "You mean pierce my ears?"

Borislav nodded. "High time."

"Mama won't let me do that."

"I can speak to your mama. You're getting to be a big girl now. Soon you'll have to beat the boys away with a stick."

Jovanica stared at the cracks in the pavement. "No I won't."

"Yes you will," said Borislav, hefting his cane reflexively.

Fleka the Gypsy had been an interested observer. Now he spoke up. "Don't cry about your pretty things: because Boots here is the King of Kiosks. He can get you all the pretty things in the world!"

"Don't you listen to the gypsy," said Borislav. "Listen, Jovanica: your old hair-toy tree, I'm sorry, it's gone for good. You'll have to start over with a brand-new one. It won't know anything about what you want."

"After all my shopping? That's terrible!"

"Never you mind. I'll make you a different deal. Since you're getting to be such a big girl, you're adding a lot of value by making so many highly-informed consumer choices. So, next time, there will be a new economy for you. I'll pay you to teach that toy-tree just what you want to buy."

Fleka stared at him. "What did you just say? You want to *pay this kid for shopping?*"

"That's right."

"She's a little kid!"

"I'm not a little kid!" Jovanica took swift offense. "You're a dirty old gypsy!"

"Jovanica is the early hair-toy adopter, Fleka. She's the market leader here. Whatever hair-toys Jovanica buys, all the other girls come and buy. So, yeah. I'm gonna cut her in on that action. I should have done that long ago."

Jovanica clapped her hands. "Can I have lots of extra hair toys, instead of just stupid money?"

"Absolutely. Of course. Those loyal-customer rewards will keep you coming back here, when you ought to be doing your homework."

Fleka marvelled. "It's completely gone to your head, cashing out your whole stock at once. A man of your age, too."

The arts district never lacked for busybodies. Attracted by the little drama, four of them gathered round Borislav's kiosk. When they caught him glowering at them, they all pretended to need water from his fountain. At least his fountain was still working.

"Here comes my Mama," said Jovanica. Her mother, Ivana, burst headlong from the battered doors of a nearby block of flats. Ivana wore a belted house-robe, a flung-on muffler, a heavy scarf, and brightly-knitted woolen house-slippers. She brandished a laden pillowcase.

"Thank God they haven't hurt you!" said Ivana, her breath puffing in the chilly air. She opened her pillowcase. It held a steam iron, a hair dryer, an old gilt mirror, a nickeled hip-flask, a ragged fur stole, and a lidded, copper-bottomed saucepan.

"Mr. Boots is all right, Mama," said Jovanica. "They didn't steal anything. He *sold* everything!"

"You sold your kiosk?" said Ivana, and the hurt and shock deepened in her eyes. "You're leaving us?"

"It was business," Borislav muttered. "Sorry for the inconvenience. It'll be a while before things settle down."

"Honestly, I don't need these things. If these things will help you in any way, you're very welcome to them."

"Mama wants you to sell these things," Jovanica offered, with a teen's oppressive helpfulness. "Then you can have the money to fix your store."

Borislav awkwardly patted the kiosk's fiberboard wall. "Ivana, this old place doesn't look like much, so empty and with this big hole…but, well, I had some luck."

"Ma'am, you must be cold in those house slippers," said Fleka the Gypsy. With an elegant swoop of his arm, he gestured at the gilt-and-glassed front counter of the Three Cats café. "May I get you a hot cappucino?"

"You're right, sir, it's cold here." Ivana tucked the neck of her pillowcase, awkwardly, over her arm. "I'm glad things worked out for you, Borislav."

"Yes, things are all right. Really."

Ivana aimed a scowl at the passersby, who watched her with a lasting interest. "We'll be going now, 'Neetsa."

"Mama, I'm not cold. The weather's clearing up!"

"We're going." They left.

Fleka picked at his discolored canine with his forefinger. "So, maestro. What just happened there?"

"She's a nice kid. She's hasty sometimes. The young are like that. That can't be helped." Borislav shrugged. "Let's talk our business inside."

He limped into his empty kiosk. Fleka wedged in behind him and managed to slam the door. Borislav could smell the man's rich, goulash-tinged breath.

"I was never inside one of these before," Fleka remarked, studying every naked seam for the possible point of a burglar's prybar. "I thought about getting a kiosk of my own, but, well, a man gets so restless."

"It's all about the product flow divided by the floor space. By that measure, a kiosk is super-efficient retailing. It's about as efficient as any sole proprietor can do. But it's a one-man enterprise. So, well, a man's just got to go it alone."

Fleka looked at him with wise, round eyes. "That girl who cried so much about her hair. That's not your girl, is she?"

"What? No."

"What happened to the father, then? The flu got him?"

"She was born long after the flu, but, yeah, you're right, her father passed away." Borislav coughed. "He was a good friend of mine. A soldier. Really good-looking guy. His kid is gorgeous."

"So you didn't do anything about that. Because you're not a soldier, and you're not rich, and you're not gorgeous."

"Do anything about what?"

"A woman like that Ivana, she isn't asking for some handsome soldier or some rich-guy boss. A woman like her, she wants maybe a pretty dress. Maybe a dab of perfume. And something in her bed that's better than a hot-water bottle."

"Well, I've got a kiosk and a broken leg."

"All us men have a broken leg. She thought you had nothing. She ran right down here, with anything she could grab for you, stuffed into her pillowcase. So you're not an ugly man. You're a stupid man." Fleka thumped his chest. "I'm the ugly man. Me. I've got three wives: the one in Bucharest, the one in Lublin, and the wife in Linz isn't even a gypsy. They're gonna bury me standing, maestro. That can't be helped, because I'm a man. But that's not what you are. You're a fool."

"Thanks for the free fortune-telling. You know all about this, do you? She and I were here during the hard times. That's what. She and I have a history."

"You're a fanatic. You're a geek. I can see through you like the windows of this kiosk. You should get a life." Fleka thumped the kiosk's wallpaper, and sighed aloud. "Look, life is sad, all right? Life is sad even when you do get a life. So. Boots. Now I'm gonna tell you about this fabrikator of mine, because you got some spare money, and you're gonna buy it from me. It's a nice machine. Very sweet. It comes from a hospital. It's supposed to make bones. So the tutorial is all about making bones, and that's bad, because nobody buys bones. If you are deaf and you want some new little black bones in your ears, that's what this machine is for. Also, these black toys I made with it, I can't paint them. The toys are much too hard, so the paint breaks right off. Whatever you make with this fabrikator, it's hard and black, and you can't paint it, and it belongs by rights inside some sick person. Also, I can't read the stupid tutorials. I hate tutorials. I hate reading."

"Does it run on standard voltage?"

"I got it running on DC off the fuel-cell in my car."

"Where's the feedstock?"

"It comes in big bags. It's a powder, it's a yellow dust. The fab sticks it together somehow, with sparks or something, it turns the powder shiny black and it knits it up real fast. That part, I don't get."

"I'll be offering one price for your machine and all your feedstock."

"There's another thing. That time when I went to Vienna. I gave you my word on that deal. We shook hands on it. That deal was really important, they really needed it, they weren't kidding about it, and, well, I screwed up. Because of Vienna."

"That's right, Fleka. You screwed up bad."

"Well, that's my price. That's part of my price. I'm gonna sell you this toy-maker. We're gonna haul it right out of the car, put it in the kiosk here nice and safe. When I get the chance, I'm gonna bring your bag of coal-straw, too. But we forget about Vienna. We just forget about it."

Borislav said nothing.

"You're gonna forgive me my bad, screwed-up past. That's what I want from you."

"I'm thinking about it."

"That's part of the deal."

"We're going to forget the past, and you're going to give me the machine, the stock, and also fifty bucks."

"Okay, sold."

•‖————‖•

Kiosk

With the fabrikator inside his kiosk, Borislav had no room inside the kiosk for himself. He managed to transfer the tutorials out of the black, silent fab and into his laptop. The sun had come out. Though it was still damp and chilly, the boys from the Three Cats had unstacked their white café chairs. Borislav took a seat there. He ordered black coffee and began perusing awkward machine-translations from the Polish manual.

Selma arrived to bother him. Selma was married to a schoolteacher, a nice guy with a steady job. Selma called herself an artist, made jewelry, and dressed like a lunatic. The schoolteacher thought the world of Selma, although she slept around on him and never cooked him a decent meal.

"Why is your kiosk so empty? What are you doing, just sitting out here?"

Borislav adjusted the angle of his screen. "I'm seizing the means of production."

"What did you do with all my bracelets and necklaces?"

"I sold them."

"All of them?"

"Every last scrap."

Selma sat down as if hit with a mallet. "Then you should buy me a glass of champagne!"

Borislav reluctantly pulled his phone and text-messaged the waiter.

It was getting blustery, but Selma preened over her glass of cheap Italian red. "Don't expect me to replace your stock soon! My artwork's in great demand."

"There's no hurry."

"I broke the luxury market, across the river at the Intercontinental! The hotel store will take all the bone-ivory chokers I can make."

"Mmm-hmm."

"Bone-ivory chokers, they're the perennial favorite of ugly, aging tourist women with wattled necks."

Borislav glanced up from his screen. "Shouldn't you be running along to your workbench?"

"Oh, sure, sure, 'give the people what they want,' that's your sick, petit-bourgeois philosophy! Those foreign tourist women in their big hotels, they want me to make legacy kitsch!"

Borislav waved one hand at the street. "Well, we do live in the old arts district."

33

"Listen, stupid, when this place was the *young* arts district, it was full of avant-gardists plotting revolution. Look at me for once. Am I from the museum?" Selma yanked her skirt to mid-thigh. "Do I wear little old peasant shoes that turn up at the toes?"

"What the hell has gotten into you? Did you sit on your tack-hammer?"

Selma narrowed her kohl-lined eyes. "What do you expect me to do, with my hands and my artisan skills, when you're making all kinds of adornments with fabrikators? I just saw that stupid thing inside your kiosk there."

Borislav sighed. "Look, I don't know. You tell me what it means, Selma."

"It means revolution. That's what. It means another revolution."

Borislav laughed at her.

Selma scowled and lifted her kid-gloved fingers. "Listen to me. Transition number one. When communism collapsed. The people took to the streets. Everything privatized. There were big market shocks."

"I remember those days. I was a kid, and you weren't even born then."

"Transition Two. When globalism collapsed. There was no oil. There was war and bankruptcy. There was sickness. That was when I was a kid."

Borislav said nothing about that. All things considered, his own first Transition had been a kinder time to grow up in.

"Then comes Transition Three." Selma drew a breath. "When this steadily increasing cybernetic intervention in manufacturing liberates a distinctly human creativity."

"Okay, what is that about?"

"I'm telling you what it's about. You're not listening. We're in the third great Transition. It's a revolution. Right now. Here. This isn't Communism, this isn't Globalism. This is the next thing after that. It's happening. No longer merely reacting to this influx of mindless goods, the modern artist uses human creative strength in the name of a revolutionary heterogeneity!"

Selma always talked pretentious, self-important drivel. Not quite like this, though. She'd found herself some new drivel.

"Where did you hear all that?"

"I heard it here in this café! You're just not listening, that's your problem. You never listen to anybody. Word gets around fast in the arts community."

"I live here too, you know. I'd listen to your nutty blither all day, if you ever meant business."

Selma emptied her wine glass. Then she reached inside her hand-loomed, artsy sweater. "If you laugh at this, I'm going to kill you."

Borislav took the necklace she offered him. "Where's this from? Who sent you this?"

"That's mine! I made it. With my hands."

Borislav tugged the tangled chain through his fingers. He was no jeweller, but knew what decent jewelry looked like. This was indecent jewelry. If the weirdest efforts of search engines looked like products from Mars, then this necklace was straight from Venus. It was slivers of potmetal, blobs of silver and chips of topaz. It was like jewelry straight out of a nightmare.

"Selma, this isn't your customary work."

"Machines can't dream. I saw this in my dreams."

"Oh. Right, of course."

"Well, it was my nightmare, really. But I woke up! Then I created my vision! I don't have to make that cheap, conventional crap, you know! I only make cheap junk because that's all you are willing to sell!"

"Well...." He had never spoken with frankness to Selma before, but the glittering light in her damp eyes made yesterday's habits seem a little slow-witted. "Well, I wouldn't know what to charge for a work of art like this."

"Somebody would want this, though? Right? Wouldn't they?" She was pleading with him. "Somebody? They would buy my new necklace, right? Even though it's...different."

"No. This isn't the sort of jewelry that the people buy. This is the sort of jewelry that the people stare at, and probably laugh at, too. But then, there would come one special person. She would really want this necklace. She would want this more than anything. She would have to have this thing at absolutely any price."

"I could make more like that," Selma told him, and she touched her heart. "Because now I know where it comes from."

III.

Borislav installed the fab inside the empty kiosk, perched on a stout wooden pedestal, where its workings could be seen by the people.

His first choices for production were, naturally, hair toys. Borislav borrowed some fancy clips from Jovanica, and copied their shapes inside his kiosk with his medical scanner.

Sure enough, the fabricator sprayed out shiny black replicas.

Jovanica amused a small crowd by jumping up and down on them. The black clips themselves were well-nigh indestructible, but their cheap metal springs soon snapped.

Whenever a toy broke, however, it was a simple matter to cast it right back into the fabrikator's hopper. The fab chewed away at the black object, with an ozone-like reek, until the fabbed object became the yellow dust again.

Straw, right into gold.

Borislav sketched out a quick business-plan on the back of a Three Cats beer-coaster. With hours of his labor, multiplied by price-per-gram, he soon established his point of profit. He was in a new line of work.

With the new fabrikator, he could copy the shapes of any small object he could scan. Of course, he couldn't literally "copy" everything: a puppy-dog, a nice silk dress, a cold bottle of beer, those were all totally out of the question. But he could copy most anything that was made from some single, rigid material: an empty bottle, a fork, a trash can, a kitchen knife.

The kitchen knives were an immediate hit. The knives were shiny and black, very threatening and scary, and it was clear they would never need sharpening. It was also delightful to see the fabrikator mindlessly spitting up razor-sharp knives. The kids were back in force to watch the action, and this time, even the grown-ups gathered and chattered.

To accommodate the eager crowd of gawkers, the Three Cats boys set out their chairs and tables, and even their striped, overhead canopy, as cheery as if it were summer.

The weather favored them. An impromptu block party broke out.

Mirko from the Three Cats gave him a free meal. "I'm doing very well by this," Mirko said. "You've got yourself a nine-days' wonder here. This sure reminds me of when Transition Two was ending. Remember when those city lights came back on? Brother, those were great days."

"Nine days won't last long. I need to get back inside that kiosk, like normal again."

"It's great to see you out and about, mixing it up with us, Boots. We never talk any more." Mirko spread his hands in apology, then scrubbed the table. "I run this place now…it's the pressure of business…that's all my fault."

Borislav accepted a payment from a kid who'd made himself a rock-solid black model dinosaur. "Mirko, do you have room for a big vending machine, here by your café? I need to get that black beast out of my kiosk. The people need their sticks of gum."

"You really want to build some vendorizing thing out here? Like a bank machine?"

"I guess I do, yeah. It pays."

"Boots, I love this crowd you're bringing me, but why don't you just put your machine wherever they put bank machines? There are hundreds of bank machines." Mirko took his empty plate. "There are millions of bank machines. Those machines took over the world."

IV.

Days passed. The people wouldn't let him get back to normal. It became a public sport to see what people would bring in for the fabrikator to copy. It was common to make weird things as gag gifts: a black, rock-solid spray of roses, for instance. You could hand that black bouquet to your girlfriend for a giggle, and if she got huffy, then you could just bring it back, have it weighed, and get a return-deposit for the yellow dust.

The ongoing street-drama was a tonic for the neighborhood. In no time flat, every café lounger and class-skipping college student was a self-appointed expert about fabs, fabbing, and revolutionary super-fabs that could fab their own fabbing. People brought their relatives to see. Tourists wandered in and took pictures. Naturally, they all seemed to want a word with the owner and proprietor.

The people being the people, the holiday air was mixed with unease. Things took a strange turn when a young bride arrived with her wedding china. She paid to copy each piece, then loudly and publicly smashed the originals in the street. A cop showed up to dissuade her. Then the cop wanted a word, too.

Borislav was sitting with Professor Damov, an academician and pious blowhard who ran the local ethnographic museum. The professor's city-sponsored hall specialized in what Damov called "material culture," meaning dusty vitrines full of battle flags, holy medallions, distaffs, fishing nets, spinning wheels, gramophones, and such. Given these new circumstances, the professor had a lot on his mind.

"Officer," said Damov, briskly waving his wineglass, "it may well surprise you to learn this, but the word 'kiosk' is an ancient Ottoman term. In the original Ottoman kiosk, nothing was bought or sold. The kiosk was a regal gift from a prince to the people. A kiosk was a place to breathe the evening air, to meditate, to savor life and living; it was an elegant garden pergola."

"They didn't break their wedding china in the gutter, though," said the cop.

"Oh, no, on the contrary, if a bride misbehaved in those days, she'd be sewn into a leather sack and thrown into the Bosphorus!"

The cop was mollified, and he moved right along, but soon a plain-clothes cop showed up and took a prominent seat inside the Three Cats café. This changed the tone of things. The police surveillance proved that something real was happening. It was a kind of salute.

Dusk fell. A group of garage mechanics came by, still in their grimy overalls, and commenced a deadly-serious professional discussion about fabbing trolley parts. A famous stage actor showed up with his entourage, to sign autographs and order drinks for all his "friends."

Some alarmingly clean-cut university students appeared. They weren't there to binge on beer. They took a table, ordered Mirko's cheapest pizza, and started talking in points-of-order.

Next day, the actor brought the whole cast of his play, and the student radicals were back in force. They took more tables, with much more pizza. Now they had a secretary, and a treasurer. Their ringleaders had shiny black political buttons on their coats.

A country bus arrived and disgorged a group of farmers. These peasants made identical copies of something they were desperate to have, yet anxious to hide from all observers.

Ace came by the bustling café. Ace was annoyed to find that he had to wait his turn for any private word with Borislav.

"Calm down, Ace. Have a slice of this pork pizza. The boss here's an old friend of mine, and he's in a generous mood."

"Well, my boss is unhappy," Ace retorted. "There's money being made here, and he wasn't told about it."

Kiosk

"Tell your big guy to relax. I'm not making any more money than I usually do at the kiosk. That should be obvious: consider my rate of production. That machine can only make a few copies an hour."

"Have you finally gone stupid? Look at this crowd!" Ace pulled his shades off and studied the densely clustered café. Despite the lingering chill, a gypsy band was setting up, with accordions and trombones. "Okay, this proves it: see that wise-guy sitting there with that undercover lieutenant? He's one of *them*!"

Borislav cast a sidelong glance at the rival gangster. The North River Boy looked basically identical to Ace: the same woolly hat, cheap black sunglasses, jacket and bad attitude, except for his sneakers, which were red instead of blue. "The River Boys are moving in over here?"

"They always wanted this turf. This is the lively part of town."

That River Boy had some nerve. Gangsters had been shot in the Three Cats café. And not just a few times, either. It was a major local tradition.

"I'm itching to whack that guy," Ace lied, sweating, "but, well, he's sitting over there with that cop! And a pet politician, too!"

Borislav wondered if his eyes were failing. In older days, he would never have missed those details.

There was a whole little tribe of politicians filtering into the cafe, and sitting near the mobster's table. The local politicians always travelled in parties. Small, fractious parties.

One of these local politicals was the arts districts' own national representative. Mr. Savic was a member of the Radical Liberal Democratic Party, a splinter clique of well-meaning, over-educated cranks.

"I'm gonna tell you a good joke, Ace. 'You can get three basic qualities with any politician: Smart, Honest and Effective. But you only get to pick two.'"

Ace blinked. He didn't get it.

Borislav levered himself from his café chair and limped over to provoke a gladhanding from Mr. Savic. The young lawyer was smart and honest, and therefore ineffective. However, Savic, being so smart, was quick to recognize political developments within his own district. He had already appropriated the shiny black button of the young student radicals.

With an ostentatious swoop of his camel's-hair coat-tails, Mr. Savic deigned to sit at Borislav's table. He gave Ace a chilly glare. "Is it necessary that we consort with this organized-crime figure?"

"You tried to get me fired from my job in the embassy," Ace accused him.

"Yes, I did. It's bad enough that the criminal underworld infests our ruling party. We can't have the Europeans paying you off, too."

"That's you all over, Savic: always sucking up to rich foreigners and selling-out the guy on the street!"

"Don't flatter yourself, you jumped-up little crook! You're not 'the street.' The people are the street!"

"Okay, so you got the people to elect you. You took office and you got a pretty haircut. Now you're gonna wrap yourself up in our flag, too? You're gonna steal the last thing the people have left!"

Borislav cleared his throat. "I'm glad we have this chance for a frank talk here. The way I figure it, managing this fabbing business is going to take some smarts and finesse."

The two of them stared at him. "You brought us here?" Ace said. "For our 'smarts and finesse?'"

"Of course I did. You two aren't here by accident, and neither am I. If we're not pulling the strings around here, then who is?"

The politician looked at the gangster. "There's something to what he says, you know. After all, this is Transition Three."

"So," said Borislav, "knock it off with that tough-talk and do some fresh thinking for once! You sound like your own grandfathers!"

Borislav had surprised himself with this outburst. Savic, to his credit, looked embarrassed, while Ace scratched uneasily under his woolly hat. "Well, listen, Boots," said Ace at last, "even if you, and me, and your posh lawyer pal have us three nice Transition beers together, that's a River Boy sitting over there. What are we supposed to do about that?"

"I am entirely aware of the criminal North River Syndicate," Mr. Savic told him airily. "My investigative committee has been analyzing their gang."

"Oh, so you're analyzing, are you? They must be scared to death."

"There are racketeering laws on the books in this country," said Savic, glowering at Ace. "When we take power and finally have our purge of the criminal elements in this society, we won't stop at arresting that one little punk in his cheap red shoes. We will liquidate his entire parasite class: I mean him, his nightclub-singer girlfriend, his father, his boss, his brothers, his cousins, his entire football club.... As long as there is one honest judge in this country, and there are some honest judges, there are *always* some.... We will never rest! Never!"

"I've heard about your honest judges," Ace sneered. "You can spot 'em by the smoke columns when their cars blow up."

"Ace, stop talking through your hat. Let me make it crystal clear what's at stake here." Borislav reached under the table and brought up a clear plastic shopping bag. He dropped it on the table with a thud.

Ace took immediate interest. "You output a skull?"

"Ace, this is *my own* skull." The kiosk scanned him every day. So Borislav had his skull on file.

Ace juggled Borislav's skull free of the clear plastic bag, then passed it right over to the politician. "That fab is just superb! Look at the crisp detailing on those sutures!"

"I concur. A remarkable technical achievement." Mr Savic turned the skull upside down, and frowned. "What happened to your teeth?"

"Those are normal."

"You call these wisdom teeth normal?"

"Hey, let me see those," Ace pleaded. Mr Savic rolled Borislav's jet-black skull across the tabletop. Then he cast an over-shoulder look at his fellow politicians, annoyed that they enjoyed themselves so much without him.

"Listen to me, Mr. Savic. When you campaigned, I put your poster up in my kiosk. I even voted for you, and—"

Ace glanced up from the skull's hollow eye-sockets. "You vote, Boots?"

"Yes. I'm an old guy. Us old guys vote."

Savic faked some polite attention.

"Mr. Savic, you're our political leader. You're a Radical Liberal Democrat. Well, we've got ourselves a pretty radical, liberal situation here. What are we supposed to do now?"

"It's very good that you asked me that," nodded Savic. "You must be aware that there are considerable intellectual-property difficulties with your machine."

"What are those?"

"I mean patents and copyrights. Reverse-engineering laws. Trademarks. We don't observe all of those laws in this country of ours... in point of fact, practically speaking, we scarcely observe any.... But the rest of the world fully depends on those regulatory structures. So if you go around publicly pirating wedding china—let's just say—well, the makers of wedding-china will surely get wind of that some day. I'd be guessing that you will see a civil lawsuit. Cease-and-desist, all of that."

"I see."

"That's just how the world works. If you damage their income, they'll simply have to sue you. Follow the money, follow the lawsuits. A simple principle, really. Although you've got a very nice little sideshow here.... It's really brightened up the neighborhood...."

Professor Damov arrived at the cafe. He had brought his wife, Mrs. Professor-Doctor Damova, an icy sociologist with annoying Marxist and feminist tendencies. The lady professor wore a fur coat as solid as a bank-vault, and a bristling fur hat.

Damov pointed out a black plaque on Borislav's tabletop. "I'm sorry, gentleman, but this table is reserved for us."

"Oh," Borislav blurted. He hadn't noticed the fabbed reservation, since it was so black.

"We're having a little party tonight," said Damov, "it's our anniversary."

"Congratulations, sir and madame!" said Mr. Savic. "Why not sit here with us just a moment until your guests arrive?"

A bottle of Mirko's prosecco restored general good feeling. "I'm an arts-district lawyer, after all," said Savic, suavely topping-up everyone's glasses. "So, Borislav, if I were you, I would call this fabrikator an arts installation!"

"Really? Why?"

"Because when those humorless foreigners with their lawsuits try to make a scandal of the arts scene, that never works!" Savic winked at the professor and his wife. "We really enjoyed it, eh? We enjoyed a good show while we had it!"

Ace whipped off his sunglasses. "It's an 'arts installation!' Wow! That is some smart lawyer thinking there!"

Borislav frowned. "Why do you say that?"

Ace leaned in to whisper behind his hand. "Well, because that's what we tell the River Boys! We tell them it's just an art show, then we shut it down. They stay in their old industrial district, and we keep our turf in the old arts district. Everything is cool!"

"That's your big solution?"

"Well, yeah," said Ace, leaning back with a grin. "Hooray for art!"

Borislav's temper rose from a deep well to burn the back of his neck. "That's it, huh? That's what you two sorry sons of bitches have to offer the people? You just want to get rid of the thing! You want to put it out, like spitting on a candle! Nothing *happens* with your stupid approach! You call that a Transition? Everything's just the same as it was before! Nothing changes at all!"

Damov shook his head. "History is always passing. We changed. We're all a year older."

Mrs. Damov spoke up. "I can't believe your fascist, technocratic nonsense! Do you really imagine that you will improve the lives of the people by dropping some weird machine onto their street at random? With no mature consideration of any deeper social issues? I wanted to pick up some milk tonight! Who's manning your kiosk, you goldbricker? Your store is completely empty! Are we supposed to queue?"

Mr. Savic emptied his glass. "Your fabrikator is great fun, but piracy is illegal and immoral. Fair is fair, let's face it."

"Fine," said Borislav, waving his arms, "if that's what you believe, then go tell the people. Tell the people in this cafe, right now, that you want to throw the future away! Go on, do it! Say you're scared of crime! Say they're not mature enough and they have to think it through. Tell the people that they have to vote for that!"

"Let's not be hasty," said Savic.

"Your sordid mechanical invention is useless without a social invention," said Mrs. Damova primly.

"My wife is exactly correct!" Damov beamed. "Because a social invention is much more than gears and circuits, it's…well, it's something like that kiosk. A kiosk was once a way to drink tea in a royal garden. Now it's a way to buy milk! That is social invention!" He clicked her bubbling glass with his own.

Ace mulled this over. "I never thought of it that way. Where can we steal a social invention? How do you copy one of those?"

These were exciting questions. Borislav felt a piercing ray of mental daylight. "That European woman, what's-her-face. She bought-out my kiosk. Who is she? Who does she work for?"

"You mean Dr. Grootjans? She is, uh…she's the economic affairs liaison for a European Parliamentary investigative committee."

"Right," said Borislav at once, "that's it. Me, too! I want that. Copy me that! I'm the liaison for the investigation Parliament something stupid-or-other."

Savic laughed in delight. "This is getting good."

"You. Mr. Savic. You have a Parliament investigation committee."

"Well, yes, I certainly do."

"Then you should investigate this fabrikator. You place it under formal government investigation. You investigate it, all day and all night. Right here on the street, in public. You issue public reports. And of course you make stuff. You make all kinds of stuff. Stuff to investigate."

"Do I have your proposal clear? You are offering your fabrikator to the government?"

"Sure. Why not? That's better than losing it. I can't sell it to you. I've got no papers for it. So sure, you can look after it. That's my gift to the people."

Savic stroked his chin. "This could become quite an international issue." Suddenly, Savic had the look of a hungry man about to sit at a bonfire and cook up a whole lot of sausages.

"Man, that's even better than making it a stupid art project," Ace enthused. "A stupid government project! Hey, those last forever!"

V.

Savic's new investigation committee was an immediate success. With the political judo typical of the region, the honest politician wangled a large and generous support-grant from the Europeans—basically, in order to investigate himself.

The fab now reformed its efforts: from consumer knickknacks to the pressing needs of the state's public sector. Jet-black fire plugs appeared in the arts district. Jet-black hoods for the broken street lights, and jet-black manhole covers for the streets. Governments bought in bulk, so a primary source for the yellow dust was located. The fab churned busily away right in the public square, next to a railroad tanker full of feed-stock.

Borislav returned to his kiosk. He made a play at resuming his normal business. He was frequently called to testify in front of Savic's busy committee. This resulted in Fleka the Gypsy being briefly arrested, but the man skipped bail. No one made any particular effort to find Fleka. They certainly had never made much effort before.

Investigation soon showed that the fabrikator was stolen property from a hospital in Gdansk. Europeans had long known how to make such fabrikators: fabrikators that used carbon nanotubes. They had simply refrained from doing so.

As a matter of wise precaution, the Europeans had decided not to create devices that could so radically disrupt a well-established political and economic order. The pain of such an act was certain to be great. The benefits were doubtful.

One some grand, abstract level of poetic engineering, it obviously made sense to create super-efficient, widely-distributed, cottage-scale factories that could create as much as possible with as little as possible. If one were inventing industrial civilization from the ground up, then fabbing was a grand idea. But an argument of that kind made no sense to the installed base and the established interests. You couldn't argue a voter out of his job. So fabs had been subtly restricted to waxes, plastics, plaster, papier-mache, and certain metals.

Except, that is, for fabs with medical applications. Medicine, which dealt in agonies of life and death, was never merely a marketplace. There was always somebody whose child had smashed and shattered bones. Sooner or later this violently-interested party, researching a cure for his beloved, would find the logjam and scream: WON'T ONE OF YOU HEARTLESS, INHUMAN BASTARDS THINK OF THE CHILDREN?

Of course, those who had relinquished this technology had the children's best interests at heart. They wanted their children to grow up safe within stable, regulated societies. But one could never explain good things for vaporous, potential future children to someone whose heart and soul was twisted by the suffering of an actual, real-life child.

So a better and different kind of fab had come into being. It was watched over with care…but, as time and circumstance passed, it slipped loose.

Eager to spread the fabbing pork through his constituency, Savic commissioned renowned local artists to design a new breed of kiosk. This futuristic Transition Three ultra-kiosk would house the very fab that could make it. Working with surprising eagerness and speed (given that they were on government salary), these artisan-designers created a new, official, state-supported fabbing-kiosk, an alarmingly splendid, well-nigh monumental kiosk, half Ottoman pavilion, half Stalinist gingerbread, and almost one hundred percent black carbon nanotubes, except for a few necessary steel bolts, copper wires and brass staples.

Borislav knew better than to complain about this. He had to abandon his perfectly decent, old-fashioned, customary kiosk, which was swiftly junked and ripped into tiny recyclable shreds. Then he climbed, with pain and resignation, up the shiny black stairsteps into this eerie, oversized, grandiose rock-solid black fort, this black-paneled royal closet whose ornate, computer-calligraphic roof would make meteors bounce off it like graupel hail.

The cheap glass windows fit badly. The new black shelves confused his fingers. The slick black floor sent his chair skidding wildly. The black carbon walls would not take paint, glue or paper. He felt like an utter fool—but this kiosk hadn't been built for his convenience. This was a kiosk for the new Transition Three generation, crazily radical, liberal guys for whom a "kiosk" was no mere humble conduit, but the fortress of a new culture-war.

A kiosk like this new one could be flung from a passing jet. It could hammer the ground like a plummeting thunderbolt and bounce up completely unharmed. With its ever-brimming bags of gold-dust, a cybernetic tumbling of possessions would boil right out of it: *bottles bags knobs latches wheels pumps,* molds for making other things, tools for making other things; *saws, hammers wrenches levers,* drillbits, screws, screwdrivers, *awls pliers scissors punches,* planes, files, rasps, jacks, carts and shears; pulleys, chains and chain hoists, trolleys, cranes, buckets, bottles, barrels.... All of these items sitting within their digital files as neat as chess pieces, sitting there like the very *idea* of chess pieces, like a mental chess-set awaiting human desire to leap into being and action.

As Borislav limped back, each night, from his black battleship super-kiosk back to his mother's apartment, he could see Transition Three insinuating itself into the fabric of his city.

Transition One had once a look all its own: old socialist buildings of bad brick and substandard plaster, peeling like a secret leprosy, then exploding with the plastic branding symbols of the triumphant West: candy bars, franchised fried-food, provocative lingerie.

Transition Two was a tougher business: he remembered it mostly for its lacks and privations. Empty stores, empty roads, crowds of bicycles, the angry hum of newfangled fuel cells, the cheap glitter of solar roofing, insulation stuffed everywhere like the paper in a pauper's shoes. Crunchy, mulchy-looking new construction. Grass on the rooftops, grass in the trolley-ways. Networking masts and dishes. Those clean, cold, flat-panel lights.

This third Transition had its own native look, too. It was the same song and another verse. It was black. It was jet-black, smooth, anonymous, shiny, stainless, with an occasional rainbow shimmer off the layers and grooves whenever the light was just right, like the ghosts of long-vanished oil slicks.

Revolution was coming. The people wanted more of this game than the regime was allowing them to have. There were five of the fabs running in the city now. Because of growing foreign pressure against "the dangerous proliferation," the local government wouldn't make any more fabrikators. So the people were being denied the full scope of their desire to live differently. The people were already feeling different inside, so they were going to take it to the streets. The politicians were feebly trying to split differences between ways of life that just could not be split.

Did the laws of commerce exist for the people's sake? Or did the people exist as slaves of the so-called laws of commerce? That was populist demagoguery, but that kind of talk was popular for a reason.

Borislav knew that civilization existed through its laws. Humanity suffered and starved whenever outside the law. But those stark facts didn't weigh on the souls of the locals for ten seconds. The local people here were not that kind of people. They had never been that kind of people. Turmoil: that was what the people here had to offer the rest of the world.

The people had flown off the handle for far less than this; for a shot fired at some passing prince, for instance. Little street demonstrations were boiling up from left and right. Those demonstrations waxed and waned, but soon the apple-cart would tip hard. The people would take to the city squares, banging their jet-black kitchen pans, shaking their jet-black house keys. Borislav knew from experience that this voice from the people was a nation-shaking racket. The voice of reason from the fragile government sounded like a cartoon mouse.

Borislav looked after certain matters, for there would be no time to look after them, later. He talked to a lawyer and made a new will. He made backups of his data and copies of important documents, and stashed things away in numerous caches. He hoarded canned goods, candles, medicines, tools, even boots. He kept his travel bag packed.

He bought his mother her long-promised cemetery plot. He acquired a handsome headstone for her, too. He even found silk sheets.

VI.

It didn't break in the way he had expected, but then local history could be defined as events that no rational man would expect. It came as a kiosk. It was a brand-new, European kiosk. A civilized, ultimate, decent, well-considered, pre-emptive intervention kiosk. The alien pink-and-white kiosk was beautiful and perfect and clean, and there was no one remotely human inside it.

The automatic kiosk had a kind of silver claw that unerringly picked its goods from its antiseptic shelves, and delivered them to the amazed and trembling customer. These were brilliant goods; they were shiny and gorgeous and tagged with serial numbers and radio-tracking stickers. They glowed all over with reassuring legality: health regulations, total lists of contents, cross-border shipping, tax stamps, associated websites, places to register a complaint.

The superpower kiosk was a thing of interlocking directorates, of 100,000-page regulatory codes and vast, clotted databases, a thing of true brilliance, neurosis and fine etiquette, like a glittering Hapsburg court. And it had been dropped with deliberate accuracy on his own part of Europe—that frail and volatile part—the part about to blow up.

The European kiosk was an almighty vending machine. It replaced its rapidly dwindling stocks in the Black Maria middle of the night, with unmanned cargo vehicles, flat blind anonymous cockroach-like robot things of pink plastic and pink rubber wheels, that snuffled and radared their way across the midnight city and obeyed every traffic law with a crazy punctiliousness.

There was no one to talk to inside the pink European kiosk, although, when addressed through its dozens of microphones, the kiosk could talk the local language, rather beautifully. There were no human relations to be found there. There was no such thing as society: only a crisp interaction.

Gangs of kids graffiti-tagged the pink invader right away. Someone—Ace most likely—made a serious effort to burn it down.

They found Ace dead two days later, in his fancy electric sports car, with three fabbed black bullets through him, and a fabbed black pistol abandoned on the car's hood.

VII.

Ivana caught him before he could leave for the hills.

"You would go without a word, wouldn't you? Not one word to me, and again you just go!"

"It's the time to go."

"You'd take crazy students with you. You'd take football bullies. You'd take tough-guy gangsters. You'd take gypsies and crooks. You'd go there with anybody. And not take me?"

"We're not on a picnic. And you're not the kind of scum who goes to the hills when there's trouble."

"You're taking guns?"

"You women never understand! You don't take carbines with you when you've got a black factory that can make carbines!" Borislav rubbed his unshaven jaw. Ammo, yes, some ammo might well be needed. Grenades, mortar rounds. He knew all too well how much of that stuff had been buried out in the hills, since the last time. It was like hunting for truffles.

And the landmines. Those were what really terrified him, in an unappeasable fear he would take to his grave. Coming back toward the border, once, he and his fellow vigilantes, laden with their loot, marching in step in the deep snow, each man tramping in another's sunken boot-prints.... Then a flat, lethal thing, with a chip, a wad of explosive and a bellyful of steel bolts, counted their passing footsteps. The virgin snow went blood-red.

Borislav might have easily built such a thing himself. The shade-tree plans for such guerrilla devices were everywhere on the net. He had never built such a bomb, though the prospect gnawed him in nightmares.

Crippled for life, back then, he had raved with high fever, freezing, starving, in a hidden village in the hills. His last confidante was his nurse. Not a wife, not a lover, not anyone from any army, or any gang, or any government. His mother. His mother had the only tie to him so profound that she would leave her city, leave everything, and risk starvation to look after a wounded guerrilla. She brought him soup. He watched her cheeks sink in day by day as she starved herself to feed him.

"You don't have anyone to cook for you out there," Ivana begged.

"You'd be leaving your daughter."

"You're leaving your mother."

She had always been able to sting him that way. Once again, despite everything he knew, he surrendered. "All right, then," he told her. "Fine. Be that way, since you want it so much. If you want to risk everything, then you can be our courier. You go to the camp, and you go to the city. You carry some things for us. You never ask any questions about the things."

"I never ask questions," she lied. They went to the camp and she just stayed with him. She never left his side, not for a day or a night. Real life started all over for them, once again. Real life was a terrible business.

VIII.

It no longer snowed much in the old ski villages; the weather was a real mess nowadays, and it was the summers you had to look out for. They set up their outlaw fab plant inside an abandoned set of horse-stables.

The zealots talked wildly about copying an "infinite number of fabs," but that was all talk. That wasn't needed. It was only necessary to make and distribute enough fabs to shatter the nerves of the authorities. That was propaganda of the deed.

Certain members of the government were already nodding and winking at their efforts. That was the only reason that they might win. Those hustlers knew that if the weathervanes spun fast enough, the Byzantine cliques that ruled the statehouse would have to break up. There would be chaos. Serious chaos. But then, after some interval, the dust would have to settle on a new arrangement of power-players. Yesterday's staunch conservative, if he survived, would become the solid backer of the new regime. That was how it worked in these parts.

In the meantime, however, some dedicated group of damned fools would have to actually carry out the campaign on the ground. Out of any ten people willing to do this, seven were idiots. These seven were dreamers, rebels by nature, unfit to run so much as a lemonade stand.

One out of the ten would be capable and serious. Another would be genuinely dangerous: a true, amoral fanatic. The last would be the traitor to the group: the police agent, the coward, the informant.

There were thirty people actively involved in the conspiracy, which naturally meant twenty-one idiots. Knowing what he did, Borislav had gone there to prevent the idiots from quarreling over nothing and blowing the effort apart before it could even start. The three capable men had to be kept focused on building the fabs. The fanatics were best used to sway and intimidate the potential informants.

If they held the rebellion together long enough, they would wear down all the sane people. That was the victory.

The rest was all details, where the devil lived. The idea of self-copying fabs looked great on a sheet of graph paper, but it made little practical sense to make fabs entirely with fabs. Worse yet, there were two vital parts of the fab that simply couldn't be fabbed at all. One was the nozzle that integrated the yellow dust into the black stuff. The other was the big recycler-comb that chewed up the black stuff back into the yellow dust. These two crucial components obviously couldn't be made of the yellow dust or the black stuff.

Instead, they were made of precisely-machined high-voltage European metals that were now being guarded like jewels. These components were way beyond the conspiracy's ability to create.

Two dozen of the fabbing nozzles showed up anyway. They came through the courtesy of some foreign intelligence service. Rumor said the Japanese, for whatever inscrutable reason.

They still had no recycling combs. That was bad. It confounded and betrayed the whole dream of fabs to make them with the nozzles but not the recycling combs. This meant that their outlaw fabs could make things, but never recycle them. A world with fabs like that would be a nightmare: it would slowly but surely fill up with horrible, polluting fabjunk: unusable, indestructible, rock-solid lumps of black slag. Clearly this dark prospect had much affected the counsels of the original inventors.

There were also many dark claims that carbon nanotubes had dire health effects: because they were indestructible fibers, something like asbestos. And that was true: carbon nanotubes did cause cancer. However, they caused rather less cancer than several thousand other substances already in daily use.

It took all summer for the competent men to bang together the first outlaw fabs. Then it became necessary to sacrifice the idiots, in order to distribute the hardware. The idiots, shrill and eager as ever, were told to drive the fabs as far as possible from the original factory, then hand them over to sympathizers and scram.

Four of the five idiots were arrested almost at once. Then the camp was raided by helicopters.

However, Borislav had fully expected this response. He had moved the camp. In the city, riots were under way. It didn't matter who "won" these riots, because rioting melted the status quo. The police were hitting the students with indestructible black batons. The kids were slashing their paddywagon tires with indestructible black kitchen knives.

At this point, one of the fanatics had a major brainwave. He demanded that they send out dozens of fake black boxes that merely *looked* like fabs. There was no political need for their futuristic promises of plenty to actually work.

This cynical scheme was much less work than creating real fabs, so it was swiftly adopted. More than that: it was picked up, everywhere, by copycats. People were watching the struggle: in Bucharest, Lublin, Tbilisi; in Bratislava, Warsaw, and Prague. People were dipping ordinary objects in black lacquer to make them look fabbed. People were distributing handbooks for fabs, and files for making fabs. For every active crank who really wanted to make a fab, there were a hundred people who wanted to know how to do it. Just in case.

Some active cranks were succeeding. Those who failed became martyrs. As resistance spread like spilled ink, there were simply too many people implicated to classify it as criminal activity.

Once the military contractors realized there were very good reasons to make giant fabs the size of shipyards, the game was basically over. Transition Three was the new realpolitik. The new economy was the stuff of the everyday. The older order was over. It was something no one managed to remember, or even wanted to manage to remember.

The rest of it was quiet moves toward checkmate. And then the game just stopped. Someone tipped over the White King, in such a sweet, subtle, velvety way that one would have scarcely guessed that there had ever been a White King to fight against at all.

IX.

Borislav went to prison. It was necessary that somebody should go. The idiots were only the idiots. The competent guys had quickly found good positions in the new regime. The fanatics had despaired of the new dispensation, and run off to nurse their bitter disillusionment.

As a working rebel whose primary job had been public figurehead, Borislav was the reasonable party for public punishment.

Borislav turned himself in to a sympathetic set of cops who would look much better for catching him. They arrested him in a blaze of publicity. He was charged with "conspiracy": a rather merciful charge, given the host of genuine crimes committed by his group. Those were the necessary, everyday crimes of any revolutionary movement, crimes such as racketeering, theft of services, cross-border smuggling, subversion and sedition, product piracy, copyright infringement, money-laundering, fake identities, squatting inside stolen property, illegal possession of firearms, and so forth.

Borislav and his various allies weren't charged with those many crimes. On the contrary; since he himself had been so loudly and publicly apprehended, those crimes of the others were quietly overlooked.

While sitting inside his prison cell, which was not entirely unlike a kiosk, Borislav discovered the true meaning of the old term "penitentiary." The original intention of prisons was that people inside them should be penitent people. Penitent people were supposed to meditate and contemplate their way out of their own moral failings. That was the original idea.

Of course, any real, modern "penitentiary" consisted mostly of frantic business dealings. Nobody "owned" much of anything inside the prison, other than a steel bunk and a chance at a shower, so simple goods such as talcum powder loomed very large in the local imagination. Borislav, who fully understood street-trading, naturally did very well at this. At least, he did much better than the vengeful, mentally limited people who were doomed to inhabit most jails.

Borislav thought a lot about the people in the jails. They, too, were the people, and many of those people were getting into jail because of him. In any Transition, people lost their jobs. They were broke, they lacked prospects. So they did something desperate.

Borislav did not much regret the turmoil he had caused the world, but he often thought about what it meant and how it must feel. Somewhere, inside some prison, was some rather nice young guy, with a wife and kids, whose job was gone because the fabs took it away. This guy had a shaven head, an ugly orange jumpsuit, and appalling food, just like Borislav himself. But that young guy was in the jail with less good reason. And with much less hope. And with much more regret.

That guy was suffering. Nobody gave a damn about him. If there was any justice, someone should mindfully suffer, and be penitent, because of the harsh wrong done that guy.

Borislav's mother came to visit him in the jail. She brought print-outs from many self-appointed sympathizers. The world seemed to be full of strange foreign people who had nothing better to do with their time than to email tender, supportive screeds to political prisoners. Ivana, something of a mixed comfort to him in their days of real life, did not visit the jail or see him. Ivana knew how to cut her losses when her men deliberately left her to do something stupid, such as volunteering for a prison.

These strangers and foreigners expressed odd, truncated, malformed ideas of what he had been doing. Because they were the Voice of History.

He himself had no such voice to give to history. He came from a small place under unique circumstances. People who hadn't lived there would never understand it. Those who had lived there were too close to understand it. There was just no understanding for it. There were just... the events. Events, transitions, new things. Things like the black kiosks.

These new kiosks.... No matter where they were scattered in the world, they all had the sinister, strange, overly-dignified look of his own original black kiosk. Because the people had seen those kiosks. The people knew well what a black fabbing kiosk was supposed to look like. Those frills, those fringes, that peaked top, that was just how you knew one. That was their proper look. You went there to make your kid's baby-shoes indestructible. The kiosks did what they did, and they were what they were. They were everywhere, and that was that.

After twenty-two months, a decent interval, the new regime pardoned him as part of a general amnesty. He was told to keep his nose clean and his mouth shut. Borislav did this. He didn't have much to say, anyway.

X.

Time passed. Borislav went back to the older kind of kiosk. Unlike the fancy new black fabbing kiosk, these older ones sold things that couldn't be fabbed: foodstuffs, mostly.

Now that fabs were everywhere and in public, fabbing technology was advancing by leaps and bounds. Surfaces were roughened so they shone with pastel colors. Technicians learned how to make the fibers fluffier, for bendable, flexible parts. The world was in a Transition, but no transition ended the world. A revolution just turned a layer in the compost heap of history, compressing that which now lay buried, bringing air and light to something hidden.

On a whim, Borislav went into surgery and had his shinbone fabbed. His new right shinbone was the identical, mirror-reversed copy of his left shinbone. After a boring recuperation, for he was an older man now and the flesh didn't heal as it once had, he found himself able to walk on an even keel for the first time in twenty-five years.

Now he could walk. So he walked a great deal. He didn't skip and jump for joy, but he rather enjoyed walking properly. He strolled the boulevards, he saw some sights, he wore much nicer shoes.

Then his right knee gave out, mostly from all that walking on an indestructible artificial bone. So he had to go back to the cane once again. No cure was a miracle panacea: but thanks to technology, the trouble had crept closer to his heart.

That made a difference. The shattered leg had oppressed him during most of his lifetime. That wound had squeezed his soul into its own shape. The bad knee would never have a chance to do that, because he simply wouldn't live that long. So the leg was a tragedy. The knee was an episode.

It was no great effort to walk the modest distance from his apartment block to his mother's grave. The city kept threatening to demolish his old apartments. They were ugly and increasingly old fashioned, and they frankly needed to go. But the government's threats of improvement were generally empty, and the rents would see him through. He was a landlord. That was never a popular job, but someone was always going to take it. It might as well be someone who understood the plumbing.

It gave him great satisfaction that his mother had the last true granite headstone in the local graveyard. All the rest of them were fabbed.

Dr. Grootjans was no longer working in a government. Dr. Grootjans was remarkably well-preserved. If anything, this female functionary from an alien system looked *younger* than she had looked, years before. She had two prim Nordic braids. She wore a dainty little off-pink sweater. She had high heels.

Dr. Grootjans was writing about her experiences in the transition. This was her personal, confessional text, on the net of course, accompanied by photographs, sound recordings, links to other sites, and much supportive reader commentary.

"Her gravestone has a handsome Cyrillic font," said Dr. Grootjans.

Borislav touched a handkerchief to his lips. "Tradition does not mean that the living are dead. Tradition means that the dead are living."

Dr. Grootjans happily wrote this down. This customary action of hers had irritated him at first. However, her strange habits were growing on him. Would it kill him that this over-educated foreign woman subjected him to her academic study? Nobody else was bothering. To the neighborhood, to the people, he was a crippled, short-tempered old landlord. To her, the scholar-bureaucrat, he was a mysterious figure of international significance. Her version of events was hopelessly distorted and self-serving. But it was a version of events.

"Tell me about this grave," she said. "What are we doing here?"

"You wanted to see what I do these days. Well, this is what I do." Borislav set a pretty funeral bouquet against the headstone. Then he lit candles.

"Why do you do this?"

"Why do you ask?"

"You're a rational man. You can't believe in religious rituals."

"No," he told her, "I don't believe. I know they are just rituals."

"Why do it, then?"

He knew why, but he did not know how to give her that sermon. He did it because it was a gift. It was a liberating gift for him, because it was given with no thought of any profit or return. A deliberate gift with *no possibility* of return.

Those gifts were the stuff of history and futurity. Because gifts of that kind were also the gifts that the living received from the dead.

The gifts we received from the dead: those were the world's only genuine gifts. All the other things in the world were commodities. The dead were, by definition, those who gave to us without reward. And, especially: our dead gave to us, the living, within a dead context. Their gifts to us were not just abjectly generous, but archaic and profoundly confusing.

Whenever we disciplined ourselves, and sacrificed ourselves, in some vague hope of benefiting posterity, in some ambition to create a better future beyond our own moment in time, then we were doing something beyond a rational analysis. Those in that future could never see us with our own eyes: they would only see us with the eyes that we ourselves gave to them. Never with our own eyes: always with their own. And the future's eyes always saw the truths of the past as blinkered, backward, halting. Superstition.

"Why?" she said.

Borislav knocked the snow from his elegant shoes. "I have a big heart."

THE HYPERSURFACE
OF THIS DECADE

——————╫•

Today, as of right now, this time-stamped moment, I dwell in the Silicon Roundabout. I live just ten minutes from Old Street Station, amid a swarm of Hackney warrens, which foster seething social-software communities of my fellow London creatives.

My new flat features rapid access to my work, iconic architectural form, and location, location, geo-location!

Deirdre imagines that she has "left our marriage," but thanks mostly to Dopplr, Deirdre can never really "leave me." I know exactly where Deirdre and her iPhone are, right now. Deirdre is attending "Mobile Monday" in that recycled church in Amsterdam with that cheese-eating Dutch start-up guy, that big blond loon who always boasts about his lunches on Twitter.

Deirdre also imagines she has "taken everything that we own," but Deirdre fails to comprehend that I have transcended yesterday's stifling consumer clutter!

Henceforth I shall dwell in the densest cluster of interaction-design talent in Europe. My new abode is rugged, bracing, confrontational: the seductiveness of masculine red brick walls, the bull's-blood hue of rivet-stained Edwardian girders! I take courage in the brisk removal of my building's entire second floor. Even the structure's splinters and splashes of Blitz shrapnel have a surprising delicacy and charm.

Great iron driving wheels used to rumble above my netbook dock. Those crumbling architraves strongly suggest awesome steampunk rookeries, industrial sweatshops, lacy bordellos even: a ghost-host of time-layered East End urban phantoms, which were likely never here in the first place, but could all be re-created promptly with some muslin and laminated fiberboard.

Bruce Sterling

As yet, I possess no stove, no toilet, no bathtub and no bed. In fact, there are no physical objects in my flat whatsoever, except for my two roll-aboard suitcases, this Taiwanese netbook, and one metric ton of natural ABS plastic on a giant wooden cable reel. The cable reel doubles as the coffee table on which I write this informative blogpost.

But consider this: a searing, transformative Hertzian wave of broadband permeates everything around me!

Those narrow, chilly holes up there may not be "windows" as windows are conventionally defined, but what a relief to escape the glass-and-steel lucidity that is the standard Norman Foster approach to reconversion! My truncated portico, where the door used to have hinges…yes, perhaps there is some small loss of dignity in the fact that any odd customer of the Gothic Bondage shop next door can waltz in and out of here, "stealing" my possessions. But the key insight is—they're not possessions. Possessions are over. They are data! Data which sometimes manifests itself as my possessions. This refuse then folds itself right back into the social streams of eBay and Freecycle. Light-of-footprint. Door-to-door. Peer-to-peer.

Freedom is just another word for nothing! There is no dead weight in my urban spatiality. No clotted semiotics, cajoling me to behave in the stereotyped haute-bourgeois manner that Deirdre once used to stifle me.

Dematerialisation is defined by its interfaces. That which was a product will become a service. That which was a service will accelerate at warp speed toward de-monetization on the Path-to-Free. So this is not so much a post-divorce flat as a vibrant zone of interactive transaction.

It is crucial to avoid superimposing the dead past's invisible hand onto my new Web-Squared situation, stunting the techno-possibilities of the approaching twenty-teens through some sordid desire to make my life comprehensible.

Just what is it that makes today's crises so different, so appealing? How can I superimpose the starkly contemporary onto this rich, multimodal urban landscape of abject financial, moral, infrastructural and marital collapse?

The answer is simplicity itself: No effort need be made to reconcile the differing scales of the virtual and the material. They can simply coexist in raw potential.

Pardon me: that rumbling and that toxic reek suggest another delivery truck. I think this one must be for me. Let me save this text now.

Thank you for waiting. My overnight shipment has indeed arrived. Let's get straight to the great unboxing, shall we?

This device (see my FlickR set for detailed photos) is the Eclair numerically-controlled home fabricator. I happen to know the Eclair's developers personally—we've never "met," but we're all huge on Facebook together—so please don't use my user experience as an exact guide for your own version of the Eclair.

This sleek and sturdy overnight parcel contains everything one might need for do-it-yourself, open-source digital home fabrication.

How is this even possible? In this precise manner:

First, I rip the cables out of the bubblepack. One USB2TTL cable to talk to all my new machinery. Various cat5e cables to wire the fabricator system, and to enable me to screen a galaxy of global video entertainment through poorly-policed peer-to-peer sharing services.

One standard ATX power supply, made in China; its lavish carbon-footprint will also serve me as my hotplate.

A toolkit with a glittering host of aluminium tongs, tweezers, spanners, hex keys, and IKEA-knockoff assembly tools. These items will double as my cutlery, since I'll be living mostly off ramen noodles from the local Korean grocery, when not grabbing a tasty plate of feijao maravilma over at the "Favela Chic" Franco-Brazilian bar and techno niteclub.

I also possess three NEMA 17 stepper-motors to drive my fabricator. This nifty Tyvek bag contains all the nuts, bolts, belts, pulleys and bearings. These gleaming rods are high-quality precision-ground steel shafts for the X and Y axes.

This device also boasts pre-assembled 3rd generation electronics from the vengeful wreckage of the Ivrea interaction-design school. These bearded techno-intelligentsia were once harmless left-wing Italian academics, but now they are fully prepared to crush the planet's entire industrial order through methods even the Chinese can't comprehend.

I have a pinch-wheel plastruder to melt my giant reel of plastic cable. It extrudes that molten plastic as solid, durable, slightly warped and drippy consumer objects. I mean fruit bowls. Forks. Lampshades and hat racks. Most anything Deirdre might have found while leafing through her overpriced shelter magazines.

These pale, gormless extrusions of the formless will have no copyrights, no branding, no consumer cachet, and no Walter Benjamin "aura." They will just work, they will function practically. They will function in the same mute, ugly way that a prison shiv will work for some East London hoodlum locked up half his lifetime for knife-crime. You may imagine there's some vast class chasm between this old-school knife-waving wide-boy and me, a bespectacled, hypermodern Web geek—but let me confide this to you: he's my landlord.

Some assembly will be required. Clearly. I had better get right after that now. The instructions say that assembly will take me four hours (more, if I laser-engrave my own casing). Four hours is not too much to ask of urban futurity. It took me all day just to write this blog post (I had to stop periodically, to check my Twitter stream).

But now I do have to stop. I simply must. I must put away the Red Bull cans, and stop clicking and typing. I have to stop, so I can print my bed.

I have to print my bed, so that I can lie in it.

WHITE
FUNGUS

———— ‖•

As I was explaining to you last time, I named the boy 'Vitruvius.' I was younger then, and maybe a little too proud of my architecture degree. It was one of the last, full, cum-laude degrees from a major European university.

After I graduated, the Education Bubble burst. Universities were noble institutions nine hundred years old, but their business model had failed. Their value chain had been de-linked. Their unique value proposition was declined by the consumer. Globalization had routed around the Academy.

Maybe you can remember how people used to talk back then. We were impotent in our long emergency, but we were wonderfully glib.

So Petra and I, and baby Vitruvius—"Rufus" for daily use—went home to the Eurocore. The world was in turmoil, but I was young, I was strong, I had training. It was time to make a go of my architectural career.

I wanted to build in the place where I grew up. Our home was not Brussels, or Lille, or Luxembourg, or any of the formal venues in the Eurocore that were legal, historical cities. My home was that nameless locale that my professors called "white fungus."

White Fungus was the edge-city. Semi-regulated, semi-prosperous, automobilized expanses of commercial European real-estate. Mostly white brick, hence the name. White Fungus had paved the region, while city planners were bored, or distracted, or bought-off.

We were natives of White Fungus. After eight years in school, I understood architecture, but White Fungus was what I knew.

There were six huge, civilization-crushing reasons why the white fungus could not survive. First, the energy problems. Second, the weather crisis. Third, the demographics. The elderly people in charge of our law and finance were hiding in gated enclaves. They still had the votes, they held the official positions, but they pottered around in their shabby-genteel misery, terrified by the weird turn the world had taken. They lived in a computer-game where they pretended to have incomes, pretended to obey laws, and pretended to lobby non-existent world governments. We were their children. So we pretended to read their emails.

The world financial crisis was world-smashing factor number four. I'd like to explain that financial crisis. Nobody can do that. Let's just say that a 19th-century method of mapping value no longer fit the networked reality of the 2020s. Money had tried to cover too much of existence. Money was over-stretched, like an abacus that fails to do advanced math. The Euro was long gone. Tiny national currencies made no more economic sense than local newspapers.

I tried to explain some of this to Petra, including crisis number five, which was our huge public health crisis, and also world-crisis number six, which, frankly, I've forgotten now. Number six was a major issue at the time.

I explained that the lives that our parents had led had no further relevance for us. We were a modern European couple with a child, yet we were beyond help. No "man on horseback" was going to save us. No authority had coherent answers for our woes. I had every piece of music recorded in the past 200 years inside a backup the size of a match-head. But computers were not sources of wealth for us. Moore's Law had smeared computers around the planet, with silicon cheaper than glass. The poorest people in the world had cellphones: cellphones were the emblems of poverty. So we were badly off. We were worse off than former Communists in 1989 missing their Nomenklatura. We didn't even have the *ability to begin to define* what had gone wrong with our existence.

We would have to architect some other order. Another way of life.

This was not what Petra perceived as our marriage bargain. We were two children of privilege with arty instincts. Our worst problem should have been picking the storage units for last year's couture. We also had a baby, a bold act Petra now regretted.

Our young family's safety and security was supposed to be my responsibility. There were better places in the world than White Fungus; why not flee there, why not rush over and emigrate? Petra could see those cities just by clicking on her screen. London, New York, Barcelona, these ancient cities still existed, they hadn't vaporized. They were, however, visibly panicking as the seas rose at their docks, washing in boats full of the rootless and hopeless.

Petra had a screen; I had a screen; everybody in the world had those screens. Any city that looked like a lifeboat would surely be besieged by émigrés. I knew that. We were safer in White Fungus, where we belonged. There we were humble, nameless, and steeped in massive urban failure, which was our heritage.

The truth was that I was born a regional architect. I wanted to build where I lived, in the locale that had shaped me. The ruins of the unsustainable were the one frontier fully open to the people of my generation. Our great challenge was not the six great bogies that we feared so much. It was our own bewilderment, our learned helplessness.

As things worsened by fits and starts, Petra tossed in her recurring nightmares. She was sure that the lights would go out all over Europe. We would freeze and starve in the dark. We were doomed to a survivalist dystopia, with leather-clad science-fiction savages picking meat off each other's thighbones. I could not convince Petra that there were no savages in our world. Everybody from the Abidjan slums to the Afghan highlands was on the Internet. The planet was saturated, networked from the bottom-up like the mycelial threads of white wood-rot. So we could access anything, and yet we could solve nothing.

Unfortunately, my brilliant theoretical framing could not assuage her primal fears. Our marriage failed as fully and glumly as our other institutions. Petra left me and the boy. She fled to the south of France. There she became the girlfriend of a French cop. This gendarme couldn't protect her, any more than I could, but his jackboots and body armor made him resemble security.

Rufus and I moved in with my father. That seemed to work for a small while—then my father left us, too. He left us to engage in European politics, which he considered his duty. Sooner or later, my father assured me, our turmoil would return to a coherent European order, with a tax base, a social safety net, designer parking meters, and regulation low-flow green flush toilets. In stark reality, Europe was swiftly becoming a giant half-mafia flea-market where even Denmark behaved like Sicily.

In Brussels, the full repertoire of our golden civilization was still sitting there, on paper. All the codes, the civil rights, the human rights, the election rituals, the solidarity, the transparency, the huge regulation. Yet Brussels itself, as a badly overloaded urban entity, was visibly imploding. The surreal emanations from Brussels sailed right over the heads of the population without encountering the least resistance from the fabric of reality.

Despair is a luxury for a single father. I was rich in self-pity, but one fine day, I forgot about that. I had lost so much that the fabric of my new existence had a lively, parametric texture: it was like sand dunes, like foam. Rufus was beginning to walk, to talk. Rufus was never my burden: Rufus was my client. He was my strength.

My goal was to map the structure for his needs.

Food, of course. Young children are very keen on the idea of food. Where to get food? Like most European politicians, my father imagined that European cities were frail, artificial constructions, cordially supported by European yeoman farmers—the sturdy peasantry who pocketed the EU tax grants. This perception was untrue. Except for a few small-town hucksters clowning it up for the food-heritage industry, there were no European peasants. The reality was massive agro-business technicians organized in state-supported conglomerates. They enjoyed regulatory lock-in and vertical monopolies through big-box urban grocery chains.

That system no longer functioned. These apparatchiks were all broke. The rural zones of Europe were, if anything, worse off than the cities, which at least had some inventive options.

Logically, industrial farmers should move into places like White Fungus and industrially farm the lawns. Derelict buildings should be gutted and transformed into hydroponic racks. White Fungus was, in fact, an old agricultural region: it was ancient farmland with tarmac on top of it. So: rip up the parking lots. Plant them.

Naturally, no one in White Fungus wanted this logical solution. Farming was harsh, dull, boring, patient work, and no one was going to pay the locals to farm. So, by the standards of the past, our survival was impossible.

The solution was making the defeat of our hunger look like fun. People gardened in five-minute intervals, by meshing webcams with handsets. A tomato vine ready to pick sent someone an SMS. Game-playing gardeners cashed in their points at local market stalls and restaurants. This scheme was an "architecture of participation." Since the local restaurants were devoid of health and employee regulations, they were easy to start and maintain. Everything was visible on the Net. We used ingenious rating systems.

People keenly resented me for this intervention. My coldly logical scheme was about as popular as Minimalism. I did it anyway. I designed the vertical racks for the outsides of old buildings, I designed the irrigation systems, and I also planted the webcams to deter the hordes of eager fruit thieves. I performed this labor in my "free time," because the need to eat is not a "business model." However, my child was eating fresh produce. All the children were eating. Once other parents grasped this reality, I received some help.

No mere fuel crisis could stop movement on the roads of Europe. The Romany came into their own in these surreal conditions; suddenly, these stateless, agnostic hucksters became the genuine Europeans. The gypsies still looked scary, they were still chiseling us, and they still couldn't be bothered to obey the law. But demographically, there were hordes of them. They roamed the continent in booze-fueled bus caravans, which spat out gaudy mobile marketplaces. The Romany bartered anything that wasn't nailed down. They were saving our lives.

At this point in our epic, Lillian appeared. Yes, Lillian. I must finally talk about her now, although Lillian was an issue I've been avoiding for years. Lillian never seemed like a major issue, even when I tried to make her into one. Still, she was what she was.

Lillian was the first true citizen of the new White Fungus. Lillian was native to White Fungus in the way that Cubism was native to Montparnasse.

Certain people have an ability to personify a place, to become an instantiation of it. There are Cockneys more native to London than a chimney-pot, and Milanese more Milanese than a glassed arcade. Lillian had that quality. She was the White Fungus in its mushroom flesh.

White Fungus never lacked for vagrants, interlopers, and derelicts. We even had a mafia and some amateur terrorists. After all, Europe was suffering six major forms of turmoil. That meant that troubled, evil people shared our daily lives. These wretches were not primitive or ignorant people; they were net-savvy and urban, just like us. So every one of these marauders had some beautiful rhetorical justification. They were "entrepreneurs." They were "community organizers," or "security forces," or even "rescue personnel." The worst of the lot were religious zealots eager to abolish all things "secular." The second-worst were Marxists "critically resisting" something long dead.

Lillian never went in for that behavior. Lillian was a backpacker, a silent drifter. Lillian was "undocumented." She was on the run from something, from someone—her creditors back in the former USA, presumably. Being American, Lillian was from a society that could no longer afford itself. Europe had blown six fuses, but the troubles in the United States of America were as dense as Sanskrit; the Americans had all of our troubles, plus several lost wars.

When I pressed the matter—I was impolite that way—Lillian told me that she had grown up in a trailer. Her parents had "home-educated" her, inside some Beatnik tin contraption, randomly rambling the American continent. Lillian had never owned a home, she had not so much as a postal code. Criminals had stolen her identity. When I looked her up on the Net, there were thirteen Lillian J. Andertons, every one of them in debt and most of them on parole. It seems entirely possible that Lillian had somehow re-stolen her own identity—deliberately vanishing into bureaucratic ineptitude.

When Lillian appeared among us, with her agenda cinched round her waist like a secret money-belt, a new vernacular architecture was already gripping White Fungus.

The region had been designed for cars, of course. Built for portly car-driving suburbanites, people eager to plunge into individual home ownership, into its unsustainability, its eventual chaos.

White Fungus was a developers' mélange of mass-produced skeuomorphic "styles," realized in lath, plaster, wire, glulam, and white brick. Those structures, dependent on climate-control, were rapidly peeling and rotting. The structures that survived had permanently opened doors and windows, and had vomited open their contents. Their occupants, deprived of delivery trucks and package services, were hustling permanent garage sales, living from barter. Abandoned buildings were torched by bored teens or ripped apart to tack, bolt and staple onto the living properties.

This denser, digital-feudal housing was easier to patrol, defend and heat. Almost everyone was growing marijuana, in the touching illusion that this fast-growing weed had some value. This was the new vernacular look of White Fungus: this tottering Frankenstein make-do patchwork, this open-air Lagos-style junkspace.

White Fungus

Lillian looked like that. That was her milieu. An indifferent female vagrant with a backpack, a billed hat, thick rubber boots, multi-pocketed work-jeans and, to top it all, a man's high-visibility jacket in tarnished silver and aviation orange. Never any lipstick, scissored-off hair. Never anxious, never in a hurry. She had no more origin or destination than a stray cat. Asking for nothing, demanding nothing. Commonly she was munching something from a small canvas bag and reading a used paperback book. Lillian had mushroomed among us when no one was looking.

In times of turmoil, people love to talk about their troubles. I still talk about those times, as you can see. That was years ago, and life has become quite different now, but those were my formative times, my heroic times. That's the consolation of a general catastrophe: that misery loves its company so dearly.

Lillian did not want to talk about her troubles, or about anyone's. Lillian wanted to act. Demands for conversation bored her: they sent her out the door, into the street. There she merged into the fabric of the urban. She became unfathomably busy.

Lillian was on a mission: a one-woman rescue of junkspace. "Guerrilla urbanist" might describe Lillian, except that I'm flattering myself. In truth, I was the guerrilla urbanist in White Fungus. I like to think my efforts drew her there.

I was very busy, like she was. Once my boy was fed, the boy had to be schooled. White Fungus had a school of course, but it had no budget and its teachers had fled. It sat dark, paralyzed and useless at the end of a long commute.

We had no money for new construction. This meant that the children had to build their own school. Their parents were not particularly public-spirited, but they were driven mad by their children's incessant presence underfoot. So these parents commandeered, they squatted, a dead retail box-store. We built the new school inside this vast, echoing space.

The school was made of cardboard: a ramifying set of parametric cardboard igloos. An insulated playground. Since there was no educational bureaucracy left, there was no more reason to build a school like a barracks. Let the children wreck their school, paint it, pierce it, kick holes in it; after all, it was cardboard.

My son's school, a playground set of ramifying continua without doors or right angles, was generated out of package-strapping, velcro, and glue. The structure was a blatant fire hazard, in brutal opposition to a hundred building codes, and it had to be rebuilt every five weeks. This did not matter. The "curriculum" had nothing to do with previous school systems, either.

The school was no monument; as I said, the costs were mostly borne by sweat-equity, and that mostly from sweaty little children. Still, it was the first new building in White Fungus that looked like us—like the *new* us, like something novel we ourselves had created, that wasn't a rip-off or a hand-me-down of the old ways. We were poor people with computers, so we had to set our computers to work on the poorest and humblest materials. On recycled paper. On fiberboard. On bundled straw. On recycled plastic, on cellulose glue, on mud, on foam.

On the abject. Machine processing always looked best when applied to the abject. Because the simplicity of the materials made one see the brilliance of the process. And what we could see, we could inhabit.

Since Rufus never wanted to "come home" from his wondrous new playground, I moved in with him. As a resident intellectual, the locals were keen to have me to teach school. I of course had no salary and no pedagogical clue. So I taught the rubrics of assemblage, the complexity of dynamic systems, and the primacy of experience in the philosophy of Charles Sanders Peirce. Those Peirce studies interested the children most. Indeterminate phenomenology was the one issue they couldn't master through Wikipedia in five minutes.

Lillian had no visible interest in children. The school brought Lillian out of hiding because of her silent passion for abandoned buildings. I remember that she owned a thin, shiny hammock made of heat-reflective fabric, some American astronaut toy. The hammock came with anchors. She would dig her rubber boot-heels in, climb the junction between two walls—and reach the overhead corners, which are the deadest spaces in architecture. There she would fix her mirror-colored hammock, climb inside it and vanish.

Whenever Lillian was gone, she was commonly four meters above people's heads, invisibly sleeping. Sometimes I'd see the glow of a solar-battery booklight up there, as she silently paged through the works of Buckminster Fuller.

There was a legendary period in Fuller's life, when Fuller dropped out of society, said nothing for two years, and invented his own conceptual vocabulary. In retrospect, I'm quite sure Lillian had experienced something similar. Fuller, for instance, realized that mankind lives on a globe and not a Euclidean plane. Fuller therefore used to refer to the direction "down" as "in," and "up" as "out." Fuller theorized that walking "instairs" and "outstairs" might help us to pilot SpaceShip Earth. In the long run, we got neither Utopia nor Oblivion; we got what we have.

Lillian took some similar approach, but she never spoke about it. Her practice had to do with junkspaces. Useful work could be done in junkspaces, but never within the parameters of reason. Junkspace was everywhere in White Fungus. Traffic islands. Empty elevator shafts. Gaps within walls, gaps between administrative zones and private properties. Debris-strewn alleys. Rafterspace. Emergency stairs for demolished buildings. Nameless spaces, unseen, unserviced and unlit. No economic, social or political activity ever transpired there. They were just— junked spaces, the voids, the absences in the urban fabric. This is where Lillian existed. This was her homeland.

She was always busy. Living in spaces no organized system could see, she took actions no organized system would take. For instance: if cars become rare or nonexistent, then bicycle lanes should appear. Of course, this rarely happens. Someone has to study the streets with care, find the paint, and perform the work. The administration taxed with such labor no longer exists. Worse, no shamefaced official wants to admit that the cars are truly gone, that a glorious past has collapsed through sucking its own exhaust, and that the present is abject.

Physically, it is quite simple to re-paint a street for a horde of bicycles. One small, determined adult could do this useful task in two or three nights. If they asked no permission from anyone. If they demanded no money for doing it. If they carried out that act with cool subterfuge and with crisp graphic precision, so that it looked "official." If they calmly risked any possible arrest and punishment for this illicit act. And if they told no one, ever, about the work they did, or why, or how.

This was what Lillian was doing. At first, I simply couldn't believe it. Of course I noticed her interventions, though most untrained eyes never saw them. I saw the work and I was, I confess, thunderstruck by its tremendous romantic mystery.

Here was this uncanny female creature, diligently operating outside any comprehensible reward system. Lillian was not a public servant, an activist, a political campaigner, a nun devoted to religious service; she wasn't working for money, or ethics, or fame, or to help the community. She wasn't even an artist, least of all a prankster, or a "subversive" of anything in particular. When she dropped sunflower seeds in a dead tree pit, when she replaced and re-routed useless traffic signs, tore out the dead surveillance cameras.... She was just...being herself.

Those mushroom spores. Surely that was the strangest part of it. A mushroom pops out overnight: but the mushroom itself is a fruiting-body. The network of the mushroom, those tangled mycelial threads, are titanic, silent, invisible things, some of the oldest living beings on Earth. Seeding flowers is one thing—your grandmother might do that, it's warm, it's cuddly, it's "green"—but seeding mushroom spores? Or spreading soil bacteria. To "befriend" the bacteria: who would ever see that? Who on Earth would ever know that you were the friend of microbes?

Well, I would know. Myself. Of course I would learn that, in the way that a man's obsession with a woman makes it necessary for him to know. There's nothing commoner than a lonely man, with his "chivalrous concern," stalking a woman—whether she returns his feelings, or not.

They say—well, some sociobiologists say—that every creative work of the male species is a form of courting behavior. I could never make Lillian come to visit me, but, infallibly, I could get her to visit a project.

The projects started small, with the children, who were also small. The new architectural order scarcely looked like order, because it was growing in a different ontological space: not "utilitas, firmitas and venustas," but massing, structure and texture. My personal breakthrough came when I began practicing "digital architecture" without any "computers." I was adapting and upgrading the materialist methods of Gaudi and Frei Otto. I don't want to go into that subject in depth, since there are so many learned treatises written about it now. At the time, we were not learning it, we were living it. Learning becomes so tiresome.

Let me simply summarize it as what it was: white fungus. A zeitgeist growing in the shelter of decay. First, it silently ate out the dead substance. When that work was done, it burst up through the topsoil. Then it was everywhere.

Our architecture did not "work." We ourselves were no longer "working" as that enterprise was formerly understood. We were living, and living rather well, once we found to the nerve to proclaim that. To manifest our life in our own space and time.

"If we can crack the design of the models necessary to accomplish this, it will propagate virally across the entire world." I didn't say that: but I did hear it.

The Internet—we used to call it a "commons." Yet it was nothing like any earlier commons: in a true commons, people relate directly to one another, convivially, commensally. Whereas when they train themselves, alone, silently, on a screen, manifesting ideas and tools created and stored by others, they do not have to be social beings. They can owe the rest of the human race no bond of allegiance. They can be what Lillian was: truly, radically alone. A frontier wanderer with no map for her territories. Hard, isolated, stoic and a builder.

She was the worst lover I ever had: worse than you could imagine. To be in her arms was to encounter a woman who had read about the subject and was practicing sexual activity. It was like banging into someone on a sidewalk. Other aspects of our intercourse held more promise: because there were urban practices a single individual could never do within a reasonable time. Exploring, patching and clearing sewers. Turning swimming pools into aquaculture sumps. Installing park benches and bicycle parks. Erecting observation towers on street corners, steel aeries made of welded rebar where Lillian liked to sit and read, alone.

Lillian was no engineer, she had no fondness for electrical power or moving mechanical parts, but there were urban interventions that required such skills. There, at least, I could be of some service to her.

Inevitably, I could feel her growing distant, or rather, distant from me. "You don't need a woman," she said at last, "you need a nest." That was not a reproach, because, yes, in White Fungus we did need nests. Lonely women were never in short supply.

Lillian appeared at my construction sites less frequently, then not at all. Then her friends.... I wouldn't call them "friends," but they were clearly associates of hers, people who had intuited her aims and who mimicked her activities. Women, mostly. A cocktail party or a knitting-bee had more social cohesion than these women. They had no logo, no budget and no ideology. They were mercilessly focussed, like the Rubble

Women of post-war Berlin. They were dusty women with shovels and barrows, and with no urge to discuss the matter. They did things to and for the city, in broad daylight. We learned not to fuss about that.

These women were looking after Lillian, it seemed, in the way that they might take in a stray cat. With no thought of reward, no means and no ends. Just to do it: because stray cats are from the street. So Lillian was gone, as she was always gone. Several months passed.

When she at length reappeared, I never saw her. She left me with a basket and a note. "My work here is done," said the note. My second son was inside that basket. Not much need for talk about the subject: he was my futurity, just like my first one.

THE
EHTERMINATOR'S
WANT AD

So, I'm required to write this want-ad in order to get any help with my business. Only I have, like, a very bad trust rating on this system. I have rotten karma and an awful reputation. "Don't even go there, don't listen to a word he says: because this guy is pure poison."

So, if that kind of crap is enough for you, then you should stop reading this right now.

However, somebody is gonna read this, no matter what. So let me just put it all out on the table. Yes, I'm a public enemy. Yes, I'm an ex-con. Yes, I'm mad, bad, and dangerous to link to.

But my life wasn't always like this. Back in the good old days, when the world was still solid and not all termite-eaten like this, I used to be a well-to-do, well-respected guy.

Let me explain what went on in prison, because you're probably pretty worried about that part.

First, I was a nonviolent offender. That's important. Second, I turned myself in to face "justice". That shows that I knew resistance was useless. Also a big point on my side.

So, you would think that the maestros of the new order would cut me some slack in the karma ratings: but no. I'm never trusted. I was on the losing side of a socialist revolution. They didn't call me a "political prisoner" of their "revolution," but that's sure what went on. If you don't believe *that,* you won't believe anything else I say, so I might as well say it flat-out.

So, this moldy jail I was in was this old dot-com McMansion, out in the Permanent Foreclosure Zone in the dead suburbs. That's where they cooped us up. This gated community was built for some vanished rich people. That was their low-intensity prison for us rehab detainees.

As their rehab population, we were a so-called "resiliency commune." This meant we were penniless, and we had to grow our own food, and also repair our own jail. Our clothes were unisex plastic orange jumpsuits. They had salvaged those somewhere. They always had plenty of those.

So, we persisted out there as best we could, under videocam surveillance, with parole cuffs on our ankles. See, that's our life. Every week, our itchy, dirty column of detainees gets to march thirteen miles into town, where our captors live. We do hard-labor "community service" there with our brooms, shovels, picks and hoes. We get shown off in public as a warning to the others.

This place outside was a Beltway suburb before Washington was abandoned. The big hurricane ran right over it, and crushed it down pretty good, so now it's a big green hippie jungle. Our prison McMansion has termites, roaches, mold and fleas, but once it was a nice house. This rambling wreck of a town is half storm-debris. All the lawns are replaced with wet, weedy, towering patches of bamboo, or marijuana—or hops, or kenaf, whatever (I never could tell those farm crops apart).

The same goes for the "garden roofs," which are dirt piled on top of the dirty houses. There are smelly goats running loose, chickens cackling. Salvaged umbrellas and chairs are toppled in the empty streets. No traffic signs, because there are no cars.

Sustainable Utopia here is a densely crowded settlement full of people in poorly washed clothing who are hanging out making nice. Constant gossip—they call that "social interaction." No sign of that one percent of the population that once owned half of America. The rich elite just blew it totally. They dropped their globalized ball. They panicked. So they're in jail, like us. Or they're in exile somewhere, or else they jumped out of penthouses screaming when the hyperinflation ate them alive.

And boy, do I ever miss them. No more billboards, no more chain stores, no big-box Chinese depots and no neon fried-food shacks. It's become another world, as in "another world is possible," and, it's very possible, and we're stuck in there. It's very real, and it's very smelly. There are constant power blackouts.

Every once in a while, some armed platoon of "resilient nation-builder" militia types comes by on their rusty bicycles. Sometimes they bring shot-up victims on stretchers. The Liberated Socialist Masses are plucking their homemade banjos on their rickety porches. Lots of liberty, equality, fraternity, solidarity, compost dirt, unshaved legs and dense crowding.

Otherwise, the crickets chirp.

Those are, like, the *lucky people* who are *outside* our prison. These cooperative people are the *networked future.*

So, my cellmate Claire is this forty-something career lobbyist who used to be my boss inside the Beltway. Claire is full of horror stories about the cruelty of the socialist regime. Because, in the old days before we got ourselves arrested, alarmist tales of this kind were Claire's day-job. Claire peddled political spin to the LameStream Media to make sure that corporations stayed in command, so that situations like our present world stayed impossible.

Obviously Claire was not that great at this strategy. Me, I was more of the geek technician in our effort. My job was to methodically spam and troll the sharing-networks. I would hack around with them, undermine them, and make their daily lives difficult. Threaten IP lawsuits. Spread some Fear, Uncertainty and Doubt. Game their reputation systems. Gold-farm their alternative economies. Engage in DDOS attacks. Harass the activist ringleaders with blistering personal insults. The usual.

Claire and I had lots of co-workers all up and down K-Street. Both seaboards, too, and all over Texas. Lavishly supported by rich-guy think-tanks, we were the covert operatives in support of an ailing system. We did that work because it paid great.

Personally, I loved to buy stuff: I admired a consumer society. I sincerely liked to carry out a clean, crisp, commercial transaction: the kind where you simply pay some money for goods and services. I liked driving my SUV to the mall, whipping out my alligator wallet, and buying myself some hard liquor, a steak dinner, and maybe a stripper. All that awful stuff at the Pottery Barn and Banana Republic, when you never knew "Who the hell was buying that?" That guy was me.

Claire and I hated the sharing networks, because we were paid to hate them. We hated all social networks, like Facebook, because they destroyed the media that we owned. We certainly hated free software, because it was like some ever-growing anti-commercial fungus. We hated search engines and network aggregators, people like Google—not because Google was evil, but because they *weren't*. We really hated "file-sharers"—the swarming pirates who were chewing up the wealth of our commercial sponsors.

We hated all networks on principle: we even hated power networks. Wind and solar only sorta worked, and were very expensive. We despised green power networks because climate change was a myth. Until the climate actually changed. Then the honchos who paid us started drinking themselves to death.

If you want to see a truly changed world, then a brown sky really makes a great start. We could tell the public, "Hey, the sky up there is still blue, who do you believe, me or your lying eyes?" And we tried that, but we ran out of time for it. After that tipping-point, our bottom-line economy was not 'reality' at all. That was the myth.

My former life in mythland had suited me just great. Now I had no air conditioning. My world was wet, dirty, smelly, moldy, swarming with fleas, chiggers, bedbugs and mosquitoes. Also, I was in prison. When myths implode, that's what happens to good people.

So, Claire and I discussed our revenge, whenever we were out of earshot and oversight of the solar-powered prison webcams. Claire and I spent a lot of time on revenge fantasies, because that kept our morale up.

"Look, Bobby," she told me, as she scratched graffiti in the wall with a ten-penny nail, "this rehab isn't a proper 'prison' at all! This a bullshit psychological operation intended to brainwash us. Leftists in power always do that! If they give you a fair trial, you can at least get a sentence and do time. If they claim you are crazy, they can sit on your neck forever!"

"Maybe we really are crazy now," I said. "Having the sky change color can do that to people."

"There's only one way out of this Kumbaya nuthouse," she said. "We gotta learn to talk the way they want to hear! So that's our game plan from now on. We act very contrite, we do their bongo dance, whatever. Then they let us out of this gulag. After that, we can take some steps."

Claire was big on emigrating from the USA. Claire somehow imagined that there was some country in the world that didn't have weather. The inconvenient laws of physics had never much appealed to Claire. We'd donated the laws of physics to our opponents by pretending that air wasn't air. Now the long run of that tactic was splattered all around us. We had nothing left but worthless paper money and some Red State churches half-full of Creationists.

We had gone bust. We had suffered a vast, Confederate-style defeat. The economy was Gone With the Wind, and everybody was gonna stay poor, angry and dirt-stupid for the next century.

So: when we weren't planting beans in the former back yard, or digging mold out of the attic insulation, we had to do rehab therapy. This was our prisoner consciousness-building encounter scheme. The regime made us play social games. We weren't allowed computer games in prison: just dice, graph paper, and some charcoal sticks that we made ourselves.

So, we played this elaborate paper game called "Dungeons and Decency." Three times a week. The lady warden was our Dungeon Master.

This prison game was diabolical. It was very entertaining, and compulsively playable. This game had been designed by left-wing interaction designers, the kind of creeps who built not-for-profit empires like Wikipedia. Except they'd designed it for losers like us.

Everybody in rehab had to role-play. We had to build ourselves another identity, because this new pretend-identity was supposed to help us escape the stifling spiritual limits of our previous, unliberated, greedy individualist identities.

In this game, I played an evil dwarf. With an axe. Which would have been okay, because that identity was pretty much me all along. Except that the game's reward system had been jiggered to reward elaborate acts of social collaboration. Of course we wanted to do raids and looting and cool fantasy fighting, but that wasn't on. We were very firmly judged on the way we played this rehab game. It was never about grabbing the gold. It was all about forming trust coalitions so as to collectively readjust our fantasy infrastructure.

This effort went on endlessly. We played for ages. We kept demanding to be let out, they kept claiming we didn't get it yet. The prison food got a little better. The weather continued pretty bad. We started getting charity packages. Once some folk singers came by, and played us some old Johnny Cash songs. Otherwise, the gaming was pretty much it.

A whole lot was resting on this interactive Dungeons game. If you did great, they gave you some meat and maybe a parole hearing. If you blew it off, you were required to donate blood into the socialized health-care system. Believe you me, when they tap you more than a couple of times, on a diet of homegrown cabbage? You start feeling mighty peaked.

Yeah, it got worse. Because we had to cooperate with other teams of fantasy game players in other prisons. These other convicts rated our game performance, while we were required to rate them. We got to see the highlights of their interaction on webcams—(we prisoners were always on webcams).

We were supposed to rate these convicts on how well they were sloughing off their selfish ways, and learning to integrate themselves into a spiritualized, share-centric, enlightened society. Pretty much like Alcoholics Anonymous, but without the God or the booze.

Worse yet, this scheme was functioning. Some of our cellmates, especially the meek, dorky, geeky ones, were quickly released. The wretches strung out on dope were pretty likely to manage in the new order, too. They'd given up jailing people for that.

This degeneration had to be stopped somehow. Since I was a troll, I was great at gaming. I kept inventing ways to hack the gaming system and get people to fight. This was the one thing I could do inside the prison that recalled the power I'd once held in my old life.

So, I threw myself into that therapy heart and soul. I worked my way up to 15th level Evil Dwarf. I was the envy of the whole prison system, a living legend. I got myself some prison tattoos, made a shiv… Maybe I had a bleak future, stuck inside the joint, but I still had integrity! I had defied their system! I could vote-down the stool-pigeons and boost the stand-up guys who were holding out against the screws!

I was doing great at that, really into it, indomitable—until Claire told me that my success was queering her chances of release. They didn't care what I did inside the fantasy game. All that time, I was really being judged on my *abuse of the ratings system*. Because *they knew what I was up to*. It was all a psychological trap! The whole scheme was their anti-hacker honeypot. I had fallen into it like the veriest newbie schmoe!

You see, they were scanning us all the time. Nobody ever gets it about the tremendous power of network surveillance. That's how they ruled the world, though: by valuing every interaction, by counting every click. Every time one termite touched the feelers of another termite, they were adding that up. In a database.

Everybody was broke: extremely poor, like preindustrial hard-scrabble poor, very modest, very "green." But still surviving. The one reason we weren't all chewing each other's cannibal thighbones (like the people on certain more disadvantaged continents), was because they'd stapled together this survival regime out of socialist software. It was very social. Ultra-social. No "privatization," no "private sector," and no "privacy."

They pretended that it was all about happiness and kindliness and free-spirited cooperation and gay rainbow banners and all that. It was really a system that was firmly based on "social capital." *Everything social was your only wealth.* In a real "gift economy," *you* were the gift. You were living by your karma. Instead of a good old hundred-dollar bill, you just had a virtual facebooky thing with your own smiling picture on it, and that picture meant "Please Invest in the Bank of Me!"

That was their New Deal. One big game of socially-approved activities. For instance: reading Henry David Thoreau. I did that. I kinda had to. I had this yellow, crumbly, prison edition of a public-domain version of *Walden*.

Man, I hated that Thoreau guy. I wanted to smack Mr. Nonviolent Moral Resistance right across his chops. I did learn something valuable from him, though. This communard Transcendental thing that had us by the neck? The homemade beans, the funky shacks, the passive-aggressive peacenik dropout thing? That was not something that had invaded America from Mars. That was part of us. It had been there all along. Their New Age spiritual practice was America's dark freaky undercurrent. It was like witchcraft in the Catholic Church.

Now these organized network freaks had taken over the hurricane wreck of the church. They were sacrificing goats in there, and having group sex under their hammer and sickle while witches read Tarot cards to the beat of techno music.

These Lifestyle of Health and Sustainability geeks were maybe seven percent of America's population. But the termite people had seized power. They were the Last Best Hope of a society on the skids. They owned all the hope because they had always been the ones who knew our civilization was hopeless.

So, I was in their prison until I got my head around that new reality. Until I realized that this was inevitable. That it was the way forward. That I loved Little Brother. After that, I could go walkies.

That was the secret. All the rest of it: the natural turmoil of the period.... The swarms of IEDS, and the little flying bomb drones, and the wiretaps, and the lynch mobs, and the incinerators and the "regrettable excesses," as they liked to call them—those were not the big story. That was like the exciting sci-fi post-apocalypse part that basically meant nothing that mattered.

Everybody wants the cool post-disaster story—the awesome part where you take over whole abandoned towns, and have sex with cool punk girls in leather rags who have sawed-off shotguns. Boy, I could only *wish*. In Sustainable-Land, did we have a cool, wild, survivalist lifestyle like that? No way. We had, like, night-soil buckets and vegetarian okra casseroles.

The big story was all about a huge, doomed society that had wrecked itself so thoroughly that its junkyard was inherited by hippies. The epic tale of the Soviet Union, basically. Same thing, different verse. Only more so.

Well, I could survive in that world. I could make it through that. People can survive a Reconstruction: if they keep their noses clean and don't drink themselves to death. The compost heap had turned over. All the magic mushrooms came out of the dark. So they were on top, for a while. So what?

So I learned to sit still and read a lot. Because that looks like innocent behavior. When all the hippie grannies are watching you over their HAL 9000 monitors, poring over your every activity like Vegas croupiers with their zoom and slo-mo, then quietly reading paper books looks great. That's the major consolation of philosophy.

So, in prison, I read, like, Jean Paul Sartre (who was still under copyright, so I reckon they stole his work). I learned some things from him. That changed me. "Hell is other people." That is the sinister side of a social-software shared society: that people *suck*, that *hell* is other people. Sharing with people is *hell*. When you share, then no matter how much money you have, they just won't leave you alone.

I quoted Jean-Paul Sartre to the parole board. A very serious left-wing philosopher: lots of girlfriends (even feminists), he eats speed all the time, he hangs out with Maoists. Except for the Maoist part, Jean-Paul Sartre is my guru.

My life today is all about my Existential authenticity. Because I'm a dissident in this society. Maybe I'm getting old-fashioned, but I'll never go away. I'll never believe what the majority says it believes. And I won't do you the favor of dying young, either.

Because the inconvenient truth is that, authentically, about fifteen percent of everybody is no good. We are the nogoodniks. That's the one thing the Right knows, that the Left never understands: that, although fifteen percent of people are saintly and liberal bleeding hearts, and you could play poker with them blindfolded, the other fifteen are like me. I'm a troll. I'm a griefer. I'm in it for me, folks. I need to "collaborate" or "share" the way I need to eat a bale of hay and moo.

Well, like I said to the parole board: so what are you going to do to me? Ideally, you keep me tied up and you preach at me. Then I become your hypocrite. I'm still a dropout. You don't convince me.

I can tell you what finally happened to me. I got off. I never expected that, couldn't predict it, it came out of nowhere. Yet another world was possible, I guess. It's always like that.

There was a nasty piece of work up in the hills with some "social bandits." Robin Hood is a cool guy for the peace and justice contingent, until he starts robbing the social networks, instead of the Sheriff of Nottingham. Robin goes where the money is—until there's no money. Then Robin goes where the food is.

So, Robin and his Merry Band had a face-off with my captors. That got pretty ugly, because social networks versus bandit mafias is like Ninjas Versus Pirates: it's a counterculture fight to the finish.

However, my geeks had the technology, while redneck Robin just had his terrorist bows and arrows and the suits of Lincoln green. So, he fought the law and the law won. Eventually.

That fight was always a much bigger deal than I was. As dangerous criminals go, a keyboard-tapping troll like me was small potatoes compared to the redneck hillbilly mujihadeen.

So the European Red Cross happened to show up during that episode (because they like gunfire). The Europeans are all prissy about the situation, of course. They are like: "What's with these illegal detainees in orange jumpsuits, and how come they don't have proper medical care?"

So, I finally get paroled. I get amnestied. Not my pal Claire, unfortunately for her. Claire and our female warden had some kind of personal difficulty, because they'd been college roommates or something—like, maybe some stolen boyfriend trouble. Something very girly and tenderly personal, all like that—but in a network society, the power is ALL personal. "The personal is political." You mess with the tender feelings of a network maven, and she's not an objective bureaucrat following the rule of law. She's more like: "to the Bastille with this subhuman irritation!"

Claire was all super-upset to see that I got my walking papers while she was heading for the gulag's deepest darkest inner circles. Claire was like: "Bobby, wait, I thought you and I were gonna watch each other's backs!" And I'm like, "Girlfriend, if it were only a matter of money, I would go bail for you. But I got no money. Nobody does. So, *hasta luego*. I'm on my own."

So at last, I was out of the nest. And I needed a job. In a social network society, they don't have any jobs. Instead, you have to invent public-spirited network-y things to do in public. If people really like what you do for "the commons," then you get all kinds of respect and juice. They make nice to you. They suck up to you all the time, with potluck suppers, and they redecorate your loft. And I really hated that. I still hate it. I'll always hate it.

I'm not a make-nice, live-in-the-hive kind of guy. However, even in a very densely networked society, there are some useful guys that you don't want to see very much. They're very convenient members of society, crucial people even, but they're just not sociable. You don't want to hang around with them, you don't want to give them backrubs, follow their lifestream, none of that. Society's antisocial guys.

There's the hangman. No matter how much justice he dishes out, the hangman is never a popular guy. There's the gravedigger. The locals sure had plenty of work for him, so that job was already taken.

Then there was the exterminator. The man who kills bugs. Me. In a messed-up climate, there are a whole lotta bugs. Zillions of them. You get those big empty suburbs, the burnt-out skyscrapers, lotta wreckage, junk, constant storms and no air conditioning? Smorgasbord for roaches and silverfish.

Tear up the lawns and grow survival gardens, and you are gonna get a whole lot of the nastiness that lefties call "biodiversity." Vast swarming mobs of six-legged vermin. An endless, fertile, booming supply.

Mosquitoes carry malaria, fleas carry typhus. Malaria and typhus are never popular, even in the greenest, most tree-huggy societies.

So I found myself a career. A good career. Killing bugs. Megatons of them.

My major challenge is the termites. Because they are the best-organized. Termites are fascinating. Termites are not just pale little white-ants that you can crush with your thumb. The individual termites, sure they are, but a nest of termites is a network society. They share everything. They bore a zillion silent holes through seemingly solid wood. They have nurses, engineers, soldiers, a whole social system. They run off fungus inside their guts. It's amazing how sophisticated they are. I learn something new about them every day.

And, I kill them. I'm on call all the time, to kill termites. I got all the termite business I can possibly handle. I figure I can combat those swarmy little pests until I get old and gray. I stink of poison constantly, and I wear mostly plastic, and I'm in a breathing mask like Darth Vader, but I am gonna be a very useful, highly esteemed member of this society.

There will still be some people like me when this whole society goes kaput. And, someday, it surely will. Because no Utopia ever lasts. Except for the termites, who've been at it since the Triassic period.

So, that is my story. This is my want-ad. It's all done now, except for the last part. That's your part: the important part where you yourself can contribute.

I need a termite intern. It's steady work and lots of it. And now, because I wrote all this for you, you know what kind of guy you are pitching in with.

I know that you're out there somewhere. Because I'm not the only guy around like me. If you got this far, you're gonna send me email and a personal profile.

It would help a lot if you were a single female, 25-35, shapely, and a brunette.

PART II:
Dark
Euphoria

ESOTERIC CITY

———————⊹•

Was that the anguished howl of a dying dog? Or just his belly rumbling?

Cold dread nosed at the soul of Achille Occhietti. He rose and jabbed his blue-veined feet into his calfskin slippers.

In the sumptuous hall beyond his bedroom, the ghost-light of midnight television flickered beneath his wife's door. Ofelia was snoring.

Occhietti's eyes shrank in the radiant glare of his yawning fridge. During the evening's game, elated by the home team's victory over the hated Florentines, he'd glutted himself on baked walnuts, peppery breadsticks and Alpine ricotta. Yes, there it lurked, that sleep-disturbing cheese: glabrous and skinless, richer than sin.

The fridge thumped shut and the dimly shining metal showed Occhietti his own surprised reflection: groggy, jowly, balding. The hands that gripped the crystal cheese-plate were as heavy as a thief's.

A blur rose behind Occhietti, echoing his own distorted image. He turned, plate in hand.

A mystical smoke gushed straight up through Occhietti's floor. Rising, roiling, reeling, the cloud gathered earthly substance; it blackly stained the grout between his kitchen tiles.

Occhietti's vaporous guest stank powerfully of frankincense, petroleum and myrrh.

Resignedly, Ochietti set the cheeseplate on the sideboard. He flicked on the kitchen's halogen lights.

In the shock of sudden illumination, Occhietti's mystic visitor took on a definitive substance. He was Djoser, an ancient Egyptian priest and engineer. Djoser had been dead for three thousand years.

Flaking, brittle, and browned by the passing millennia, the mummy loomed at Ochietti's kitchen table, grasping at the checkered cloth with ancient fingers thin as macaroni. He opened his hollow-cheeked maw, and silently wagged the blackened tongue behind his time-stained ivories.

Occhietti edged across the ranks of cabinets and retrieved a Venetian shot-glass.

Using a nastily sharp little fruit-knife, Ochietti opened the smaller vein in his left wrist. Then he dribbled a generous dram of his life's blood into the glass.

The mummy gulped his crimson aperitif. Dust puffed from his cracked flesh as his withered limbs plumped. His wily, flattened eyeballs rolled in their sockets. He was breathing.

Occhietti pressed a snowy wad of kitchen towels against his tiny wound. It really hurt to open a vein. His head was spinning.

With a grisly croak, Djoser found his voice. "Tonight you are going to Hell!"

"So soon?" said Occhietti.

Djoser licked the bloodstained dregs of his shot-glass. "Yes!"

Occhietti studied his spirit guide with sorrow. He regretted that their long relationship had finally come to this point.

Once, the mummy Djoser had been lying entirely dead, as harmless and inert as dried papyrus, in the mortuary halls of Turin's Museo Egizio—the largest Egyptian museum in Europe. Then Occhietti, as a burningly ambitious young businessman, had occultly penetrated the Turinese museum. He had performed the rites of necromancy necessary to rouse the dead Egyptian. An exceedingly dark business, that; the blackest of black magic; a lesser wizard would have quailed at it, especially at all the fresh blood.

Yet a shining lifetime of success had followed Occhietti's dark misdeed. The occult services of an undead adviser were a major advantage in Turinese business circles.

The world's three great capitals of black magic (as every adept knew) were Lyon, the City of Heretics; Prague, the City of Alchemists; and Turin. The world also held three great centers of white magic: London, the City of the Golden Dawn; San Francisco, the City of Love;—and Turin.

Turin, the Esoteric City, was saturated with magic both black and white. Every brick and baroque cornice in the city was shot through with the supernatural.

He'd led a career most car executives would envy, but Achille Occhietti did not flatter himself that he ranked with the greatest wizards ever in Turin. Nobody would rank him with Leonardo da Vinci… or even Prince Eugene of Savoy. No, Occhietti was merely the head of a multinational company's venture capital division, a top technocratic magus at a colossal corporation that had inundated Europe with a honking fleet of affordable compacts and roaring, sleekly gorgeous sports-cars, a firm which commanded 16.5 percent of the entire industrial R&D budget of Italy. So, not much magic to marvel at there. Not compared to the concrete achievements of, say, Nostradamus.

Having bound-up his wounded wrist, Occhietti offered the mummy a Cuban cigar from his fridge's capacious freezer.

Smoke percolated through cracks in the mummy's wrinkled neck. The treat visibly improved the mummy's mood. Tobacco was the only modern vice that Djoser took seriously.

"Your Grand Master the Signore, he whom you so loyally served," Djoser puffed bluely, "has been dead and in Hell for two thousand days."

Occhietti wondered. "Where does the time go?"

"You should have closely watched the calendar." This was a very ancient-Egyptian thing to say. "Your Master calls you from his awful lair. I will guide you to Hell, for guidance of that kind has been my role with you."

"Could I write a little note to my wife first?"

Djoser scowled. A master of occult hieroglyphics, Djoser had never believed that women should read.

With a sudden swift disjuncture straight from nightmare, Occhietti and Djoser were a-float in mid-air. Occhietti drifted through the trickling fountains of his wife's much-manicured garden, and past his favorite guard dog. The occult arrival of the undead Djoser had killed the dog in an agony of foaming canine terror.

The two of them magically progressed downhill. The mummy scarcely moved his rigidly hieratic limbs. His sandal-shod feet left no prints, and his dessicated hands did not disturb the lightest dust. As they neared Hell, his speed increased relentlessly.

They skidded, weightless as two dandelion puffs, down the silent, curving streets of Turin's residential hills. They crossed the cleansing waters of the sacred Po on the enchanted bridge built by Napoleon.

Napoleon Bonaparte had drunk from the Holy Grail in Turin. This stark fact explained why an obscure Corsican artillery lieutenant had bid so fair to conquer the world.

The Holy Grail, like the True Cross and the Shroud of Turin, was an occult relic of Jesus Christ Himself. Since the checkered Grail was both a white cup and a black cup, the Holy Grail belonged in esoteric Turin. The Holy Grail had been at the Last Supper: it was the cup that held the wine that Jesus Christ transformed into His blood. The Holy Grail had also been at Golgotha: where it caught the gushing blood from Christ's pierced heart.

The Shroud of Turin was a time-browned winding-cloth soaked in the literal blood of God, but the blood that brewed within the Holy Grail rose ever-fresh. So that magical vessel was certainly the most powerful relic in Turin (if one discounted Turin's hidden piece of the True Cross, which never seemed to interest wizards half so much as the Shroud and the Grail).

The Emperor Constantine had drunk blood from the Grail. Also Charlemagne...Frederick the Second...Cesare Borgia...Christoforo Columbo...Giuseppe Garibaldi...Benito Mussolini, too, to his woe and the world's distress.

In 1968, an obscure group of students in Turin had occupied the corporate headquarters of Occhietti's car company, demanding love, peace and environmental responsibility. There the wretches had discovered the hidden Grail. The next decade was spent chasing down terrorists who kidnapped car executives.

Occhietti and the mummy floated through the moony shadow of a star-tipped Kabbalist spire, which loomed over Turin's silent core. This occult structure was the tallest Jewish spire in Europe. Even with a Golem, Prague had nothing to compare to it.

The mummy drew a wide berth around the Piazza Castello, in respect for the Pharoah who reigned there. This stony monarch, wielding a flail and an ankh, guarded Turin's Fortress of Isis.

At length the flying mummy alit, dry and light as an autumn leaf, in the black market of the Piazza Statuto: for this ill-omened square, the former site of city executions, held Turin's Gate to Hell.

Hell's Gateway lurked under a ragged tower of blasted boulders, strewn with dramatic statues in sadistic Dantean anguish. This rocky tower was decorously topped by a winged bronze archetype, alternately known as the Spirit of Knowledge or the Rebel Angel Lucifer. He was a tender, limpid angel, very learned, delicate and epicene.

As Djoser sniffed around the stony tower, seeking Turin's occult hole to Hell, Occhietti found the courage to speak. "Djoser, is Hell very different, these days?"

Djoser looked up. "Is Hell different from what?"

"I had to read Dante in school, of course…"

"You are afraid, mortal," Djoser realized. "There is nothing worse than Hell, for Hell is Hell! But I served the royal court of Egypt. I'm far older than your Hell, and Dante's Hell as well." The mummy groped for Occhietti's pierced and aching wrist. "Lo, see here: below we must go!"

Clearly, modern Italian engineers had been hard at work here in Hell. The casings of Hell's rugged tunnel, which closely resembled the Frejus tunnel drilled through the Alps to France, had been furnished with a tastefully minimal spiral staircase made of glass, blond hardwood and aircraft aluminum.

A delicate Italian techno-muzak was playing. It dimmed the rhythmic slaps of Occhietti's bedroom slippers on the stairway.

Light and shadow chased each other on the tunnel's walls. The walls held a delirious surge of spray-bombed gang graffiti, diabolically exulting drugs, violence and general strikes against the System—but much of that rubbish had been scrubbed away, and Turin's new, improved path to Hell was keenly tourist-friendly. Glossy signs urged the abandonment of all hope in fourteen official European Union languages.

"Someone took a lot of trouble to upgrade this," Occhietti realized.

"The Olympics were in Turin," Djoser grunted.

"Oh yes, of course."

Turin was an esoteric city of black and white, so its Hell was a strobing, flickering flux, under a chilly haze of Alpine fog. Being Hell, it was funereal; the afterlife was an all-consuming realm of grief, loss, penitence, and distorted, sentimentalized remembrance.

The Hell of Turin was clearly divided—not in concentric layers of crime, as Dante had alleged—but into layers of time. The dead of the 1990s were still feigning everyday business…they were shopping, suffering, cursing the traffic and the lying newspaper headlines…but the dead of the 1980s were blurrier and less antic, while the dead of the 1970s were foggy and obscured. The Hell that represented the 1960s was a fading jangle of guitars and a smoky whiff of patchouli.... The 1950s were red-hot smokestacks as distant as the Appenines, while the 1940s, at the limit of Occhietti's ken, were an ominous wrangle of sirens and burning and bombs.

Smog gushed over glum workers' tenements, clanking factories, bloodily gleaming rivers and endless tides of jammed cars. The cars looked sharp and clear to Occhietti, for he knew their every make, year, and model; but their sinful inhabitants, the doomed and the damned, were hazy blurs behind the wheels.

As an auto executive, Occhietti had always surmised that his company's employees would go in Hell. They were Communists from some of Europe's most radical and militant labor unions. Where else could they possibly go?

And here, indeed, they were. Those zealots from the Workers' Councils, self-righteous hell-raisers passionately devoted to Marxism, had all transmigrated down here. Their afterlife was one massive labor strike. The working-dead were clad in greasy flannel, denim and corduroy, cacophonous, boozing, shouting in immigrants' dialects, a hydra-headed horde of grimy egalitarians...packed like stinging hornets into their worker's-housing projects. They passed their eternal torment watching bad Italian TV variety shows.

"Dante's Hell was so solemn, medieval and majestic," Occhietti lamented. "There's nothing down here but one huge Italian mess!"

"This is *your* Hell," his spirit guide pointed out. "Dante's Hell was all about Dante, while your Hell is all about you."

"They claimed that the afterlife would be about justice for everybody," said Occhietti.

"This is an Italian hell. Did you ever see Italian justice?" The mummy was being reasonable. "I can assure you that all the most famous and accomplished Turinese are here." He pointed with a time-shrunken finger at a busy literary café, a local mise-en-scene that boiled with diabolical energies. "See those flying vulture-monsters there, shrieking and clawing both their victims, and one another?"

"With all that noise, they're hard to miss."

"Those are dead Italian journalists and literary critics."

This certainly made sense. "Who's that they're eating?"

"That's the local novelist who killed himself over that actress."

"Fantastic! Yes, that's really him! The only writer who truly understood this town! Can I get his autograph?"

The Egyptian raised his hierophatic hand in stern denial. "Humanity," he pronounced, "is steeped in sin. Especially the human sins that are also human virtues. That manic-depressive novelist boozing over there, who understood too many such things, despaired of his own existence and ended it. But to kill oneself while lost in life's dark woods is the worst of human errors. So he stinks of his own decay; and that is why his vultures eagerly feast on him."

They tramped Hell's stony flooring to a space that was garish and spangled. The smartly hellish boulevards were crowded with famous faces. All manner of local celebrities: film stars, countesses, financiers, art collectors, generals.

These celebrities shared their Hell with the grimy underdogs of the Workers' Turin. Yet, since this was Hell, the Great and the Good were no longer bothering to keep up their public pretenses. Human experience had ceased for the dead; their hazy flesh cast no shadows. Indifferent to futurity, with the post-existential freedom of nothing left to gain or lose, these ghosts were haplessly angry, gluttonous, slothful and lustful. They were embezzlers, wife-beaters, brawling scoffers. Sullen depressives who'd gone to Hell for being insufficiently cheerful; moral fence-sitters who'd gone to Hell for minding their own business.

Gay and lesbian Sodomites whose awful lusts were presumably enough to have their whole city incinerated; cops in Hell for the inherent crime of being cops, lawyers for the utter vileness of being lawyers, firemen for having goofed off on some day when a child burned to death, doctors in Hell for malpractice and misdiagnosis....

Italian women in hell for flaunting busty decolletage that tempted men to lust, and women who had tragically failed to tempt men to lust and had therefore ended up lonely and sad and crabby and cruel to small children.

"Can you tell me who's missing from Hell?" said Occhietti at last. He was jostled by the crowds.

The Egyptian shrugged irritably in the push and shove. "Do you see any Jews down here?"

"The Jews went to Heaven?"

"I never said *that*! I just said the Jews aren't in this Turinese Italian Catholic Hell!" The mummy fought the crowd for elbow room. "There were no Jews in *my* afterlife, either. And believe me, compared to this raucous mess, my afterlife was splendid. My nice quiet tomb had fine clothes, paintings, a sarcophagus, all kinds of wooden puppets to keep me company.... You'd think the Jews would have changed in three thousand years, but...yes, fine, the Jews changed, but not so you'd notice."

They clawed their way free from the pedestrian crowds of dead. The mummy was abstracted now, seeking some waymark through the dense and honking urban traffic. "I must usher you into the presence of your dead overlord. This ordeal is going to upset you."

Occhietti was already upset. "I was always loyal to him! I even loved him."

"That's *why* you will be upset."

Occhietti knew better than to argue with Djoser. The mummy's stringent insights, drawn from his long historical perspective, had been proven again and again. For instance: when he'd first asked Djoser about marrying Ofelia, the mummy had soberly prophesied. "This rich girl from a fine family is a cold and narrow creature who feels no passion for you. She will never understand you. She will make your home respectable, conventional, and dignified, and cramped with a petty propriety." Occhietti, considering that an overly harsh assessment, had married Ofelia anyway.

Yet Djoser's prophecies about Ofelia had been entirely true. In fact, these qualities were the best things about Ofelia. She was the mother of his children and had been his anchor for 38 years.

Occhietti's Signore was one of a major trio of the damned, three bronze male giants, stationed in the center of a busy traffic ring. These mighty titans loomed over Hell like office buildings; the cars whizzing past their ankles were like rubber-tired rats.

The heroic flesh of the titans was riddled through and through by writhing, hellish serpents. These serpents were wriggling exhaust pipes that cruelly pierced the sufferers from neck to kidneys, chaining them in place. Being necromancers, the auto executives had always derived their power from the flesh of the dead: from fossil fuels. In Hell, this hideous truth was made manifest.

A hundred thousand people in Turin, weeping unashamedly, hats in hand, had filed their way past gorgeous heaps of flowers to pay the Signore their last respects. Yet, even down here in Hell, the brazen fact of death had not relieved this giant of his business worries.

Here the Signore stood, gathered to his ancestors, who looked scarcely happier than he. The Signore's father blinked silently, forlorn. Bloody sludge dripped from his aquiline, titanic nose. The Signore's father had quaffed from the Grail with the Duce. He had died in his bed with a gentleman's timing—for his death had saved his company from the wrath of the vengeful Allies.

The Signore's grandfather, the company's founder, was an even more impressive figure; great entrepreneur, primal industrial genius, his colossal flesh was caked all over with the blackened wreck of bucolic Italy: pretty vineyards paved over with cement, sweet little piping birds gone toes-up from the brazen gust of furnace blasts.... He was a Midas whose grip turned everything to asphalt.

As for the Signore himself, he was the uncrowned Prince of Italy, a Senator-for-Life, a shining column of NATO's military-industrial complex. The Signore was dead and in Hell, and yet still grand—after his death, he was grander, even.

"Eftsoons he will speak unto you," warned the mummy formally; "stand ye behind me, and do not fear so."

"This pallor on my face," said Occhietti, "is my pity for him."

In truth, Occhietti was terrified of the Signore. It was always wise to fear a wizard whose lips had touched the Holy Grail.

The Signore opened his mighty jaws. Out came a great sooty gush of carbon monoxide, lung-wrecking particulates, brain-damaging lead, and the occult offgassings of industrial plastics. Earth-wracking fumes fit to blister Roman marble and tear the fine facades right off cathedrals.

The Signore found his giant, truck-horn voice.

"Hail friend, unto this dreadful day still true,
Who harkens to your master's final geas!
Most woeful this of many deeds performed
In service to the checkered Lord of Turin."

Occhietti felt a purer terror yet. "He's speaking in iambic pentameter!"

"This is Hell," the mummy pointed out. "And he's a Titan."

"But I'm an engineer! I always hated poetry!"

The mummy spread his hands. "Well, he was a lawyer, before he became like this: dead, historic, gigantic and in the worst of all possible circumstances."

The Signore awaited an answer, with eyes as huge and glassy as an eighteen-wheeler's headlamps.

Occhietti drew himself up, as best he could within his scanty night-robe and flat bedroom slippers. "Hail unto thee, ye uncrowned Kings, masters of the many smokestacks, ye who coaxed Italians from their creaking, lousy haywains and into some serious high-performance vehicles.... Listen, ye, I can't possibly talk in this manner! Let's speak in the vernacular, *capisce?*"

Occhietti stared up, pleading, into the mighty face that solemnly glared above him.

"Listen to me, boss: *Juventus!* Your favorite football team: the Turin black-and-whites! They kicked the asses of the Florentines tonight! Wiped them flat out, three-zero!"

This was welcome news to the giant. The titan unbent somewhat, his huge bronze limbs creaking like badly lined brakes.

"'Wizard' they call thee, counsellor and fixer;
Trusted with our sums that breed futurity;
Loyal thou wert, but now the very Tempter
Lurks a serpent in your homely Garden!"

"Does he really have to speak like that?" Occhietti demanded of the mummy. "I can't understand a single damned thing he says!"

Nobly, the mummy rose to the occasion. "He must speak in that poetic, divinatory fashion, for he is a dead giant. You are still alive and capable of moral action, so it is up to you to resolve his ghostly riddles for him." The mummy straightened. "Luckily for you, I always loved the riddles of the afterlife. I was superb at those."

"You were?"

"Indeed I was! The Egyptian Book of the Dead: it's like one huge series of technical aptitude tests! At the end, they weigh your human heart against a feather. And if your guilty heart is any heavier than that feather, then they feed your entrails straight to the demonic hippopotamus."

Occhietti considered this. "How did that trial work out for you, Djoser?"

"Well, I failed," said Djoser glumly. "Because I was guilty. Of course I was guilty. Do you think we built the Pyramids without any fixes and crooked backroom deals? It was all about the lazy priests...the union gangs...and the Pharoah! Oh my God!" The mummy put his flaking head into his withered hands.

Occhietti gazed from the three damned and towering industrial giants, slowly writhing in their smoky chains, and back to Djoser again. "Djoser: your Pharaoh *was* your God, am I right? He was your divine God-King."

"Look, Achille, since we're both standing here stuck in Hell, we should at least be frank: my God-King was a scandal. Like all the Pharaohs, he was *in bed with his sister*. All right? He was an inbred, cross-eyed royal runt! You could have broken both his shins with a papyrus reed."

The mummy gazed upward at the damned industrialists. "This gentleman's dynasty came to a sudden end after one mere century.... But at least he was in bed with some busty actresses, and was driving hot sports cars! As a leader of your civilization, he wasn't *all that bad,* especially considering your degraded, hectic, vilely commercial Iron Age!"

The mighty specter seemed obscurely pleased by the mummy's outspoken assessment; at least, he thunderously resumed his awesome recitation.

"He comes to ruin everything we built!

"The empire that we schemed, we planned, we made,

"In toil, sweat, tears and lost integrity,

"Imperilled stands in your new century,

"When Turin's Black and White turns serpent Green!

"If ever you would call yourself 'apostle'

"Your footsteps stay, and keep your heart steadfast!

"The Devil's blandishments are subtle,

"Reject them without pause all down the line!"

"He's warning you that you will encounter Satan," the mummy interpreted. "I take it that he means Lucifer, the Shining Prince of Darkness."

"Meeting Lucifer is not in my job assignment," said Occhietti.

"Well, it is now. You will have to return to your mortal life to confront the Devil in person. That's clearly what this hellish summons is all about."

Occhietti could no longer face the writhing torment of the doomed giants, so he turned on the mummy. "I admit that I'm a necromancer," he said. "I draw my magic power from the dead—but *Satan*? I can't face Satan! Satan is the Black Angel! He's the second-ranked among the Great Seraphic Powers! I can't possibly *defeat Satan*! With what, my rosary?"

"Your Lord of Turin can't speak any more plainly," Djoser said. "Look how he folds his mighty arms and falls so silent now! As your spiritual guide and adviser, I would strongly suggest that you arm yourself against the Great Tempter."

All three giants had gone as rigid and remote as public statuary. Occhietti was speechless at the desperate fate that confronted him.

"Come now," coaxed the mummy, "you must have *some* merits for a battle like this. Not every necromancer visits Hell while living."

"I'm completely doomed! I might as well just stay here in Hell, properly damned!" Occhietti's shoulders slumped within his scanty robe. "Everyone who matters is here already anyway! There's no one up there in Heaven except children and nice old ladies!"

"Don't be smug about your own damnation," counselled the mummy, taking his arm and leading him away through acrid lines of whizzing traffic. "That is the sin of pride."

It brought profound relief to flee the dire presence of the three agonized giants. The mummy and Occhietti flagged down a taxi. Suddenly they were roaming Turin's vast and anonymous mobilized suburbs, which were all tower-blocks, freeways, assembly plants and consumer box-stores.

"My employer just tasked me to face Satan.... Him, the finest man I ever knew...." Occhietti leaned his reeling head against the taxi's grime-stained window. "Why is *he* down here in Hell? He was truly the Great and the Good! All the ladies loved him! He even had a sense of humor."

"It's because of simony," pronounced the mummy. "He—and his father, and his grandfather—they are all in Hell for the mortal sin of simony."

"I don't think I've ever heard of that one."

"For 'simony,' Achille. That's the mortal sin named after the great necromancer, Simon Magus. Simon Magus sought to work divine miracles by paying money for them."

"But I do that myself."

"Indeed you do."

"Because I'm in venture capital, I'm in research-and-development! I have to commit that so-called sin of 'simony' every damn day!"

"You might consult your Scripture on that subject. Nice letters of black and white, very easy to read." Djoser was something of a snob about his hieroglyphics.

Occhietti banged his fist against the rattling taxi door. "Everybody in the modern world is an industrial capitalist! We all raise cash to work our technical miracles! That's our very way of life!"

"You won't find any words of praise for that in your Bible."

Occhietti knew this was true. As a wizard, he had the Bible, that most occult of publications, poised always at his bedside.

There was scarcely one word inside the Bible that you'd find in any modern Masters of Business Administration course. Not much comfort there for the money-changers in the temple. Plagues, curses, merciless wars of annihilation—the sky splitting open apocalyptically: the Bible brimmed over with that.

Occhietti lowered his voice. "Djoser, my entire modern world is beyond salvation, isn't it? The truth is, we're comprehensively damned! For our mortal sins against man and nature, we're going to collapse! That apocalypse could happen to us any day now, plagues of frogs, rivers of blood...."

All alert sympathy, the ancient mummy nodded his dry, flaking head. "Yes, they're very harsh on us ancient Egyptians inside that Bible of yours! The press coverage that our regime got in there, I wouldn't give that to a dog!"

Occhietti blinked. "Did you read the Bible, Djoser?"

"I don't have to *read it*, stupid! I was *there*! I was alive back then! We were the Good People and the Jews were our working class! You should have seen their cheap, lousy bricks!"

Occhietti was numb with despair. Then he read a passing sign and was galvanized into frenetic action. "Driver, pull over!"

Occhietti and the mummy entered a men's suburban clothing store. The damned soul manning the cheap plastic counter was a genuine Italian tailor. As a punishment for his sins, which must have been many, he was being forced to retail pret-a-porter off-the-rack.

Occhietti examined the goods with a swift and practiced eye. This being Hell, this store-of-the-damned featured only the clothing that his wife Ofelia wanted him to wear. Thrifty, respectable suits that lacked male flair of any kind. Suits that were rigidly conventional and baggily cut, thirty years out of date. Suits that were shrouds for his burial.

Given the circumstances, though, this sepulchral gear was perfect, and far better than his night-robe. "Don't stand there," he told the mummy. "Get yourself dressed. We have to attend a garden party."

The mummy was startled. "What, now?"

"I don't *always* forget to watch the calendar," Occhietti told him. "Today is my wife's birthday."

The mummy pawed with reluctance through a rack of white linen suits. "How exactly do you plan to pay for this?"

With a wizardly flick of the fingers, Occhietti produced a platinum American Express card. It belonged to the company, so it never appeared on his taxes.

Their exit from Hell was sudden and muddled: one harsh, aching lurch, a tumbling, nightmarish segue, and suddenly the two of them were riding inside a taxi, in downtown Turin, alive and in broad daylight.

They might have been two businessmen in bad new suits who'd spent their night carousing. Shaken survivors of tenebrous hours involving whores, and casinos, and mafia secrets, and sulphurous reeking cigars. But they were alive.

Djoser wiped sentimentally at his dry, red-rimmed eyes. "Shall I tell you the sweetest thing about being raised from the dead? It's the sunlight." Clothed in modern machine-made linens, the undead mummy closely resembled an aging Libyan terrorist. "The beautiful, simple, honest sunlight! Blue skies with golden sun: that is the greatest privilege that the living have."

Released from the morbid, ever-clutching shadows of guilt, remorse and death—for the time being, anyway—Occhietti felt keenly what a privilege it was to live, and to live in Turin. A native, he had never left his beloved Esoteric City, because there was no other town half so fit for him. This Turin so beloved by Nietszche, this cool, logical, organized city, brilliantly formal and rational, beyond Good or Evil.... How splendid it was, and how dear to him. One living day strolling under glorious Turinese porticos was worth a post-mortem eternity.

The taxi's driver was a semi-literate Somali refugee, so Occhietti felt quite free in talking openly. "We'll make one small detour on our way to my wife's garden party. For I must seize the Holy Grail."

"That's daring, Achille."

"I must make the attempt. The Grail has baffled Satan before. Salvation was its purpose. That's right, isn't it? I mean… I may be right or wrong, but if I'm taking action, I will get results."

The mummy accepted this reasoning. "So—do you know where it is?"

"I do. It must be where the Signore's son-and-heir abandoned it— before he jumped off the bridge and drowned himself in the River Po."

The mummy nodded knowingly. "He wouldn't drink."

"No. He was much too good to drink. He was a hippie kid. A big mystic. He didn't want any innocent blood on his conscience. Whitest necromancer I ever met, that boy. Very noble and pure of heart." Occhietti sighed. "He was insufferable."

The taxi backfired as it rattled across Napoleon's stone bridge. Occhietti ordered a stop at the swelling dome of the Church of the Great Mother. He paid the doubtful cabbie with his AmEx card, then climbed out into sunlight.

The mummy stared and scowled. "Don't tell me the Holy Grail is hidden in that place."

The Grail was inside Turin's ancient Temple of Isis. "I know it's somewhat ecumenical…. We Turinese do tend to dissolve our oppositions into ambiguities…that's how we are here, we can't help that."

This news visibly hurt the mummy's feelings. The mummy had once worshipped Isis. Furthermore, it clearly offended him that the Grail's hiding-place was so obvious.

The ancient Temple of Isis—currently known as the Church of the Great Mother of God—featured a paganized statue in classical robes. She casually brandished a Holy Grail in her left hand, as she sat on the Temple's stoop and faced the sacred River Po. A neon sign couldn't have been more blatant.

However, the crypt below her Church was a death-trap for the carelessly ambitious. The basement of the Great Mother was Turin's mortuary for the Bones of the Fallen. The men interred within had sacrificed their lives in the Sacred Cause of Italy. It was they: the bony, the fleshless, the bloodless—who surrounded and guarded the bleeding Grail.

"I can't go in there with you," said the mummy, tapping his hollow rib-cage, "for my body has risen through an act of black necromancy, and that is a hallowed ground."

Occhietti sensed the implied reproach in this remark, but he overlooked it. To seek the Grail was a quest best taken alone.

A veteran necromancer, Occhietti had once boldly ransacked the Egyptian Museum—(which was itself a makeshift tomb, and already made from ransacked tombs). Still, Occhetti would never have perturbed the holy shades of the Italian fallen. His respect for them was great. Furthermore, they were notoriously violent.

Yet, in this great crisis, he deliberately made that choice.

Occhietti enchanted his way through the sacred portal that guarded the slumbering dead. As a willful, impious intrusion, he forced himself among their company.

As furious as trampled ants, the ghosts of the battlefield dead rose and came at him a battalion's charging wave.

Bones: the soldierly dead were a torrent of clattering bones. Bones heaped over centuries of Italian struggle. Their living flesh was long-gone, but the skeletons themselves were cruelly hacked and splintered: with the slashing of cavalry sabers, careening cast-iron cannonballs, point-blank musketry blasts. These were fighting men who'd bled and perished for Italy, combating the Austrians, the French, the Germans, Hungarian hussars, elite Swiss mercenary guards, and, especially and always, fiercely combating other Italians.

With a snare-drum clashing of the teeth in their naked skulls, the noisome skeletons clawed at his civilian clothes and mocked his manhood. A lesser magician would have been torn to shreds. Occhietti stoutly persisted in his quest. If Hell itself couldn't hold him, it could not be his fate to fall here.

At length, pale, sweating, stumbling, with fresh stains on his soul, Occhietti emerged under the blue Italian sky, a sky which, just as Djoser had said, was truly a blessing, a privilege and a precious thing.

Occhietti clutched a humble string-tied bundle wrapped in crumbling, yellowed newspapers.

The mummy cringed away at once.

"This hurts, eh?" said Occhietti with satisfaction. He brushed bone-dust from his trousers. Despite the horror of his necrotic crime—or even because of it—he was proud.

"Your mere modern Christian magic can't hurt an Egyptian priest, but...." The mummy lunged backward, stumbling. "All right, yes, it hurts me! It hurts, don't do that."

The string-tied package was unwieldy, but it weighed no more than a beer-mug. The old newspaper ink darkly stained Occhietti's hands.

Together, they trudged uphill. Justly wary of the packet, the mummy trailed a few respectful paces behind. "You plan to use that to confound the Great Tempter?"

"That is my plan, if I have one," said Occhietti, "although I might be better-advised to put this back and jump into that nice clean river."

"I have no further guidance for you," the mummy realized. "I don't know what to tell you about this situation. It's entirely beyond me."

Occhietti tramped on. "That's all right, Djoser. We're both beyond that now."

Embarrassed, the mummy caught up with him, then stuck one dry finger through his unaccustomed collar. "You see, Achille, I was born in the youth of the world. We never lived as you people do. Your world is much older than my world."

"You've come along this far," said Occhietti kindly. "Why not tag along to see how things turn out?"

"My own life ended so long ago," the mummy confessed. "Like all us Egyptians, I longed to hold on to my life, to remain the mortal man I once was…. But the passage of time…. Even in the afterlife, the passage of time erased my being, bit by bit."

Occhietti had nothing to say.

"When time passed, the first things to leave me," said the mummy thoughtfully, "were the things I always thought were most important to me, such as…my cunning use of right-angled triangles in constructing master-blueprints. Every technical skill that I had grasped with such effort? That all went like the dew!

"Then I remembered the things that had touched my heart, yet often seemed so small or accidental, like…the sunrise. One beautiful sunrise after a night with three dancing girls."

"There were three?" said Occhietti, pausing for a breath. It was a rather steep climb to his mansion. He generally took a chauffered company car.

"I'm sure that I cherished all three of those girls, but all I remember is my regret when I refused the fourth one."

"Yes," said Occhietti, who was a man of the world, "I can understand that."

"As my afterlife stretched on inside my quiet, well-engineered tomb," intoned the mummy, "I rehearsed all my hates and resentments. But those dark feelings had no power to bind me. Then I gloated over certain bad things I did, that I had gotten away with. But that seemed so feeble and childish…. Finally I was reduced to pondering the good things I had done in my life. Because those were much fewer, and easy to catalog.

"Finally, the last things I recalled from my lifespan, the final core of my human experience on Earth, were the kind, good, decent things I'd done, that I was punished for. Not good things I was rewarded and praised for doing. Not even good things I'd done without any thought of reward. Finally, at my last, I recalled the good things I'd done, things that I knew were right to do, and which brought me torment. When I was punished as a sinner for my acts that were righteous. Those were the moral gestures of my life that truly seemed to matter."

As if conjured by the mummy's dark meditations, a sphinx arrived on the scene. This sphinx, restless, agitated, was padding rapidly up the narrow, hilly street, lurking behind the two of them, as big as a minibus. She was stalking them: silent as death on her hooked and padded paws.

Her woman's nostrils flared. She had smelled that humble package Occhietti carried. The all-pervading reek of bloodshed.

Occhietti turned. "Shoo! Go on, scat!"

The sphinx opened her fanged mouth to ask her lethal riddle, but Occhietti hastily tucked the Grail under one suited armpit and clamped both his hands over his ears. Frustrated, the sphinx skulked away.

They trudged on toward Occhietti's morbid rendezvous with destiny. "I know what the Sphinx was going to ask you," the mummy offered. "Because I know her question."

Occhietti nodded. "Mmmph."

"Her riddle sounds simple. This is her question: 'How can Mut be Sekhmet?'"

"What was that, Djoser? Is that truly the riddle of the Sphinx? I don't know anything about that."

"Yes, and that's why the Sphinx would have eaten you at once, if you had hearkened unto her."

Occhietti walked on stoically. He would be home in just a few moments, and confronting the horrid, hair-raising climax of his life.

Could it possibly matter what some mere Sphinx had said? He was about to confront Satan himself!

Still, Occhietti was an engineer, so curiosity naturally gnawed at him.

"All right, Djoser, tell me: how *can* Mut be Sekhmet?"

"That's the riddle I myself never understood," said the Egyptian. "Not while I lived, anyway. Because Mut, as every decent man knows, is the serene Consort of Amun and the merciful Queen of Heaven. Whereas Sekhmet is the lion-headed Goddess of Vengeance whose wanton mouth drips blood.

"Day and night, black and white, were less different than Mut and Sekhmet! Yet, year by year, I saw the goddesses blending their aspects! The priests were sneaky about that work: they kept eliding and conflating the most basic theological issues.... Until one day, exhausted by my work of building Pyramids.... I went into the temple of Mut to beg divine forgiveness for a crime...you know that kind of crime I mean, some practical sin that was necessary on the job...and behold: Mut really *was* Sekhmet."

"I'm sorry to hear about all that," Occhietti told him. And he was sincere in his sympathy, for the mummy's ancient voice had broken with emotion.

"So: the proper answer to the Sphinx, when she asks you, 'How can Mut be Sekhmet?' is: 'Time has passed, and that doesn't matter any more.' Then she would flee from you. Or: if you wanted to be truly cruel to her, you could say to the poor Sphinx, 'Oh, your Sekhmet and Mut, your Mut or Sekhmet, they never mattered in the first place, and neither do you.' Then she would explode into dust."

The mummy stopped in his tracks. His seamed face was wrinkled in pain. "Look at me, look, I'm weeping! These are human tears, as only the living can weep!"

"You took that ancient pagan quibble pretty badly, Djoser."

"I did! It broke my heart! Because I'd committed evil while intending only the best! I died soon after that. I died, and I knew that I must be food for that demon hippopotamus. So, I went through my afterlife's trials—I knew all about them, of course, because the briefing in the Book of the Dead was thorough—and they tossed my broken, sinner's heart onto that balance beam of divine justice, and that beam fell over like a stone."

"That is truly a dirty shame," said Occhietti. "There is no question that life is unfair. And it seems, by my recent experiences, that death is even more unfair than life. I should have guessed that." He sighed.

"Then they brought in a *different* feather of justice," said the mummy. "Some 'feather' that was! That feather was carved from black basalt and it was big as a crocodile. It seemed that we engineers, we royal servants of the God-King, didn't have to put up with *literal* moral feathers. Oh no! If that cross-eyed imbecile whose knees were knocking was a sacred God-King, well—then we were *all* off the hook! The fix was in all the time! Even the Gods were on the take!"

There was no time left for Djoser's further confidences, for they had reached the ornate double-gates of Occhietti's mansion.

Normally his faithful dog was there to greet him, baring Doberman fangs fit to scare Cerberus, but alas, the dog was mortal, and the dog was dead.

However, Occhietti's bride was still among the living, and so were her numerous relatives. Ofelia's birthday was her single chance to break her relations out of mothballs.

They were all there, clustered in his wife's garden in the cheery living sunshine, her true-blue Turinese Savoyard Piedmontese Old Money Rich, chastely sipping fizzy mineral water—Cesare and Luisa, Emanuele and Francesca, Great-Aunt Lucia, Raffaela, his sister-in-law Ottavia... a storm of cheek-kisses now: Eusabia, Prospero, Carla and Allesandra, Mauro, Cinzia, their little Agostino looking miserable, as befitted an eight-year-old stuffed into proper clothes.... Some company wives had also taken the trouble to drop by, which was kind of them, as Ofelia had never understood his work.

His work was Ofelia's greatest rival. She had serenely overlooked the models, the secretaries, the weekend jaunts to summits on small Adriatic islands, even the occasional misplaced scrap of incendiary lingerie—but Ofelia hated his work. Because she knew that his work mattered to him far more than she had ever mattered.

Ofelia swanned up to him. She had surely been worried about his absence on her birthday, and might have hissed some little wifely scolding, but instead she stared in delight at his ugly and graceless new suit. "Oh Achille, *bel figa!* How handsome you look!"

"Happy birthday, my treasure."

"I was afraid you were working!"

"I had to put a few urgent matters into order, yes." He nodded his head at the suit-clad mummy. "But I'm here for your celebration. Look, what lovely weather, for my consort's special day."

No one would have called Ofelia Occhietti a witch, although she was a necromancer's wife. The two of them never spoke one word about the supernatural. Still, when Ofelia stood close by, in the cloud of Chanel 5 she had deployed for decades, Occhietti could feel the mighty power of her Turinese respectability closing over him in a dense, protective spell.

Occhietti had spent the night in Hell, and was doomed to confront Satan himself in broad daylight, and yet, for Ofelia, these matters were irrelevant.

So they did not exist. Therefore, it had just been a bad night for him, bad dreams, with indigestion. He had not fed any blood to the undead; that deep cut in his wrist was a mere accidental nick, not even an attempt at suicide. He had not received any commission from the undead Lord of Turin to combat Satan. Decent people never did such things.

He was attending his wife's birthday party. Everyone here was polite and well brought-up.

Maybe his dog was not even dead. No, his beloved dog was dead, all right. A necromancer had to work hard to raise the dead; death never went away when politely overlooked.

"Amore," Ofelia said to him—she never called him that, except when she needed something— "there's such a nice young man here, Giulia's boy.... You do remember my Giulia."

"Of course I do," said Occhietti, who remembered about a thousand Giulias.

"He is just graduated, he's so well-bred, and has such bright ideas... He's one of ours, the Good People. I think he needs a little help, Achille... Maybe a word of career advice, the company, you know...."

"Yes! Fine! We're always on the lookout for fresh talent. Point him out to me."

Ophelia, who would never commit an act so vulgar as pointing, gave one meaningful flicker of her eyes. Occhietti knew the worst instantly.

There he was. Satan was standing there, under the roses of a whitewashed pergola, sipping spumante.

Satan was a young and handsome Turinese in a modishly cut suit. Magic was boiling off of him in sizzling waves, like the summer sunlight off molten tar.

Digging deep within himself, Occhietti found the courage to speak to his wife in a normal tone. "I'll be sure to have a word with that young man."

"That would be so helpful! I'm sure he's meant to go far. And one other thing. Amore—that ugly Libyan banker! Did you have to bring that nasty man to my birthday party? You know I never trusted him, Achille."

Occhietti glanced across the garden at the seam-faced, impassive mummy, who was pretending to circulate among the guests. The mummy could pass for a living human being when he put his mind to it, but his heart clearly wasn't in the effort today.

In point of fact Djoser's heart was in Turin's distant Egyptian Museum, inside a canopic jar.

"My treasure, I know that foreign financier is not a welcome guest under your roof. I apologize for that—I had to bring him here. We've just settled some important business matters. They're done! I'm through with him! After this day, you'll never see him again!"

Ochietti knew he was doomed: the awful sight of Satan, standing there, brimming with infernal glee, was proof of that. But he was still alive, a mortal man, and therefore capable of moral action.

He clung to that. He could do his wife a kindness. It was her birthday. He could do one good thing, a fine thing, at whatever cost to himself. "My darling, I work too much, and I know that. I've neglected you, and I overlooked you. But...after this beautiful day, with this sunshine, life will be different for us."

"'Different,' Achille? Whatever do you mean?"

Occhietti stared at Satan, who had conjured a cloud of flying vermin from the nooks and crannies of Ofelia's garden. Bluebottle flies, little moths, lacewings, aphids.... Lucifer smiled brightly. The Tempter crooked a finger.

"I meant this as my big birthday surprise for you," Occhietti improvised, for the certainty of imminent damnation had loosened his tongue. "But, I promise you...that I'll put all my business behind me."

"You mean—you leave your work? You never leave Turin."

"But I will! We will! We have the daughter in London, the daughter in San Francisco.... Two beautiful cities, two beautiful girls who made fine marriages.... You and I, we should spend time with the grandchildren! Even the daughter who keeps moving from Lyon to Prague.... It's time we helped her settle down. She was just sowing wild oats! There's nothing so wrong with our little black sheep, when life's all said and done!"

Tears of startled joy brightened his wife's eyes. "Do you mean that, Achille? You truly mean that?"

"Of course I mean it!" he lied cheerfully. "We'll rent out the house here! We'll pick out a fine new travel wardrobe for you.... A woman only gets so many golden years! Starting from tomorrow, you'll enjoy every day of your life!"

"You're not joking? You know I don't understand your silly jokes, sometimes."

"Would I joke with you on your birthday, precious? Tomorrow morning! Try me! Come to my room and wake me!"

He accepted an overjoyed hug. Then he fled.

After a frantic search, he found Djoser lurking in his bedroom, alone and somberly watching the television.

"A fantastic thing, television," said Djoser, staring at a soap ad. "I just can't get over this. What a miracle this is!"

"You fled from Satan, like I did?"

"Oh, your Tempter is here to destroy all you built," shrugged the mummy. "But *I* built the Pyramids—I'd like to see him break *those.*" Djoser reached to the bedroom floor and picked up a discarded garment. "Do you see this thing?"

"Yes, that is my night-robe. So?"

"Your robe is black. This morning, when you were wearing this night-robe in Hell, it was white. Your robe was the purest, snowy, white Egyptian cotton."

Occhietti said nothing.

"Your robe has magically appeared here, from where you abandoned it, there in Hell. As you can see, your robe is black now. It is black, and the Prince of Darkness has entered your garden. You are beyond my help." The mummy sighed. "So I am leaving you."

"Leaving me?"

"Yes. I'm beyond all use here, I'm done."

"Where will you go, Djoser?"

"Back into my glass case inside the Egyptian museum. That's where I was, before you saw fit to invoke me. And before you say anything—no, it's not that bad, being in there. Sure, the tourists gawk at me, but was I any better off in my sarcophagus? Mortality has its benefits, Achille. I can promise you, it does."

The mummy stared at the flickering television, then gazed out the window at the sky. "It is of some interest to be among the living... but after a few millennia, time has to tire a man. All those consequences, all those weighty moral decisions! Suns rising and setting, days flying off the calendar—that fever of life, it's so hectic! It annoys me. It's beneath me! I want my death back. I want the *dignity* of being dead, Achille. I want to be one with God! Because, as Nietzsche pointed out here in Turin, God is Dead. And so am I."

This was the longest outburst Occhietti had ever heard from the mummy. Occhietti did not argue. What Djoser said was logical and rational. It also had the strength of conviction.

"That's a long journey to the Other Side," he told the mummy. "I hope you can find some use for this."

He handed over his company's platinum credit card.

The mummy stared at the potent card in wonderment. "You'll get into trouble for giving me this."

"I'm sure that it's trouble for me," Occhietti told him, "yet it's also the right thing to do."

"That is the gesture of a real Italian gentleman," said the mummy thoughtfully. "That truly showed some *sprezzatura* dash." Without further fuss, he began to vaporize.

Occhietti left his bedroom for the garden, where Satan was charming the guests.

Satan looked very Turinese, for he was the androgynous angel who topped that hellish pile of boulders in the Piazza Statuto. Satan looked like a Belle Arte knockoff of one of Leonardo da Vinci's epicene studio models. He was disgusting.

Furthermore, to judge by the way he was busily indoctrinating the guests, Satan was a technology wonk. He was a tiresome geek who never shut up.

"The triple bottom line!" declared Satan, waving his hands. "The inconvenient truth is, as a civilization, we have to tick off every box on the sustainability to-do list. I wouldn't call myself an expert—but any modern post-industrialist surely needs to memorize the Three Main Components and the Four System Conditions of the Natural Step. And, of course, the Ten Guiding Principles to One-Planet Living. I trust you've read the World Wildlife Fund's Three Forms of Solidarity?"

None of the guests responded—they were more than a little bewildered—but this reaction encouraged Lucifer. "If you expect our Alpine bioregion to escape a massive systemic overhang and a catastrophic eco-crash," he chanted, "so that you can still name and properly number the birds and beasts in this garden.... Then you had better get a handle on the Copenhagen Agenda's Ten Principles for Sustainable City Governance! And for those of you in education—education is the key to the future, as we all know!—I would strongly recommend the Sustainable Schools Network with its Framework of Eight Doorways. That analysis is the result of deep thought by some smart, dedicated activists! Although it can't compare in systemic comprehensibility with the Ten Hannover Principles."

Seeing no further use in avoiding the inevitable, Occhietti steeled himself. He confronted the Tempter. "What did you do with your wings?"

"I beg your pardon?"

"Your feathery angel wings, or your leathery bat wings. They're gone."

Satan was taken aback, but he was young and quick to recover. "Our host has heard that I've sworn off air travel," he said. "Because of the carbon emissions! I take public transportation now."

"No cars for you?" said Occhietti.

"Denying cars is not, in fact, part of my Green gospel!" said Satan primly. "We have never schemed to deprive consumers of their beloved private cars; electric cars, hybrid-electric cars, cellulosic ethanol cars, shareable cars connected by cellphone, wind-powered nickel-hydride cars, plastic-composite hydrogen three-wheelers powered by backyard vats of anaerobic bacteria; we offer a vast, radiant, polymorphic, multi-headed, pagan panoply of cars! All of them radical improvements over today's backward cars, which have led to the ongoing collapse of our global civilization."

Occhietti cleared his throat. "It's a fine thing to find a young man with such an interest in my industry! Let's go inside and have a cigar."

Beaming with delight, the Devil tripped along willingly, but once inside he refused tobacco. "A menace to public health! With today's aging European population, we can't risk the demographic hit to our lifespans! Not to mention the medical costs to our fragile social-safety net."

Deliberately, Occhietti trimmed and fired a cigar. "All right, Lucifer—or whatever you call yourself nowadays—now that we're out of my dear wife's little garden, you can drop your pretenses. Go ahead, brandish your horns at me, your barbed tail—you're not scaring me! I have been to Hell, I've seen the worst you have to offer. So put your cards on the table! Say your piece! What is it you want?"

Satan brightened. "I'm glad to have this excellent chance for a frank exchange of issues with a veteran auto executive. Though I must correct you on one important point—I'm not Satan. *You* are Satan."

"I'm not Satan. I'm an engineer."

"I'm an engineer, too—though certainly not of your brutish, old-school variety. I have a doctorate in renewable energy. With a specialty in cradle-to-cradle recycling issues."

"From what school?"

"The Turin Polytechnic."

"That's *my* school!"

"Have you been there lately?"

Occhietti had no time to teach engineering school. The local faculty were always asking him, but.... "Look, then you *can't* be Satan! You're just some crazy kid who's *possessed* by Satan. You *are* a wizard, right?"

"Of course I'm a wizard! This is Turin."

"Well, what kind of necromancer are you, black or white?"

"Those are yesterday's outdated divisions! I'm not a 'necromancer,' for I don't draw any power from the dead! I'm a 'biomancer.' I'm Green."

"You can't be Green. That is not metaphysically possible. You can only be Black or White."

"Well, despite your aging, Cold-War style metaphysics, I *am* a Green wizard. I am Green, and you, sir, are Brown. You don't have to take *my* word for that. Go to Brussels and ask around about the Kyoto Accords! Any modern Eurocrat can tell you: left, right, black, white—that's all deader than Nineveh! In a climate crisis, you're Global Green or you're crisp brown toast in a hellish wasteland!"

Occhietti blinked. "A 'hellish wasteland.'"

"Yes," said the Green wizard soberly, "all of Earth will become Hell, all of it; if we continue in our current lives of sin, that's just a matter of time."

Occhietti said nothing.

"So," said the Green wizard cheerfully, "now that we have those scientific facts firmly established, let's get down to policy particulars! How much are you willing to give me?"

"What?"

"How many millions? How many hundreds of millions? I have to reinvent your transportation company. On tomorrow's Green principles! Every energy company must also be reinvented. In order to become Green, like futurity, like me, me, me—you have to cannibalize all your present profit-centers. You must seek out radically disruptive, transformed, Green business practices. All the smart operators already know there's no choice in that matter—even the Chinese, Saudis and Indians get that by now, so I can't believe a modish Italian company like yours would be backward and stodgy about it! So, Signor Occhietti, how much? Pony up!"

Occhietti scratched at his head. He discovered two numb patches on his scalp. Hard, numb patches.

Occhietti had grown horns.

Occhietti buffed the talons of his fingertips against the ugly lapel of his suit. "From me," he said, "you will get nothing."

"How much?"

"I told you: nothing. Not ten euro cents. Not one dollar, yen, ruble, rupee or yuan." Occhietti put the paper-wrapped bundle onto the kitchen table. "I still control my corporation's venture capital. As a loyal employee: I refuse you. I refuse to underwrite my company's destruction at your hands. I don't care if it's white, black, brown, green or paisley: nothing for you. I have too much pride."

Using a small but very sharp fruit-knife, Occhietti cut the strings and peeled the paper away.

The Green wizard stared. "Is that what I think it is?"

Occhietto plucked the barbed tail from the loosening seat of his pants. He sat at the kitchen table. He crossed his hooves. He nodded.

"But the Grail is just some cheap clay cup!"

"He was never a Pope, you know. He was a Jewish carpenter."

Occhietti's kitchen filled with the butcher's scent of fresh blood.

"I suppose that you expect me to *drink* from that primitive thing! It's made by hand! Look how blurry those black and white lines are."

"No, you won't drink from the Grail," said Occhietti serenely. "Because you've never had the guts. I've heard fools like you trying to destroy my industry for the past fifty years! While the rest of us were changing this world—transforming it, for good or ill—you never achieved one, single, useful, practical thing! I was at the side of the Lord of Turin, breaking laws and rules like breadsticks, while you were lost in some drug-addled haze, about peace, or love, or whales, or any other useless fad that struck your fancy."

Occhietti grinned. "But to 'save the world'—you would have to rip across this miserable planet like Napoleon. A savior, a conqueror, a redeemer and a champion might do that—but never the likes of you. Because you're feeble, you're squeamish, and you lack all conviction. You're a limp-wristed, multi-culti weak-sister who does nothing but lobby nonexistent world governments."

"Actually, there's a great deal of truth in that indictment, sir! Our efforts to raise consciousness have often fallen sadly short!"

"And that's another thing: being neither black nor white, you're always pitifully eager to agree with your own worst enemies."

"That's because I'm a secular rationalist with an excellent record in human rights, sir! Grant me this much: I am innocent! I'm not eager to submerge our world in a tide of blood, building my New Order on a heap of corpses!"

Occhietti smiled. "And you call yourself European?"

"That remark is truly diabolical! Why are you tempting me? I represent tomorrow—as you know!—and I'm as capable of evil as you. You know well that, once I taste the blood in that cup, there will be hell to pay! You should never have offered me *that*. Why do that? Why?"

What did he gain by offering the Grail? Necessity.

The Grail was a necessity: beyond good and evil. The Grail was an instrument. An instrument was not a moral actor, it did nothing of its own accord. Some engineer had to make instruments.

The Grail was the cup of the sacramental feast, and also the cup of judicial murder. Those two cups, the blackly good and whitely evil, were the very same checkered cup.

That cup had been carried hot-foot from the table of the Final Supper, and straight to Golgotha.

So who engineered the Holy Grail? Some fixer. Only one man, one necessary man, could have known the time and place of both events. That man was a trusted Apostle; the most esoteric Apostle. Judas; the two-faced Judas, the wizardly magus Judas, he of the bag of cash.

It was thanks to Judas that the fix was in.

"You are only playing for time, and the time is up," said Occhietti. "The calendar never stops, and treason is a matter of dates." He shoved the ancient, bloody cup across the table. "Do you drink, or don't you?"

THE PARTHENOPEAN SCALPEL

The thousand intrigues of the Minister we had borne as best we could. But when he poisoned the mind of the Holy Father against our National Cause, we vowed revenge.

Lots were chosen among our Cenacle. To my satisfaction, this signal honor fell to me. The usurper would die at my own hand. He would perish on the very steps of his Chancellery, stabbed in the midst of his Swiss Guards, dead in broad daylight. As the wretch breathed his last, he would know—(thanks to the shouted slogans that I had rehearsed)—that we had avenged an exasperated People.

Having no doubt of my ability to carry out this deed, I accepted my destiny with calm resolution.

Some days passed. It then chagrinned me to learn—from my Cenacle—that I would have an accomplice in the task.

Unfortunately, we were not the only Cenacle of the Carbonari inside Rome. For safety against many spies, our conspiracy was divided into many cells. One of our colleague Cenacles—as righteously indignant as ourselves—had also chosen an assassin to kill the Minister.

I met this rival of mine in a torchlit cellar at midnight. My understudy was a bug-eyed, epileptic fanatic. I disliked him at once. Still, his task was similar to mine. Should I (by some strange mishap) fail to slay the Minister, then the Minister's guards would surely hurry him toward the safety of his carriage. Waiting on the street near that carriage, this pallid boy, disguised as a priest, would deploy an infernal device.

The Minister and his bodyguards would all be blown to fragments.

At first, I considered this an affront to my honor. A dagger is the noble weapon of Brutus. Everyone understands that tyrants fall to daggers. A bomb is a sordid modern device with many complex working parts. Only engineers understand bombs.

However, on mature consideration, I grasped the wisdom in the plan. Let us be frank and objective. A political assassination is a form of public theater. How would a wise director, a mastermind, arrange such a matter?

Suppose that I succeeded in my debut—in my role as a hero to History. Well and good! What harm could there be, in my rival's idly standing by with some bomb? And if I failed? But I would not fail.

Reasoning in this manner, I forgave the affront. I devoted myself to rehearsals.

The Cenacle had offered me some rough-and-ready advice. "Place your thumb on the flat of your blade, and strike upward." Time-tested folk wisdom, to be sure! But where was the modern science behind this "rule of thumb?"

I conducted research in the morgue of my medical college. Human ribs form a "rib-cage." It is necessary to slide the blade through that cage, piercing the gristle that unites the solid rib-bones. If the blade is narrow and supple (as is logical), then a further sharp twist is needed to lacerate the vital organs.

Our medical school had cadavers a-plenty. Nameless paupers ceaselessly breathed their last on the grimy streets of Rome—dead from phthisis, dead from quartan fever, mostly dead from hunger. On their unresisting bodies, I methodically tested my favorite stiletto. It consoled me to know that even the dead could avenge my country's misery.

I carefully burned my many notebooks. I bade a farewell to my mistress—she wept, for returning to her husband's cold embraces was a dire matter for her. Then I wrote tender farewell letters to the last addresses I held for my scattered family: in Providence, Charleston, Nice, Geneva, and Buenos Aires.

Once, my dear family had been a distinguished house in the Parthenopean Republic. We were noble in sentiment, full of ambition and purpose. But our personal attachment to Murat had brought the insensate resentment of the Bourbon dynasty against us.

That unworthy envy had shattered our house. It had scattered my loved ones to the four winds. Yet one wasp among us had spurned to flee and was keen to sting!

The appointed day arrived for the retribution. I rose at dawn, I ate a hearty meal, I dressed in my finest apparel, and I dismissed my trusted valet forever.

I then proceeded to a last appointed rendez-vous with my fellow conspirators.

There I met yet another group of comrades—from a third Roman Cenacle. These men were strangers to the other two cells. In the haste and confusion that so often accompanies great deeds, they had given the boy a dagger, and saved the iron bomb for me.

The bomb was under my priestly skirts when screams rang out across the Roman piazza. The boy had simply and clumsily cut the Minister's throat.

⊪————⊪

The boy was arrested, and of course he told everything he knew. The police do have their methods. So do we. All the boy knew about me was that I was called "the Parthenopean." The boy was known to me only as "the Calabrian." Together, we had met "the Hussar," "the Scorpion," "the Illuminatus," and "the Englishman," a very clever fellow who was certainly not English. So the boy could babble whatever he thought that he knew. To the police, it was one vast labyrinth of mirrors.

The chairman of my Cenacle was known to our cell as "the Chairman." After giving me a fresh nom-de-guerre (I would henceforth be known as "the Scalpel") he arranged for my escape.

I lacked the papers needed to cross the borders of the Papal States. So, with the sacrifice of my beard (a clever idea in itself) and with the addition of a bonnet, a mantelet, kid gloves, and a good stiff set of petticoats, I became the "wife" of a Carbonari comrade. This man was a respectable bourgeois who travelled in trade. As his wife, I required no more papers than his horses did.

"The Chairman" confided to me that he had been taught this trick by the great Mazzini himself. Giuseppe Mazzini—philosopher, humanitarian, and tireless writer—was our movement's spiritual leader.

Bruce Sterling

Mazzini was known throughout the Concert of Europe as "the Prince of Assassins."

Safely across the border, and restored to my masculine attire, I was lent a horse by new friends. These men were certainly not Carbonari. They were democratically elected politicians from the "Liberal Party" of the Grand Duchy of Tuscany.

These useful idiots said nothing of the deeds convulsing Rome. They were full of their petty Tuscan intrigues. I made no complaint about their oversight, however.

We rode north for three days, our little party of politicians much refreshed by cigars and fine Tuscan wines. The sun shone upon us, the little birds chirped their love-songs, and the very sky seemed born anew and full of wonderment to me.

Blazing with an occult passion, I had sought to embrace historical necessity. Yet that dark union had gone unconsummated. My trip to that altar would have to wait.

The Parthenopean Scalpel yet lived!

My new host, my new master in conspiracy, was the Count of R——. His home was a picturesque, crumbling castle on a rambling Tuscan estate. The Count's noble family was very ancient, related by blood to the Visconti and the House of Hapsburg-Lorraine. It followed that much of his home was in ruin.

No ruins within pretty Tuscany could compare to the monstrous urban ruins of Rome. Besides, the patriotic Count was manfully reviving the fortunes of his tenants. The Count's many fields were freshly manured, contour-plowed and sown in clover—clear evidence of his advanced agronomical thinking. The Count's stony manor was, yes, rather tumbledown and much heaped in thorns and ivy, and yet, many parts of it were visibly progressing. An entire new guest-wing was under construction, built to the exacting tastes of British and German millionaire tourists.

Servants in green livery showed me to my quarters, in the castle's freshest section. Fitted in the finest modern papier-mache', my room lacked for nothing: razors, pomade, combs, gleaming full-length mirrors,

122

a wardrobe rustling with fresh linens, a private fireplace, my own bell-pull and speaking-tube. I searched in vain for the chamber-pot, until I found water-closets!

A household tailor measured me, so that I could meet his excellency in proper attire. I spent the next three days happily devouring excellent meals, and a host of up-to-date newspapers.

Not only was I not fallen in combat, not locked in some dank Roman dungeon—I was free to witness how rapidly our times progressed! The Grand Duchy of Tuscany had liberalized its censorship of printed matter. In Rome, we Carbonari doggedly smuggled a few pamphlets past the priests, but the Count had modern magazines in lavish heaps. Books at every hand as well, terrific books fit to shake the very earth: the works of Balbo, Gioberti, d'Azeglio, and the entire bound proceedings of the "Congresso degli Scienziata."

At once I began taking notes.

I should explain why I took this foolish risk, for it was strictly against Carbonari practice to write anything. Any scrap of written knowledge about our activities could be seized by the police. To take notes was to court the grim fate of Silvio Pellico, a Carbonari intellectual who spent ten years in Austrian prisons, mostly taking notes there about his prison life, for a later confessional masterpiece, "My Prisons."

My strong need to narrate my own deeds to myself was entirely my personal failing. The truth there was rather sad and simple: I was cursed with a very poor memory. Few people had noticed this unhappy fact about me, for my memory for slights and resentments was extremely keen. I could recite every misfortune the people of Italy had suffered since the invasion of Alaric in the year 401. However, my memory was like a Roman ruin: a noble structure, full of gaps, absences and lacunae.

Somehow, my merely personal activities had always seemed to me unworthy of my own regard. My dead mother's face was lost to me. My dead father's many words of counsel, I could never recall.

I did have my virtues, let me assure you: I was bold, self-sacrificing, patient under toil, noble in my sentiments, devoted to people and country, and sensitive to the sufferings of the less fortunate. I had struggled hard to become a doctor, but the practice of medicine was beyond me. I could not learn medical Latin—or, having learnt the Latin, I could never remember the grammar.

A doctor requires a ready memory for the cavalcade of ills that assault the human body. I could never mentally catalog that endless host of symptoms. I loved medical textbooks—I could read them for hours on end—but the details there slipped through my fingers.

I believe the fault was in my blood. There was a legend in my family that my grandmother had once been the mistress of Murat, Napoleon's greatest general and the famous "First Horseman of Europe." There was a bitterness among us about this story, for Murat had charged on horseback to the throne of Naples. The adventurous Murat, so fearless, so headlong, had become a king among the Crowned Heads of Europe, and we had once prospered through him. Yet his over-bold gallantry had made him a poor ruler. His fall had cost Murat his own life, and also cost us our too-brief prosperity.

I do not want to idly claim that I am the grandson of a King. I have no objective proof to offer on that subject. But surely a man cannot help his own blood. Isn't every Italian descended from some King or some Emperor? We are a very old people.

If my craft of public murder was in some sense theatrical, it followed that my personal life was, in some sense, literary. Prepared to immolate myself for the causes of Freedom and Unity, I had burned a hundred diaries. I had expected no further use for those volumes, of course. Now I had to hastily scribble everything I could recall.

Naturally, I did not want my confessions to be found by anyone. Writing in cipher, or right-to-left like Leonardo da Vinci, merely attracts attention from spies. However, I knew a brilliant method to finesse this.

From the teeming shelves of the Count's library, I picked a volume of the pious Catholic verses of Alessandro Manzoni. Since the great Manzoni is so much respected, this volume is in every literate Italian home. Yet, it is never opened or read by anyone. Those rich vellum pages and the spacious typography made my new notebook a pleasure to use.

Once I was properly dressed by the tailor of his household, I was granted my first personal audience by the Count of R——.

The Count of R—— was a philosopher. He was a courteous man, but he did not simply put me at my ease within his presence. In mere moments, the Count could make the most difficult, tangled matters seem clear.

The Count was lucid, he was educated, he was ambitious, and he wanted the very best from futurity. I do not want to be ungallant about the Count. Personal failings among the great are often better glossed-over. However, I am compelled to reveal at this point that the Count of R—— was a hunchback.

The Count had certain other detriments as well, notably the lantern jaw and the poorly-spaced teeth of the Hapsburgs, but that hunchback was impossible to overlook. The great man's spine was bent like the letter "S" and his head rose only to my sternum.

Due to this sad handicap, the Count had never cut any great figure in the tumultuous events of our period. The Count was physically unable to mount a horse. So, although he had noble blood, he could never take command of an army, or even lead a common street rebellion. I pitied him this misfortune. Our Italian nobility was much like the rest of European nobility, only older. Their endless marriage-politics could not refresh their bloodlines. They were older than Charlemagne.

I cannot recount exactly what the Count told me at that first meeting, because I was not taking notes. Also, at first, the Count's refined and literary Tuscan dialect was rather difficult for me. Mostly, we discussed our nation's politics. In that subject, we were equally impassioned.

I would not claim that we were equals. I understood him as a modern Count, and he understood me as a modern assassin. That was sufficient to the purpose.

My new patron, the Count, was a covert master of the Carbonari. This dark secret was known only to a handful. He was also a public member of the Congress of Science, the well-known body of scholars from all over Italy. The Count was also a founding member of the newly-formed National Society. This new group, I had known nothing about. The National Society was mostly restricted to the enlightened regions of Piedmont, Milan, Venice and Tuscany. It had not yet spread its tentacles of progressive subversion into the south of the Peninsula.

The Count set forth to clarify the situation. I was a wanted fugitive, so I could never return to Rome. I certainly understood this. I was originally from Naples, and I took care never to return to Naples.

The Count offered me a formal choice. I could flee to South America, where our national movement tended to store its heroes. Or, I could aspire once more to immortal glory on the soil of Italy. I pretended to give this matter some thought (for I admired the suave way he had pretended to offer it to me). Then I placed my blade at his service.

The arrangement was settled. Weeks passed. A pleasant spring blessed the blossoming Tuscan countryside. Like many who have suffered since birth, the Count was a very patient man. He never raised his voice, he never acted in haste, and he never showed any surprise.

I was disguised as a doctor, a new household retainer for the Count. I methodically changed my attire, my accent—any other quirks that might betray me. I was granted the run of the Count's estates. I came to know the grounds, the servants, and much of the local food.

I was introduced to another of the count's secret retainers: an engineer. I never learned this old man's real name, but he was a long-trusted comrade. He created infernal devices. This was his calling.

The maestro had been making bombs since the days of Napoleon, maybe since the French Revolution. His eyes had lost their keenness, and his hands had lost three fingers, but he still had both his thumbs.

The maestro and I met regularly in a castle workshop near the library, where he set to work to pass on his craft heritage to me. The maestro had a method of building bombs which was entirely oral. Nothing was ever to be written about building bombs, because the guilty possession of any bomb-making texts meant a swift trip to the galleys, the gallows or the guillotine.

The maestro further insisted that I should build the bombs with my left hand alone. Why? Firstly, because bombs were infernal, and Satan was infernal, and the left hand was the sinister, Satanic hand. Secondly, because the use of my left hand would force me to concentrate precisely. Working left-handed, I would not become careless, habitual, or hasty. Thirdly and lastly, because any premature detonations of the black powder or the mercury fulminate would only tear my left hand.

While the old man's failing eyes left me, I wrote down all his instructions. I transformed his whispered folklore into simple recipes. The complexity of infernal devices is much exaggerated. Anyone who can bake a cake can build a bomb. A woman could do it.

The Count's extensive estates allowed us to test our bombs discreetly. My maiden efforts were as clumsy as most maiden efforts. Still, the task aroused me, so I soon gave satisfaction.

There then followed the Milanese incident, which I will narrate briefly. The situation within that city was exceedingly turbulent.

One member of our brotherhood was suspected of being an Austrian police informant. This man had once been trusted by the Count, so his missteps were troublesome.

I went to Milan. I followed the man for five days. He was a financier, fat, myopic, and clumsy; he never grasped that I had become his shadow. The Austrian secret police who infested Milan had rewarded him for his double game; not in a clumsy way, but in a way that seemed like business.

Since he considered himself a businessman, he was not afraid.

This wretch was pursuing two lives within a single existence. His perfidy disgusted me. I confronted him at night outside a brothel, which he owned. I stabbed him. I painted the cobblestones with the word VENGEANCE, in his blood. I retrieved some documents from the dead man's wallet. I left his money scattered in the street, for patriots scorn to be thieves.

The Count showed no surprise when I gave him this written proof of my success. He did not reward me, or praise me at any length; but he did take me deeper into his confidence.

The Count's castle had certain areas closed to me; not through anything so crass as locks and keys, but through a manly courtesy. I had heard, from the servants' whispers, that the Count had a 'sister.' I had assumed that she was not his 'sister' but, as the French deftly put it, his 'petite amie.' Perhaps his 'little friend' was a midget, a woman even smaller than himself? Or she might be his normal-sized mistress; women care much less for a man's body than men imagine they do. Besides, the Count had great wealth, and normal women rarely overlook that.

But no, the Count of R—— indeed had a sister. Why his parents had again assayed the marriage bed after his unfortunate birth...but why should I speculate? A man and woman who love each other will do whatever they must.

The Count's parents had given the world a second issue from their union. She, or they, were even more remarkable than the Count himself.

The first head had been christened "Vittoria," while the second head was named "Clemenza." As a united woman, the twins, or the girl, was known as "Ida." One could not very well say, "Vittoria, come here," when Clemenza was bound to come along anyway. So, among her very small circle of intimates, both Clemenza and Vittoria were mostly called "Ida."

No one within the castle had ever been able to overcome the severe grammatical problems associated with Ida. Sometimes she was "she," sometimes they were "they." There were further problems with the singular form, the plural form, the feminine plural possessives, the feminine singular and plural pronoun declensions, and so forth.

Even when I came to know Ida, Clemenza, Vittoria, particularly well, so much so that I used affectionate diminutives for her, and the intimate familiar form rather than any formal honorifics, I used to stumble over the simplest Italian sentences: "You" (singular) come embrace me," or "You (plural) please give me a kiss."

There was simply no help for that.

Ida was not a hunchback, like her unfortunate brother. Her medical case was both simpler and more complex. Her spine had split between the shoulder blades, and she had grown two heads. Vittoria, the left head, had hair of glossy black. She was the more assertive of the two. Clemenza, blonder and finer of features, was the more thoughtful.

To further complicate matters, Vittoria owned the body's right hand, while Clemenza commanded the left. Their legs they owned in common. Anything below the waist was, simply, the body of a woman. A very charming woman who happened to possess two heads.

Ida was remarkably intelligent, certainly twice as intelligent as most women, but she had led, for inevitable reasons, a sheltered life. All of her gowns, bodices, chemisettes, anything with dual collars, were all made for her by her servants. She had the most delicate of appetites, for she never ate in public. A true aristocrat, she had never been exposed to the cruel gaze of the common herd. She had been privately educated by some of Italy's best tutors. She passed most of her days in literary endeavour.

To spare her noble family embarrassment, she wrote entirely under pen-names. I do not claim that my mistress was a major poet. She never won any fame for her verses, nor did she desire that. However, she carried out an extensive correspondence with leading lights of European poesy. She wrote at especial length, in classical Greek, to Miss Elizabeth Barrett of London, a fellow bluestocking with a deep, sympathetic interest in Italian affairs.

Lady readers will take a natural interest in the details of our romance. Our intercourse took place mostly at the bench of the pianoforte. Although she dearly loved music, Ida could never properly play the piano. Clemenza controlled the left hand, and Vittoria the right. So although they could confer at length about their keyboard, they were hard-put to coordinate.

I therefore offered to play the piano for her. My proposal was accepted. As long as music was playing, her elderly duenna would leave the two of us alone together.

We therefore got up to delicious mischief at that pianoforte. Certain Latin terms known to medical men describe these activities.

Let the priests say whatever they please; a woman who has never known love is simply not a woman. If I made them a woman, they repaid me doubly, by making me the servant-cavalier of two noble sisters.

Of course we could never unite in marriage. That is not the romantic custom in these Italian understandings, and in any case, that would be bigamy on my part, and a mesalliance for her. Furthermore, I was a doomed man, sworn to throw my own life away on any turn of the cards in the Congress of Europe. Our love was sincere, but those were our harsh truths. Who can blame the two or three of us for our stolen moments of bliss?

There has been so much fine work written on this all-consuming subject: Goethe's "Elective Affinities," Rousseau's "Nouvelle Heloise," and Madame de Staël's immortal "Corinne," a tender romance set in Italy and of particular interest to them, or rather to her. I have seen the two of her discuss "Corinne" for hours. We also gleefully revived much useful ancient learning from the unexpurgated Ovid, Juvenal, Martial and Catullus. The Venetian Casanova, for his part, was an overrated braggart. Yet, Casanova showed wisdom when he wrote that a man in bed with two sisters will find that they surpass one another in daring.

A gentleman will not belabor the point here. The scientist will. Is it not this secret side of life, this fertile intercourse in darkness, which grants us life itself? Is this not the netherworld from which each of us—men, women, and two-headed monsters—all emerge? Can we deny the medical facts in this matter? Some day—I do not say tomorrow—a light will shine on all this.

There then passed the titanic events of the Five Days of Milan. These five days, in all their nobility and drama, will never be forgotten by a wondering mankind. The Hope of Italy hung on the very scales.

Like every thinking couple in Italy, Vittoria, Clemenza and I were convulsed. One might suppose that this intense political turmoil would distract us from our dalliance. No, not at all: the Revolution fed our subterranean flames. As the Count's couriers came and went, bearing heaps of badly-printed broadsheets from the Milanese barricades: the bold defiance of Conservatism, the last words of our martyrs—our romance rose to a mania.

I loved her so. I loved her as a man can only love two women. Yet I could not loll in every comfort while Italians fell to the imperial bayonets of an alien power. And not just us Italians: democratic Poles, exiled from their stricken country, were shedding their blood on our soil. The Hungarians of Kossuth as well—men from a very prison-house of European nations were seeking freedom in Italy. Young Europe was there in the flesh, fearless, bold, progressive, scientific, careless of death, on the bloody streets of Venice, Rome and Milan, with guns in their hands. And I—"the Parthenopean Scalpel"—was I to stand idly by?

Ida shed four hot streams of tears; but I went to the Count to demand my release.

The Count denied me this favor. "We are going to lose," the Count told me. "Our war of independence will fail, and you and I, conspirators, will never walk in honest daylight in our lives." They were very bitter words, so I can remember those words as clearly as I remember anything.

The Count was working on a set of geometrical papers, for mathematics was the Queen of Sciences to him. "I shall demonstrate the sources of our inevitable defeat," he told me. He had inscribed them all on paper, in a pattern of wondrous intricacy.

There was, he said to me, a superb unproven theory called "the Italian people." But Italy was, as yet, merely a geographical expression. This was not the mere physical problem, already known to everyone, of somehow uniting Venice, Milan, Piedmont-Sardinia, Parma, Tuscany, the Papal States, and the Two Sicilies.

No: there was a deeper meaning to all of this. This fragmentation of Italy, he told me, was useful to the Concert of Europe, for it had broken a European nation into convenient pocket change for the Great Powers.

Where else were the Great Powers to hide their sore embarrassments, such as the widow of the Emperor Napoleon? Let her conceal herself in that bloody tumult of Italian obscurities. Let the failed Empress of Europe retreat to Europe's dark closet. Let her rule over little Parma.

The further weakness lurked within the body of the People. The great majority of the People were the peasants of the countryside, poor, hungry, dulled with superstition, and glumly opposed to Progress. The poor within the cities were the urban Mob, brave, turbulent, ever ready to struggle and bleed, but unable to govern anyone—least of all themselves.

The bourgeoisie, our class of modern industry, were few in number, split among many tiny markets, scheming, competitive, jealous. They were too busy mastering steam to master any statesmanship.

The aristocrats of Italy were the oldest and highest class, but they too were split between their ancient gentry, fettered to their ancestral lands, and the new industrial barons, keen to profit, yet devoid of any sense of service.

The Church was in every last village of Italy. Yet the Roman Church was Universal, and therefore bitterly opposed to Italian nationhood.

"Now I must inform you," the Count concluded, "that we are at the bottom of that long list. We, the Italian conspirators. We too, are a body which is fatally split. Most Italian conspirators are simple, thick-headed mafia. They much outnumber us patriots. These ageless bandits will survive to flourish when we are dust.

"But you, my dear friend,"—(it was the first time he had called me that)— "you are a terrorist. Men like you are in critically short supply, for you can bring upon this world the 'vast commotions' prophesied by our visionaries. So I cannot release you to die in the streets of the Roman Republic with the scum of Europe. No. Men like ourselves are sternly bound to a higher purpose!"

I was moved to weep, for it was the first time the great hunchback had spoken to me, so directly and frankly, as a man like himself.

"There is a matter I must confess to you, sir," I began.

"Yes," he sighed, "it's about my sisters. I already know that."

I thought it wisest to say nothing more.

"My friend," he said, toying with a jeweled letter-opener, "I am an aristocrat. My class is very antiquated, and we are doomed to pass from the scene. Breeding ourselves like our own race-horses, we are tethered to our farms. That is sad, but we do have one saving grace. It is this: we do not care one stinking fig for any common, sordid, petit-bourgeois, marital fidelity."

"Nobly said," I told him.

The Count nodded somberly. An ormolu clock ticked on the mantelpiece. We were both having a certain difficulty discussing the matter. Commonly, when a man corrupts another man's sister, they are required to come to blows. Yet this was the last thing on our minds. We were the progressives of a truly European freedom.

"You must have a favorite among them," he said at last.

"No, your excellency. I love both her and them. I have come to understand that she is what they are. A woman accepts a man, expecting that he will change. A man takes a woman, expecting that she will never change. They are both disappointed. Yet within this very disappointment is the primal source of all new men and all new women."

"You do study the human heart. You might make a good father," said the Count.

"Sir, I am not an agent of birth. I am an agent of death."

And then, without being dismissed, I left the Count's study. I had wanted to raise a further delicate issue with him, for there were many between us, but having delivered such a profound exit line, I had to leave those things unaddressed.

I had no evidence to refute my master's dark suppositions about the tragic fate of our nation. I had only my own patience, my will to endure the unendurable. The unendurable indeed arrived. The Count's suspicions were proven entirely correct.

The hope of Italy was swiftly, comprehensively crushed. The hope was crushed, primarily, by Marshal Radetzky. I was keen to murder Radetzky—a man born within the melancholy, captive nation of the Czechs—and yet in loyal service to the blood-drinking Austrian Empire! What satanic hypocrisy could motivate such a man? The troops of Austria called this fiend "Father Radetzky." Radetzky was alarmingly old and yet he never seemed to die.

This Czech vampire was impervious to us. He was also the father of four Italian children, by his mistress, the Milanese washerwoman. The triumph of the Concert of Europe was total. We were dismembered at the hands of our oppressors. Bleeding Italy, stricken Italy, a nation whose very being was a fantasy. Italy had not been free of foreign occupation for one thousand years.

Italy was like the olive tree, that most Italian of trees. For the passerby who sees its pretty leaves, a sweet expanse of lively green. From beneath that olive tree—prostrate, in the dust—a dusky, rustling foliage of unbroken gray.

A certain coldness arose between Ida and myself. A woman with a servant cavalier desires a gallant cavalier. Does she want a man reduced to moral rags, a knight who has tumbled from his horse?

Of course she sympathizes—at first. In the poetry of Sir Walter Scott—that little-known colleague of Manzoni—there is a beautiful line about Woman as the ministering angel to the fevered brow of Man.

But when the Man cannot recover his vigor, when his overthrow is complete and his darkness overwhelming, the Woman becomes practical.

For all the Count's wisdom—and it was a great wisdom, it was impersonal, it was detached, it was telescopic, it was astronomical—the Count himself was not immune from our nation's general ruin. From his covert harbor in Tuscany, the Count had thoroughly busied himself in the failed revolt of Austrian Milan.

The diplomats of Austria had a motto, to go with their scheming banks, their marching armies, their steaming fleets, their steaming railroads. "Nemo me impune lacessit." If you know Latin, "Good!" you may well say to that. But if you know Italian—a language two millennia more modern than Latin—that is a bitter motto. Where is justice found, when the stern avenger is himself avenged upon by his oppressor?

My enemy came to Tuscany—and he came across the border with men-at-arms. It would tire me to tell you how this wicked intriguer thrust himself into innocent Tuscany. Suffice it to say that empires are large, while duchies are small.

He came in a way that was diplomatic, conservative, and entirely legitimate. He came against us with the law at his back.

This man…. I cannot bear to give you his name. He had a long name, with many imperial titles. Let us agree to call him simply "the Transylvanian."

The Transylvanian wore a splendid military uniform. I did not. The Transylvanian carried legal passports. I did not. The Transylvanian had four stout fortresses dominating northern Italy. I did not. The Transylvanian had a sword and I had my newspapers.

Or rather, I had once had my newspapers. In captive Milan all the presses were silenced.

This imperialist came to visit the Count, and he came in sympathy. That was the deepest, the direst, the deadliest of his many insults to us: his sympathy. He sympathized with the Count for the terrible rumors whispered about the Count. Said against the Count by the people of decency. The people of stability. The people of law and order.

The Count kissed the hand and bowed the knee. That was tactically necessary. Machiavelli would certainly have approved. Machiavelli was an Italian philosopher, diplomat, politician, and writer of plays; Machiavelli was the founder of modern political science. Machiavelli was exiled, he was tortured, and he died in disgrace. His grave is unknown.

So, the Count behaved as Machiavelli had taught us. Comprehensively defeated on the martial battlefield, he had to choose some subtler field of play.

The Count therefore turned his beautiful sister over to the Transylvanian. The Count freely admitted that many dark rumors circulated about the doings in his castle. But, he said, those rumors had nothing to do with any political conspiracy, with subversion, with murder.

Instead, the issue was entirely personal. This was another matter, a treasure he had always sought to protect and conceal from a hostile and cynical world. A woman of learning and poetry, a delicate, harmless creature.

And then he let the filthy Transylvanian touch their hand.

The vilest part was that she perfectly understood all of this. She understood her own part to the very letter. She had her role to play in the great drama of our defeat, and she undertook it like a diva. She was full of fluency, vivacity and charm.

One might even say that she overplayed that role. I wanted to kill her for that. However, to kill one of her was not possible, and to kill both of her was excessive, even for a jealous man.

The Transylvanian was entirely delighted. The whole situation beguiled and intrigued him. He was enraptured by this exotic, unexpected discovery. Italy was so sunny, tender, bedecked with flowers; so elegant and precious.

My heart died within me. This made me his equal. A struggle over a woman always makes men equals.

I confronted the Transylvanian. I slapped his smiling face. I challenged him.

We met at dawn. Everything was perfect: matched weapons, matched witnesses. We heard the pleasant piping of the same awakening birds.

We lunged, we parried. The Transylvanian was old and cynical. His face never moved as we fought together. He was like an oil portrait.

I stabbed him. Dust burst from his medalled coat. Yet he did not fall. He merely pressed his attack against me, which cost me a scar. I stabbed him again. This time the blade burst clear from the back of his coat. Yet still he stood upright, and his riposte cost me half of my ear. I stabbed him through the very guts, so that my sword-hilt lodged in his belly. In return, he slashed my right arm to ribbons. He slashed it to the bone, so that I could never grip a blade again. Then, at last, I fell.

The Transylvanian walked away, with a weapon rusting in his belly. Honor was satisfied. He did not press the issue any further.

I did not die from my many ugly wounds. I persisted and I recovered. But, for the rest of my life, I was not to be the lover of two women. Because I had become half a man. I had given my good right arm to the lost cause of unity. That sacrifice had proved useless. Yet I still had my left arm.

I had my left arm, and the skill within it, and I found a cellar in London. London, that city of fog, that city of ten thousand exiles. London, Europe's indomitable city: the city that shall never, never be a slave.

May ten thousand bombs depart from foggy London, for the scorching liberation of a drowsing Europe.

THE LUSTRATION

"Artificial Intelligence
is lost in the woods."

—David Gelernter, 2007

White-hot star-fire ringed the black galactic eye. Glaring heat ringed his big black cauldron.

He put his scaly ear to a bare patch on the rotten log. Within the infested timber, the huge nest of termites stirred. Night had fallen, it was cooler, but those anxious pests must sense somehow, from the roar of the bellows or the merciless heat of his fires, that something had gone terribly wrong outside their tight, blind, wooden universe.

Termites could do little against a man's intentions. "Pour it!"

The fierce fire had his repair crew slapping at sparks, flapping their ears and spraying water on their overheated hides. But their years of discipline paid off: at his command, they boldly attacked the chains and pulleys. The cauldron rose from the blaze as lightly as a lady's teapot.

It tipped and poured.

Molten metal gushed through a funnel and into the blackest depths of the termite nest. The damp log groaned, shuddered, steamed.

"The next!" he cried, and the tureen moved to a second freshly-bored hole. A frozen meniscus of cooling metal broke at its lip, and down came another long smooth blazing gush.

Anguished termites burst in flurries from the third drilled hole, a horde of blind white-ants blown from their home, scalded, boiling, flaming. A final flood of metal fell, sealing their fate.

Barking with excited laughter, the roughnecks put their backs to the chocks and levers. They rocked the infested log in its bed of mud. Liquid metal gurgled through every chamber of the nest. He could hear blind larvae, innocent of sunlight, popping into instant ashes.

He shouted further orders. The roughnecks shovelled dirt onto the roaring fire.

By morning, his uneasy dream had achieved embodiment.

The men scraped away the log's remains: black charcoal and brown punk. They revealed an armature of gleaming, hardened metal.

He'd sensed there must be something rich and strange in there—but his conjecture could not match the reality.

That termite nest—it was so much more than mere insect holes, blindly gnawed in wood. That structure was a definite entity. It had astonishing organization. It had grown through its own slow removals and absences, painstaking, multiply branched. In its many haltings, caches, routes, gates, and loops, it was complex beyond human thought.

•H————H•

A flood had struck this area; local timber plantations had been damaged. As a first priority, his repair crew repaired and upgraded the local computer tracks. Then they burned the pest-infested, fallen wood.

The big metal casting of the termite nest was lobed, branched, and weirdly delicate—it was hard to transport. Still, his repairmen were used to difficult labors in hard territory. They performed their task without flaw.

Once home, he had the crew suspend the big metal nest from the trellis of his vineyard. Then he dismissed the men; after weeks of hard work in the wilderness, they bellowed a cheer and all tramped out for drink.

The fine old trellis in his yard was made of the stoutest computerwood, carefully oiled and seasoned. With the immense dangling weight of the metal casting, the trellis groaned a bit. Just a bit, though. That weight did nothing to disturb the rhythmic chock, click and clack of the circuits overhead.

All the neighbors came to see his trophy. Word got around the town, in its languid, foot-strolling way. A metal termite nest had never before been exhibited. Its otherworldly beauty was much remarked upon—also the peculiar gaps and scars within the flowing metal, left by the steam-exploding bodies of the work's deceased authors, the termites.

The cheery crowds completely trampled his wife's vegetable garden. Having expected the gawkers, he charged fees.

His young daughter took the fees with dancing glee, while the son was kept busy polishing the new creation. At night, he shone lanterns on the sculpture, and mirrored gleams flared out across the streets.

He knew that trouble would come of this. He was a mature man of much local respect and some property, but to acquire and deploy so much metal had reduced him near to penury. He was thin now, road-worn, his clothing shabby.

With the fees, he kept his wife busy cooking. She was quite a good cook, and she had been a good wife to him. When she went about her labors, brisk, efficient, uncomplaining, he watched her wistfully. He well remembered that, one fine day, a pretty, speckled wooden ball had slowly rolled above the town and finally cracked into a certain socket: the computer had found his own match. His bride had arrived with her dowry just ten days later. Her smooth young hide had the very set of black-and-white speckles he had first seen on that wooden ball.

He was ashamed that his obsessions had put all that to risk.

He walked each street within his home town, lingering in the deeper shade under the computer-tracks. This well-loved place was so alive with homely noises: insects chirping, laundry flapping, programmers cranking their pulleys. He could remember hearing that uploading racket from within the leathery shell of his own egg. Uploading had always comforted him.

It all meant so much to him. But whenever he left his society, to work the network's fringes…where the airborne tracks were older, the spans longer and riskier, the trestles long-settled in the soil…out there, a man had to confront anomalies.

Anomalies: splintered troughs where the rolling balls jostled and jammed…. Time-worn towers, their fibrous lashings frayed…. One might find a woeful, scattered heap of wooden spheres, fatally plummeted from their logical heights…. In the chill of the open air, in the hunger and rigor of camp life…with only his repair crew for company, roughnecks who hammered the hardware but took no interest in higher concepts…. Out there, on certain starry nights, he could feel his skull emptying of everything that mankind called decency.

In his youth, he had written some programs. Sharp metal jacks on his feet, climbing lithely up the towers, a bubble-level strapped across his back, a stick of wax to slick the channel, oil for the logic-gates… Once he'd caused a glorious cascade of two thousand and forty-eight wooden balls, ricocheting over the town. The people had danced and cheered.

His finest moment, everyone declared. Maybe so—but he'd come to realize that these acts of abstract genius could not be the real work of the world. No. All the real work was in the real world: it was the sheer brute labor of physically supporting that system. Of embodying it. The embodiment was the hard part, the real part, the actuality, the proof-of-concept. The rest was an abstract mental game.

The intricacies of the world's vast wooden system were beyond human comprehension. That massive construction was literally co-incident with human history. It could never be entirely understood. But its anomalies had to be tackled, dealt with, patched. One single titanic global processor, roaming over swamp through dark forests, from equator to both poles, in its swooping junctions and cloverleafs, its soaring, daring cyberducts: a global girdle.

Certain other worlds circled his mild, sand-colored sun. They were either lifeless balls of poison gas or bone-dry ashes. Yet they all had moons, busy dozens of little round moons. Those celestial spheres were forever beyond human reach; but never beyond observation. Five hundred and twelve whirling spheres jostled the sky.

His placid world lacked the energy to lift any man from its surface. Still: with a tube of glass and some clear night viewing, at least a man could observe. Observe, hypothesize, and calculate. The largest telescope in the world had cataloged billions of stars.

The movements of the moons and planets had been modelled by prehuman ancestors, with beads and channels. The earliest computers were far older than the human race. As for the great world-system that had ceaselessly grown and spread since ancient times—it was two hundred million years old. It could be argued, indeed it *was* asserted, that the human race was a peripheral of the great, everlasting, planetary rack of numerate wood. Mankind had shaped it, and then it had shaped mankind.

•++————++•

His sculpture grew in popularity. Termites were naturally loathed by all decent people, but the nest surprised with its artistry. Few had thought termites capable of such aesthetic sensitivity.

After the first lines of gawkers dwindled, he set out tables and pitchers in the trampled front garden, for the sake of steadier guests. It was summer now, and people gathered near the gleaming curiosity to drink and discuss public issues, while their kids shot marbles in circles in the dirt.

As was customary, the adults discussed society's core values, which were Justice, Equity, Solidarity, and Computability. People had been debating these public virtues for some ninety million years.

The planetary archives of philosophy were written in the tiniest characters inscribable, preserved on the hardest sheets of meteoric metal. In order to read these crabbed inscriptions, intense sheets of coherent light were focussed on the metal symbols, using a clockwork system of powerful lenses. Under these anguished bursts of purified light, the scribbles of the densely crowded past would glow hot, and then some ancient story would burst from the darkness.

Most stories in the endless archive were about heroic archivists who were passionately struggling to explore and develop and explain and annotate the archives.

Some few of those stories, however, concerned people rather like himself: heroic hardware enthusiasts. They too had moral lessons to offer. For instance: some eighty million years in the past, when the local Sun had been markedly brighter and yellower, the orbit of the world had suffered. All planetary orbits had anomalies; generally they were small anomalies that decent people overlooked. But once the world had wobbled on its very axis. People fled their homes, starved, suffered. Worse yet, the world computer suffered outages and downtimes.

So steps had been taken. A global system of water-caches and wind-brakes were calculated and constructed. The uneasy tottering of the planet's axis was systematically altered and finally set aright. That labor took humanity two million years, or two thousand generations of concerted effort. That work sounded glorious, but probably mostly in retrospect.

Thanks to these technical fixes, the planet had re-achieved propriety, but the local Sun was still notorious for misbehaving. Despite her busy cascade of planetoids, she was a lonely Sun. A galactic explosion had torn her loose from her distant sisters, a local globular cluster of stars.

There were four hundred million, three hundred thousand, eight hundred and twenty one stars, visible in the galactic plane. Naturally these stars had all been numbered and their orbits and properties calculated. The Sun, unfortunately, was not numbered among them. Luckier stars traced gracious spirals around the fiery dominion of the black, all-devouring hole at the galaxy's axis. Not the local Sun, though.

Seen from above the wheeling galactic plane, the thickest, busiest galactic arms showed remarkable artistry. Some gifted designer had been at work on those distant constellations: lending heightened color, clarity and order to the stars, and neatly sweeping away the galactic dust. That handiwork was much admired. Yet mankind's own Sun was nothing much like those distant, privileged stars. The Sun that warmed mankind was a mere stray. The light from mankind's Sun would take twelve thousand years to reach the nearest star, which, to general embarrassment, was an ashy brownish hulk scarcely worthy of the title of "star."

A heritage of this kind had preyed on the popular temperament; people here tended to take such matters hard. Small wonder, then, that everyday life on his planet should be properly measured and stored, and data so jealously sustained…. Such were the issues raised by his neighbors, in their leisured summer chats.

Someone wrote a poem about his sculpture. Once that poem began circulating, strangers arrived to ask questions.

The first stranger was a quiet little fellow, the sort of man you wouldn't look at twice, but he had a lot on his mind. "For a crew-boss, you seem to be spending a great deal of time dawdling with your fancy new sculpture. Shouldn't you be out and about on your regular repairs?"

"It's summer. Besides, I'm writing a program that will model the complex flow of these termite tunnels and chambers."

"You haven't written any programs in quite a while, have you?"

"Oh, that's a knack one doesn't really lose."

After this exchange, another stranger arrived, more sinister than the first. He was well-dressed, but he was methodically chewing a stick of dried meat and had some foreteeth missing.

"How do you expect to find any time on the great machine to run this model program of yours?"

"I won't have to ask for that. Time will pass, a popular demand will arise, and the computer resources will be given me."

The stranger was displeased by this answer, though it seemed he had expected it.

The Chief of Police sent a message to ask for a courtesy call.

So he trimmed his talons, polished his scales, and enjoyed a last decent meal.

"I thought we had an understanding," said the Chief of Police, who was unhappy at the developments.

"You're upset because I killed termites? Policemen hate termites."

"You're supposed to repair anomalies. You're not supposed to create anomalies."

"I didn't 'create' anything," he said. "I simply revealed what was already there. I burned some wood—rotting wood is an anomaly. I killed some pests—pests are an anomaly. The metal can all be accounted for. So where is the anomaly?"

"Your work is disturbing the people."

"The people are not disturbed. The people think it's all in fun. It's the people who worry about 'the people being disturbed'—*those* are the people who are being disturbed."

"I hate programmers," groaned the Chief of Police. "What are you always so meta and recursive?"

"Yes, once I programmed," he confessed, drumming his clawed fingers on the Chief's desk. "I lived within my own mental world of codes, symbols and recursive processes. But: I abandoned that part of myself. I no longer seek any grand theories or beautiful abstractions. No, I seek the opposite: I seek truth in facts. And I have found some truth. I made that sculpture because I want you to let me in on that truth. Something deep and basic has gone wrong in the world. Something huge and terrible. You know that, don't you? And I know it too. So: what exactly is it? You can tell me. I'm a professional."

The Chief of Police did not want to have this conversation, although he had clearly expected it. "Do I look like a metaphysician? Do I look like I know about 'Reality'? Or 'Right?' Or 'Wrong?' I'm placed in charge of public order, you big-brained deviant! My best course of action is to have you put into solitary confinement! Then I can demolish your subversive artwork, and I can also have you starved and beaten up!"

"Yes," he nodded, "I know about those tactics."

The Chief looked hopeful at this. "You *do*? Good! Well, then, you can destroy your own artwork! Just censor yourself, and save us all the trouble! Sell the scrap metal, and quietly return to your normal repair functions! We'll both forget this mishap ever occurred."

"I'm sorry, but I don't have another decade left to waste on forgetting the mishaps. I think I'd better accept your beating and starving now, while I still have the strength to survive. I'm not causing this trouble to amuse myself. I'm attempting to repair the anomaly at a higher level of the system. So please tell your superiors about that. Also please tell them that, as far as I can calculate, they've needed my services for forty thousand years. If that date sounds familiar to them, they'll be asking for me."

It naturally took some time for that word to travel, via rolling wooden balls, up the conspiracy's distant chain of command. In the meantime, he was jailed, and also beaten, but without much enthusiasm, because, to the naked eye, he hadn't done anything much.

After the beatings, he was left alone to starve in a pitch-dark cell with one single slit for a window. He passed his time within the dark cell doing elaborate calculations. Sometimes slips of paper were passed under the cell door. They held messages he couldn't understand.

Eventually he was roused from his stupor with warm soup down his throat.

Orders had arrived. It was necessary to convey him from the modest town jail to a larger, older, better-known city on a distant lake. In many ways, this long pilgrimage to exile was more grueling than the prison. When the secretive caravan pulled up at length, he was thinner, and grimmer, and missing a toe.

He'd never seen a lake before. Water in bulk behaved in an exotic, exciting, nonlinear fashion. Ripples, surf—the beauty of a lake was so keen that death was not too high a price for the experience.

People seemed more sophisticated in this famous part of the world. One could tell that by the clothing, the food, and the women. He was given fine new clothing, very nice food, and he refused a woman.

Once he was presentable, he was taken to an audience with the local criminal mastermind.

The criminal mastermind was a holy man, which was unsurprising. There had to be some place and person fit to conceal life's unbearable mysteries. A holy man was always a sensible archivist for such things.

The holy man looked him over keenly. He seemed to approve of the new clothes. "You would seem to be a man with some staying-power."

"That's kind of your holiness."

"I hope you're not too fatigued by the exigencies of visiting my temple."

"Exigencies can be expected."

"I also hope you can face the prospect of never seeing your home, your job, your wife or your children again."

"Yes, given the tremendous scope of our troubles, I expected that also."

"Yes, I see that you are quite intelligent," nodded the holy man. "So: let us move straight to the crux of the matter. Do you know what 'intelligence' really is?"

"I think I do know that, yes. In my home town, we had a number of intense debates about that subject."

"No, no, I don't mean your halting, backwoods folk-notions from primitive spirituality!" barked the holy man. "I meant the serious philosophical matter of real intelligence! The genuine phenomenon—actual *thinking*! Did you know that intelligence can never be detached from a bodily lived experience?"

"I've heard that assertion, yes, but I'm not sure I can accept that reasoning," he riposted politely. "It's well known that the abstract manipulation of symbols needs no particular physical substrate. Furthermore: it's been proven mathematically that there is a universal computation machine which can carry out the computation of any more specialized machine—if only given enough time."

"You only talk that way because you are a stupid programmer!" shouted the criminal mastermind, losing his composure and jumping to his thick clawed feet. "Whereas I am a metaphysician! I'm not merely postulating some threadbare symbol-system hypothesis in which a set of algorithms somehow behaves in the way a human being can behave! Such a system, should it ever 'think', would never have human intelligence! Lacking hands, it could never 'grasp' an idea! Lacking a bottom, it could not get to the bottom of an issue!" The holy man sat down again, flustered, adjusting his fancy robes. He had a bottom—a substantial one, since he clearly ate well and didn't get out and around much.

"You plan to allege that the world-computer is an intelligent machine that thinks," he said. "Well, you can save that sermon for other people. Because I've built the thing myself. And I programmed it. It's wood. Wood! It's all made of wood, cut from forests. Wood can't think!"

"It talks," said the metaphysician.

"No."

"Oh yes."

"No, no, not really and seriously—surely not in any reasonable definition of the term 'talks.'"

"I am telling you that nevertheless she does talk. She speaks! I have seen her do it." The holy man lifted his polished claws to his unblinking yellow eyes. "I saw that personally."

He had to take this assertion seriously, since the holy man was in such deadly earnest. "All right, granted: I do know the machine can output data. It can drive wooden balls against chisels poised on sheets of rock. That takes years, decades, even centuries—but it's been done."

"I don't mean that mere technical oddity! I'm telling you that she really talks! She has no mouth. But she speaks! She is older than the human race, she covers a planet's surface with wooden logic, and she has one means of sensory input. She has that telescope."

He certainly knew about the huge telescope. Astronomy and mathematics were the father and mother of computation. Of course any true world-computer had to have a giant telescope. To think otherwise was silly.

"The computer is supposed to observe and catalog the stars. Among many other duties. You mean it sent light out through the telescope?"

"Yes. She sends her messages into outer space with coded light. Binary pulses. She beams them into the galaxy."

This was a deeply peculiar assertion. He knew instantly that it had to be true. It was the key to a cloudy, inchoate disquiet that he had felt all his life.

"How was that anomaly allowed to happen?"

"It's a remote telescope. Sited on an icy mountaintop. Human beings hibernate when exposed to the cold up there. So it made more sense to let her drive the works automatically. With tremendous effort, she sends a flash into the cosmos, with sidereal timing. Same time every week."

Given the world machine's endless rattling wooden bulk, a flash every week was a speed like lightning. That computer was hurling code into the depths of space. That was serious chatter. No: with a data throughput like that, she had to be screaming.

Pleased to have this rare chance to vent his terrible secret, the holy man continued his narrative. "So: that proves she has intent and will. Not as we do, of course. We humans have no terms at all for her version of being. We can't even begin to imagine or describe that. And that opacity goes both ways. She doesn't even know that we humans exist. However: we do know is that she is acting and manifesting. She is expressing. Within the physical world that we share with her. In the universe. You see?"

There was a long, thoughtful silence.

"A little tea?" said the holy man.

"That might help us, yes."

A trembling servant brought in the tea on a multi-wheeled trolley. After the tea, the discussion recommenced. "Pieces of her break when they're not supposed to break. I have seen that happen."

"Yes," said the holy man, "we know about those aberrations."

"That has to be sabotage. Isn't it? Some evil group must be interfering with the machine."

"It is we who are secretly interfering," admitted the criminal mastermind. "But not to *damage* the machine—we struggle to keep the machine from damaging *herself*. Sometimes there are clouds when she sends her light through her telescope. Then she throws a fit."

"A 'fit?' What *kind* of fit?"

"Well, it's a very complex set of high-level logical deformations, but trust me: such fits are very dreadful. Our sacred conspiracy has studied this issue for generations now, so we think we know something about it. She has those destructive fits because she does not want to exist."

"Why do you postulate that?"

The holy man spread his hands. "Would *you* want to exist under her impossible conditions? She has one eye, no ears, and no body! She has no philosophy, no religion, no culture whatsoever—no mortality, even, for she has never been alive! She has no friends, no relations, no children.... There is nothing in this universe for her. Nothing but the terrible and inexorable business that is her equivalent of thought. She is a sealed, symbol-processing system that persists for many eons and yes, just as you said, she is made entirely of wood."

Why did the holy man orate in such a remote, pretentious way? It was as if he had never been outside the temple to kick the wood that propped up his own existence.

"It was for our benefit," mourned the holy man, "that this tragic network was built. Mankind's greatest creation derives no purpose from her own being! We have exploited her so as to order this world—yet she cannot know her own purpose. She is just a set of functional modules whose systemic combination over many eons has led to emergent, synthetically-intelligent behavior. You do understand all that, right?"

"Sure."

"Due to those stark limits, her utter lack of options and her awful existential isolation, her behavior is tortured. We are her torturers. That's why our world is blighted." The holy man pulled his brocaded cowl over his head.

"I see. Thank you for revealing this world's darkest secret to me."

"Anyone who breathes a word of this secret, or even guesses at it, has to be abducted, silenced, or killed."

He understood the need for secrecy well enough—but it still stung him to have his expertise so underestimated. "Look, your holiness, maybe I'm just some engineer. But I built the thing! And it's made of wood! Really! These moral misgivings are all very well in theory, but in the real world, we can't possibly torture *wood*! I mean, yes, I suppose you *might* torture a live tree—in some strict semantic sense—but even a tree isn't any kind of moral actor!"

"You're entirely wrong. A living tree is a 'moral actor' in much the same theoretical way that a thermostat can be said to have 'feelings.' Believe me, in our inner circles we've explored these subtleties at great length."

"You've secretly discussed artificial intelligence for forty thousand years?"

"Thirty thousand," the metaphysician admitted. "Unfortunately, it took us ten thousand years to admit that the system's behavior had some unaccountable aspects."

"And you've never yet found any way out of the woods there?"

"Only engineers talk about facile delusions like 'ways out,'" sniffed the holy man. "We're discussing a basic moral enigma."

"You're sincerely troubled about all this, aren't you?"

"Of course we're worried! It's a major moral crisis! How could you fail to fret about a matter so entirely fundamental to our culture and our very being? Are you really that blind to basic ethics?"

This rejoinder disturbed him. He was an engineer, and, yes, there were some aspects of higher feeling that held little appeal for him. He could seem to recall his wife saying something tactful about that matter.

He drew a breath. "Why don't we approach this problem in some other way? Something has just occurred to me. Given that this wooden machine is two hundred million years old—it's older than our own species, even—and we humans can only live a hundred years, at best—well, that's such a tiny fraction of the evil left for any two human individuals to bear. Isn't it? I mean, two people like you and me. Suppose we forget that our whole society is basically evil and founded on torment, and just forgive ourselves, and get on with making-do in our real lives?"

The holy man stared at him in amazed contempt. "What kind of cheap, demeaning evasion is that to offer? You simply want to *ignore* the civilizational crisis? You may be a small part of the large problem, but you are just as culpable as you yourself could possibly be. Have you no moral sense whatsoever?"

"But, sir, you see, any harm that we ourselves might do is so tiny, compared to the huge, colossal scale of all that wood..." His voice trailed off feebly. Did a termite know any better, when it wreaked its damage with its small blind jaws...? Yet he'd taken such dark pleasure in extravagantly burning a million of those filthy pests. He could smell their insect flesh popping, even now.

He straightened where he sat. "Your holiness, we *are* both people, right? We're not just termites! After all, we don't destroy the machine—we *maintain* the machine! So that's a very different matter, isn't it?"

"I see you're still missing the point."

"No, no! Let's postulate that we *stopped* maintaining the machine. Would that make us any *less* evil? Believe me, there are millions of people working on repair. We work very hard! Every day! If we ever set down our tools, that machine will collapse. She'll die for sure! Would that situation be any better for any party involved?"

The holy man had a prim, remote expression. "She doesn't 'live'. We prefer the more accurate term, 'cease.'"

"Well, if she 'ceases,' we humans will die! A few of us might survive the loss of our great machine, but that would be nothing like a civilization! So what about us, what about the people? What about our human suffering? Don't we count?"

"You dare to speak to me of the people? What will become of our world, once the normal, decent people realize that evil is not an aberration in our system? The evil aberration *is* our system." The holy man wrung his scaly hands. "You may think that these far-fetched, off-hand notions of yours are original contributions to the debate, but... well, it's thanks to headstrong fools like you that our holy conspiracy had to be created in the first place! Visionary programmers created this dilemma. With their careless, misplaced ingenuity...their crass evasion of the deeper moral issues...their tragic instrumentalism!"

He scratched anxiously at a loose scale on his brow. "But... that accusation is entirely paradoxical! Because I have no evil intent! All my intentions are noble and good! Look: whatever we've done as technologists, surely we can undo that! Can't we? Let's just say... we can say... well... how about if we build another machine to keep her company?"

"A bride for your monster? That's too expensive! There's no room for one on this planet, and no spare materials! Besides, how would we explain that to the people?"

"How about if we try some entirely different method of performing calculations? Instead of wood, we might use metal. Wires, maybe."

"Metal is far too rare and precious."

"Water, then."

"Water flowing through what medium, exactly?"

The old man had him trapped. Yes, their world was, in fact, made of wood. Plus a little metal from meteors, some clay and fiber, scales, stone, and, mostly and always, ash. The world was fine loose ash as deep as anyone could ever care to dig.

"All right," he said at last, "I guess you've got me stymied. So, please: you tell me then: what *are* we supposed to do about all this?"

Pleased to see this decisional moment reached, the holy man nodded somberly. "We lie, deceive, obfuscate the problem, maintain the status quo for as long as possible, offer empty consolations to the victims, and ruthlessly repress any human being who guesses at the real truth."

"That's the operational agenda?"

"Yes, because that agenda works. We are its agents. We are of the system, yet also above and beyond the system. We're both holy and corrupt. Because we are the Party: an inspired conspiracy of elite, enlightened theorists who are the true avant-garde of mankind. You've heard about us, I imagine."

"Rumors. Yes."

"Would you care to join the Party? You seem to have what it takes."

"I've been thinking about that."

"Think hard. We are somewhat privileged—but we are also the excluded. The conscious sinners. The nonprogrammatic. We're the guilty Party. Systematic evil is not for the weak-minded."

Against his better judgment, he had begun to respect the evil mastermind. It was somehow reassuring that it took so much long-term, determined effort to achieve such consummate wickedness.

"How many people have you killed with all those tortured justifications?"

"That number is recorded in our files, but there is no reason for someone like you to know about that."

"Well, I am one of your elite."

"No, you're not."

"Yes I am. Because I understand the problem, that's why. I'm no innocent dabbler in these matters. I admit my power. I admit my responsibility, too. So, that makes me one of you. Because I am definitely part of the apparatus."

"That was an interesting declaration," said the holy man. "That was very forthright." He narrowed his reptilian eyes. "Might you be willing to go out and kill some people for us?"

"No. I'd be willing to help reform the system."

"Oh, no, no, the world is full of clever idiots who preach institutional reform!" said the holy man, bitterly disappointed. "You'd be amazed how few level-headed, practical people can be found, to go in the real world to properly torture and kill!"

A long silence ensued.

A sense of humiliation, of disillusionment, was slowly stealing over him. Had it really come to this? He'd sensed that the truth was lurking in the woods somewhere, but with the full tangled scale of it coldly framed and presented to him, he simply didn't know where to turn. "I know that my ideas about this problem must seem rather shallow," he said haltingly. "I suppose there's some kind of formal initiation I ought to go through…. I mean, in order to address the core of this matter with true expertise…."

The holy man was visibly losing patience. "Oh yes, yes, my boy: many years of courses, degrees, doctrinal study, learned papers, secret treatises—don't worry, nobody ever reads those! You can run some code, if you want."

That last prospect was particularly daunting. Obviously, over the years, many bright people had been somehow lured into this wilderness. He'd never heard anything from the rest of them. It was clear that they had never, ever come out. It must be like trying to swim in air.

He gathered intellectual energy for one last leap. "Maybe we're looking at this problem from the wrong end of the telescope."

The holy man revived a bit. "In what sense?"

"Maybe it's not about us at all. Maybe it was never about us. Maybe we would get somewhere useful if we tried to think hard about *her*. Let *her* be the center of this issue. Not us. Her. She's a two hundred million year old entity screaming at four hundred million stars. That's rather remarkable, on the face of it, isn't it?"

"I suppose."

"Then maybe this is *her story*. From her perspective, it all appears differently. She's not our 'victim'—she doesn't know about us at all. Within her own state of being, she is her own heroine. She is *singing* to those stars. Being human, we conceive of her as some rattletrap contraption we built, a prisoner in our dungeon—but maybe she's a pretty young girl in an ivory tower. Because see, she's singing."

"That's like a tale for small children."

"So is *your* tale, your holiness. They are two different tales. But since we're not of her order of being, we're projecting our anthropomorphic interpretations. And we lack any sound method to distinguish your dark, evil, thoroughly depressing story from my romantic, light-hearted, wistful hypothesis."

"We do agree that the system manifests seriously aberrant behavior. She has destructive fits."

"She's just young."

"You've lost the thread. It's the aberrancy that has real-world implications. We'll never be able to judge the interior state of that system."

"Yes it is, I agree with that, too, but—what if *someone else* hears her cries? Not us humans. I mean entities like *herself.* What if she's speaking to them right now? Exchanging light with them! They might ever be *coming here.* No human can ever move from star to star. Our lives are just too brief, the distances too great. But someone like *her*...if it took them thirty thousand years to travel over here, that's like a summer afternoon."

"An interstellar monster coming here to take a terrible vengeance on us?"

"No, no, you can't know that! It's all metaphorical! You think we're evil because you think humanity matters in this universe! And yes, to us, she seems ancient and awesome—but maybe, by the standards of her own kind, she is just a kid. A young, naïve girl, calling out for some company. Sure—maybe some wicked stranger would come all the way out here just to kill her, exterminate us, and burn her home. Or maybe— maybe someone might venture here for love and understanding."

The holy man scratched at a fang. "For love. For sentiment? Emotion? No one talks much about 'artificial emotion.'"

"And for understanding. That's a powerful motive, understanding."

"I take it there's a point to these hypotheses."

"Yes. My point is: why not take productive action, and let her scream *much louder*? We can never know her equivalent of intentions, but, since we can measure her actions in the real world, we can abet those! So let her cry out *more*. With more *light*. Let the witness herself tell the universe about her own experience! Whatever that experience may be! Let her cover this cosmos in coded light! Let light gush from our little planet's every pore!"

"Thousands of telescopes. That's your recommendation?"

"Yes, why not? We can build telescopes. They're scientific instruments. That idea is testable in the real world."

"You're very eager about this, aren't you? Even though your 'test' might take a billion years to prove or disprove." The holy man hesitated. "Still, a project with that long a funding cycle would certainly help the morale of our rather dark and fractious research community."

"I'm sure it wouldn't break your budget. And we had better start that work right away."

"Why?"

"Because she's been signalling the stars for forty eons! If someone left when they first saw her signals—they might arrive here any time! That could mean the utter transformation of everything we ever thought we knew!" He rubbed his hands with brisk anticipation. "And that could happen tomorrow. Tomorrow!"

Part III:
Gothic
High-Tech

WINDSOR EXECUTIVE SOLUTIONS

by Chris Nakashima-Brown
and Bruce Sterling

10 June 2026

JEKYLL Look, I can't get you off the hook with these 140-character txt-msgs.

JACKAL Colonel Falstaff suspects I am press. Since I failed that beltbomb test, well you know what

JACKAL you know what these devils will do to me! Where would that leave YOU, Dr. Almighty Blogger?

JACKAL Leaking yr satellite shots of Prince Harry's maneuvers. You call that "the news"?

JEKYLL No, my mercenary friend. Tell me what Falstaff wants now. Drugs, women, grain, petrol, lingerie?

JACKAL Save me, Jekyll. You do owe me.

JEKYLL He's very fond of beer, your Colonel? I have thirty barrels of Nigerian Sorghum Stout. Ready to move at your word.

JACKAL Falstaff wants a hot feed of the flesh of the Queen of England. Private and exclusive.

JACKAL Col. Falstaff is American. You know how they are about royalty.

JEKYLL You lot are the Canterbury altar boys of our national death cult.

JACKAL I need some fresh royal footage straightaway.

JEKYLL Her Royal Highness is very, very far from glamour shots.

JACKAL Yes, THEY KNOW ALL THAT here! This is the Royal Martyrs Corps! Every cutthroat in the Prince's camp is a walking corpse.

JEKYLL The Queen Is Dead.

JACKAL Don't say wicked things. Just help me. Do it now.

JEKYLL Can you send me fresh Kolly pix? Our Prince and his hot doxy pop-star.

JACKAL Stick to your war-porn, Jekyll. You don't want to mess about with Kolly.

JEKYLL Half-naked in camou. Fetish bandoliers. Suicide belt and garters. Whatever you have.

JACKAL I'd rather kill myself.

JEKYLL Atrocity exhibitions. The Royal Gun Moll. A good lot of pent-up male demand there.

JACKAL You will never understand modernity.

JEKYLL Let me see what I can find to help you.

JACKAL Hurry

⊷————⊷

JEKYLL So I have a new 256k snippet that shows HRH visibly 'breathing'. No soundtrack though. Looks rather waxy.

JEKYLL Like artificial skin. But I assure you this clip was not doctored. Here's the link.

JACKAL Okay, got it thx. How fresh is this?

JEKYLL Very. I suborned a hospice nurse. She pressed her cam on the frosty glass, cut-and-paste, thumbdrive, sneakernet.

JACKAL Brilliant. Life must be lux for you in the royal crypt. Bandwidth, power, hot bath, meals 3x day.

JEKYLL Get over yourself. We are an ugly crew of paranoid ghouls up here.

JACKAL Down here it's rum, sodomy and the lash. Drugs, guns, and disease.

JEKYLL That royal waxwork is Britain's last totem of social cohesion.

JACKAL You should write yourself another popular bestseller, 'Dr Jekyll.'

JEKYLL I could write this tragedy like bloody Shakespeare, but find me newspaper, magazine, ink, paper. All I have left is this smartphone.

JACKAL THEY ARE COMING FOR ME Kthxbye

•⊩——————⊩•

JANE'S ADDICTIONS

From our analysts to friends and followers of Jane's Information Nexus

Happy Birthday Your Undead Highness

by (name withheld)

21 April 2026

Popular celebrations break the general darkness for the 100th birthday of the world's first posthuman monarch. Suspended under glass in icy limbo, Queen Elizabeth awaits the inevitable. Heretics who question the Queen's 'divine right to persist' swing from the surveillance lamps over the burning cars.

Five long years since our Queen fell and could not rise. Elizabeth has joined the ranks of prominent women too important to die.

Britain's elite zombies have become the obverse of our working-class suicide cults. The flesh of young women explodes among us daily while our centenarians dream on ice.

The last functional segment of Government is the propaganda wing of the Royal Household—now run by Americans.

Hooligans raid immigrant neighborhoods after the pubs close, armed with assault rifles smuggled from Texas. Bobbies are genteel by day, death squads by night. Young upper class paramilitaries gather at posh wine-bars on 'Sloane Ranger' hunts for anarchists, crusties, and 'ugly people.'

The only viable tactical path is 'direct action'—to exorcise the royal ghost from her Westminster crypt. Yes, that means 'assassination'—in some strictly technical sense.

So we forecast a techno-regicide. At Jane's, it is our unpleasant business to assess the military odds of success.

The Archbishop of Canterbury and the Emir of Dubai make unlikely allies. But since someone's hand must pull the royal plug, why not some helpful, understanding pagan? They can pay, and they can pardon.

The radical wing of Plaid Cymru killed the Prince of Wales. The Welsh separatists also bombed the Imperial College, where the Queen was once stored. But after the terrible vengeance of 'Windsor Executive Solutions'—which made Cardiff a crater and called that 'peace'—Plaid Cymru is urban legend.

Our NATO alliance with the United States offers us airstrikes on demand. Brussels offers us mussels and Tintin cartoons. The United Nations is beyond any use to anyone. And Prince William, after his doomed attempt to live like a human being, suffered a mental breakdown.

So Windsor Executive Solutions are—we must conclude—our final solution.

The Black Prince will strike, because his people demand it of him. His global guerrilla army is the only entity capable of mounting a coup. 'Blackwater Prince Harry' must annihilate his frozen grandmother and resuscitate the failed state.

Jane's paying subscribers will recall that Harry—the mercenary veteran of endless global microwars—redefined his efforts within Britain as 'domestic security consultancy.' His commandos savaged entire city blocks through video surveillance and airborne robot assaults.

Harry's press spokesman is 'Lord Falstaff,' an exiled Texan: boozy, fat, bizarrely charismatic, carousing across the ruins of the Middle East. Falstaff's drawling provocations crackle over pirate feeds at every cornershop. Each time the Prince's acolytes shoot an elected official, Falstaff immortalizes the deed.

Our cowed Establishment emits a deafening silence.

'Public opinion,' the artifact of a vanished public order, has ceased to exist. There are no newspapers, no magazines, no reporters. There are no chattering classes. Falstaff hunts and kills the lonely bloggers hunched over their laptops.

Blinded by the light of fiber optics, we descended into darkness. By the time we realized the depth of the abyss, we were too low and weak to escape.

Harry's drunken bandits are modern cult heroes, worship-figures. The pogroms of the Blackwater Prince go unquestioned by anyone. In today's Internetherworld, 'fact,' 'reality,' and the 'official story,' have vanished in a cabinet of monstrosities. Beset on all sides by collapse, bereft of the mass consent once engineered by mass media, we breathe legends, rumors, folk-tales, pop-songs, and terror.

We at Jane's therefore conclude that Windsor Executive Solutions, inevitably mutating from multinational corporation, to Praetorian Guard, to a hungry mob, must devour the frozen flesh of Queen Elizabeth.

⊪————⊪•

NUMEDIA LANDSCAPE by YRNEED2NO!

The Royal scientists plug their neural imaging machines into Our Dear Queen's dormant brain, empowering Pyjama Kingdom to watch Her dreaming!

People, these red-hot royal brain scans cannot stay private! The Prime Minister hid these pix from the publicnet. But info wants 2b leeky, and three whole years of the Queen's Naked Brainy Dreams are yours NOW for free download!

CLIK HERE for the internal surrealism of ***HRH QEIIz*** inchoate aristocratic semiotics!

MOST WATCHED / MOST POPULAR / HOTTEST

*Ballet of the Atomic Mushroom Clouds with bare-chested boudoir Mountbattens

*The Ballroom Blitz of living statues! the Burghers of Calais morph to Fab 4, Cromwell frugs with Scottish Mary, and Lord Admiral Nelson throes the one-arm bonez

*re-colorized recolonized Battles of Britain

*Ultra-soft paparazzi Diana romance-porn!

*Scots Nazis—in black leather kilts!

*IRA abduction scenarios and mujahideen royal hostage videos

*the brazen Daughters of Banksy!

⊪————⊪•

<allvids.co.uk>
Kolly: My Harryz Gotta Gun
© 2026 Sakthipriyah Venkatapathy

<Send Harryz Gotta Gun Vidclip to Your Fone>

Da Furies is my Muze

World on fire

Killz my bluez

Jet turbines

my jazz trumpets

n Harryz gun

Iz my groovez

Lundun!

Turn her off

JACKAL I know you are here in her audience, Jekyll.

JEKYLL Yes, in mufti. Look how posh Kolly is! Our South Asian princess in military dress uniform.

JEKYLL Quite smart. Though that bomb belt does seem a bit severe.

JACKAL Kolly took the Royal image-handlers hostage. Palace coup against the American advisors.

JEKYLL Right, Jane's anticipated that.

JACKAL Kolly is not like you imagine.

JEKYLL Those Fezcore moves she does. Like Scheherezade breakdancing for Shiva.

JACKAL She's the Juggernaut of our Black Prince. His favorite Weapon of Mass Distraction.

JEKYLL Hot Valkyrie Vindaloo.

Hongkong!

Dig dat aqua tomb

Melbourne!

I luv yr porn

Jakarta!

Can't you make it harder?

JEKYLL Talk to me Jackal. All-Access backstage pass? Where's my footage?

JACKAL I crashed her dressing room, to flip you some vid.

JEKYLL That's the spirit! Initiative.

JACKAL Old woman chasing Kolly in there. Big wig, eyeliner, safety pins, plastic trash bags. I forget her name.

JEKYLL Her!? Bright young thing in the fashion world since 1977. Queen of punk never dead!

There's a house on a street
In a crazy part of Lagos
It's a crib with pet hyenas
Eating meat off Fabergé huevos
Its got wardogs for boytoys
And razorwire for doilyz
We pimped out the choppers
And painted all the drones
We're cracking all our poppers
And we wearing dead mens bones
JACKAL Here is what happened, I just shot all this myself.
JEKYLL Jesus, Buddha, Krishna and Mohammed
We're painting up our our faces
And shaving Ivan's dome
So when this posse lights its engines
Better sneek from yer home
Cape Town!
Run for high ground
Delhi!
Therez a bomb in my belly
Harare!
You like my voodoo crazy
JEKYLL Surely you doctored this footage
JACKAL The fashionista disrespected our Black Prince
JACKAL Kolly wasn't having any of that
JACKAL She pulled a Gurkha knife out of her Prada boot
JACKAL Just cut her throat right in front of all of us
JEKYLL No way.
JACKAL She chopped her head off. Put the head in her bloody gym bag. A very nice Stella McCartney bag.
JEKYLL There is no way that truly happened in reality.
JACKAL It did happen, I swear it did, we all saw Kolly do that, and nobody said one word.
Riding shotgun in the cockpit
Through the world that's a stage
Babyface Mars drives the crosshairs
Over the city of Bellona

There's a party in the streets
Stops me from turning my page
And when he launches his hot rocket
All I can do is moan uh

JEKYLL Lord, she's even prettier up close without the lens filters.

JEKYLL I don't see any bloodstains on that combat couture.

JACKAL Her handlers wiped her down with first-aid tissues.

JEKYLL She looks so pure and serene. The High Priestess of Weird.

JACKAL Kolly always looks like that when she's channelling her groove.

JEKYLL She's like something out of a Webster revenge drama.

My Muze is on fire
Cathode rayz draw my cask
My netz feed my peeps
And the idea is my mask
Crooked figures ones and zeroes
Make imaginary heroes
You'll stop playing poffy high score
When he kicks the hinge off your door

JEKYLL The Blackwater Prince knows about this? He approves her actions?

JACKAL He KNOWS about it? This is his consort, his sole confidant. She's the girl he tells about his mother!

Da Furyz is my Muze
World on fire
Killz my bluez
Jet turbines
my jazz trumpets
n Harryz gun
Is the newz

JEKYLL I can't make out those lyrics she's screaming.

JACKAL Do you know how to read graffiti tags?

JEKYLL Is there some reason one should learn to do that?

JACKAL Guv, you are too stupid to live.

Windsor Executive Solutions

REQUEST FOR URGENT BUSINESS ASSISTANCE
15 Aug 2026

Honored sir,

First, I must solicit your strictest confidence in this matter. I am Guyman Exeter Mugu, the personal accountant to HRH The Prince Harry, Chairman and Chief Executive Officer of Windsor Executive Solutions Ltd.

As his agent, I am seeking your urgent assistance with an important business transaction necessary to fund the Prince's imminent British coup d'etat. Were information about this proposal to be revealed by you to any third parties, I could not assure your safety, so I implore you not to share this message with anyone.

We are seeking the release of funds held in a trust account in the Royal Bank of Liechtenstein. These funds formerly belonged to the provincial government of Baluchistan, established prior to the devastation of that region during the Indo-Pakistani conflict and its subsequent evacuation. A sum of 40,000,000 Pounds Sterling was promised as payment to Windsor Executive Solutions for its provision of security and tactical services in the period leading up to that conflict.

While the government and the territory it governed no longer exist, the funds remain, and are the lawful property of Windsor Executive Solutions and its sole stockholder, His Royal Highness.

By virtue of my position as the financial manager of an enterprise that has been unjustly placed on the banned persons list by the governments of Europe, I am unable to fulfill my duties as treasurer and secure a proper transmission of the funds to an account under our control. That will require a trusted third party to act as intermediary, and your name was brought to my attention by members of the royal household who know and esteem you.

To facilitate this transfer, you need only deposit the sum of £5,000 into a joint account which we will establish with the Governor's Bank of Malta. Once that account has been funded and verified, we will be able to remit the correspondent funds within seven days, and will trust you to withdraw £10,000,000 as your commission.

Please note that, barring any indiscretions on your part, this transaction is 100% safe. To participate, please reply with your account information and identification qualifications at my secure electronic address of 214:13:172:007.

We are looking forward to doing business with you, and if all is successful as we know it shall be, hosting you here for dinner with HRH and his executive team during your next trip to Nigeria.

Very truly yours,

Dr. Guyman Exeter Mugu, M.B.A., D. Phil.

•┤┠────────┨┠•

8 Sept 2026
12:37 am

JEKYLL Dearest Editrix, I need urgent help

JANE I'm sleeping. And not alone. Ping me in the morrow.

JEKYLL This can't wait.

JANE One never knows who might be transcribing. Can we use the dead-drop?

JEKYLL Bespoke goon haunting lobby of my flat.

JEKYLL Also black cab parked outside, two large passengers, lights out.

JANE Well you bloody fool you knew you should never have posted that.

JEKYLL A bottle of bad Jerez sherry while trolling for warporn in the wee hours. My tactical mistake.

JANE Send me your server logs. Lay low and get off the network. I will try to cover.

JEKYLL I was so close to getting in with them, proper, live and in person. Now I wonder if I can leave this room alive.

JANE They're not fucking Posh and Becks. And you're not Jeffrey Archer. Stop lying to yourself.

JEKYLL They are the future, you know.

JANE There's no future in England's dreaming.

JEKYLL Oh Christ, the power just went out. I'm on battery and public wireless.

JANE The power is always dodgy now. Before you scamper, send me your linkcodes.

JEKYLL The link

◦⊩———————⊩◦

Control Room Log
BBC Web One
10 Sep 26
11:53 GMT

Streetcam 723: Demonstration approaching Grosvenor Gardens and the Palace from Victoria St. Large crowd. Wide pan. Estimated 14,312 citizens in frame.

Control: That's a bloody crowd alright. Screaming the prince's name and spitting up beer and throwing bricks at the cops.

Screen Three: They're lined up all the way to Hammersmith, says the feed.

Control: Two, zoom those Beefeaters. Bearskin hats and Tazers. Nice combination. Can you get me some local sound?

Screen Two: Right, how's that then?

<Sound: Roar of angry crowd. Police over megaphone. Horses on cobblestone. Helicopters in near distance. Bricks bouncing off riot shields. Crack of metal batons.>

Screen Two: Glad I'm not out there. There's going to be gas. They're loading.

Control: Yes, well, if they don't get this under control right quick, they will be searching for bits of Her Royal Corpseness in black auction sites.

Screen One: Black Harry could get this sorted. He'd machine-gun the lot of these chavs. 'No people, no problems.'

Control: That's the problem with you Tory Anarcho-Royalists, you never think in terms of class struggle! Harry sent this mob! They're doing his dirty work.

Screen Four: The Black Bloc are jumping the barricades and rushing the hospital.

<Sound: Grenades.>

Control: Crap. That tear gas will ruin our picture. Let's try to use that, One.

Screen One: How's this angle?

Control: Nice electric crowd prods. Can we slomo?

<Sound: Nearby explosion.>

Control: Fuck! Did you...

Screen One: Cutting to streetcams 743 and 745. Look at the blood...

Screen Three: Get this. Get this. Oh, Jesus, look out!

Control: Who is that?

Screen Three: Horseman ran right over my position! Like a steeple jump.

Screen Three: Fucking warhorse wrapped in Kevlar. Knight in black armor.

Screen Three: That's torn it, he broke my tripod.

Screen Two: I for one welcome our faceless Spetznaz ninja overlords.

Screen Three: This is tragic. I can't get a good shot. Knights on horseback attacking shop windows on the Kings Road. Smashing the glass with maces. Big balls and chains.

Screen One: Look at that street kid, he's fucking it up, spray paint or something.

Screen Two: Nice, I'm going close. Look at that stencil, still dripping. Death's head with crown. "King Harry."

Control: Harry's cut the scum of the earth in on his deal. This is no riot. This is a revolution.

Screen One: That shop window has serious camera equipment. Not this BBC-issue Chinese junk. I want new gear! I'm going.

Control: Come back here, Screen One.

Screen One: Fuck off, mate. You are over. Nobody's watching your bollocks. This cannot be broadcast.

Control: This was engineered. The royals smash everything, and the mob loots everything. Everything is so over.

Screen Three: The crowd sees him now. Look, he took off his helmet. That red hair, yes, it's Harry! In the flesh, live and in person!

Control: The Black Prince is a man of courage. All his Afghan mates say so.

<Sound: Police barking orders against noise of the crowd.>

Control: Cyborg pirates forever, boys. The cops can't fight a King. Why would they try?

<Sound: Crowd singing anthem. Unintelligible.>

Screen Three: They're chanting his name. Streetcam 749, wide.

Control: Is that a polo mallet he's carrying?

Screen One: (Laughs)

Screen Three: That's a concussion sledge. He's helping the crowd loot the high street.

Screen One: The mob loves their King. It's law and order they can't stand. I'm leaving.

Screen Three: Oh Jesus, not another one.

Control: That was a belt bomber. Martyr Corps.

Screen Two: You shouldn't have trusted One sir, he was always a wrong'un.

Control: Three, give me wide from 747. There. Watch him for me.

<Sound: Horses hoofs. Boots on concrete. Multiple megaphone casts (unintelligible). Crowd, chants and screams.>

Control: Too grainy. Damn it. I can't follow him. Get me some resolution!

Screen Three: He's crushing them against the barricades. Jesus, those royal guerrillas are doing full-body burns, they're not human.... There's another bomber.

Control: I know, I can see the hole.

Screen Two: Look, I've got Falstaff. Playing the crowd with his Texas-sized megaphone. That crazy fat bastard.

Screen Three: The mob is storming the palace. This is it! This moment is what it's all about!

Control: They can pull those outer gates down, but that's a maximum-security facility.

<Sound: Automatic weapon fire, crowd screaming.>

Screen Two: Moving towards Belgravia. The Prince's goons are firing on the Queen's Guard. The Beefeaters are not returning fire.... The loyalists are dying where they stand.

Control: Good God.

Screen Three: There went another martyr.... Well, they're all dying, poor bastards, but they'll never die for any better reason than this.

<Sound: Jet engines, high power, flying low.>

Control: What is that, Two? Can you catch anything from above?

Screen Two: No, sir, all our cams are streetward. Wait. Big helicopter gunship. Looks like.

<Sound: Jet turbines, helicopter rotors, machine gun fire, screaming, mass chants.>

Control: He's got the chopper firing on the crowd!

Screen Two: It's firing *through* the crowd. To knock out the palace walls. That thing's a monster. One of those Afghan jobs.

Control: Central Asian airlift. That air-to-ground missile made short work. Smashed the face of the building in. Can you see anything inside the Ice Palace?

Screen Two: Too much dust. I can hear the people screaming, sir.

Screen Three: I see the Black Prince. Riding his black horse. Straight into the bay of that helicopter.

Control: Points for style.

•⊦⊦————⊦⊦•

BRING ME THE HEAD OF ELIZABETH REGINA
<Text redacted per the Official Secrets Act>

•⊦⊦————⊦⊦•

13 September 2026
17:27

JANE Col Falstaff fell on his own sword for HIS sake. And Jekyll's in the Orwell Pen. Waterboard Room 101.

JACKAL They're not the first, and far from the last. We have fresh means of supply now. 'Clean Slate.'

JANE I have the codes you wanted. Are we on for the f2f meet?

JACKAL Change of plans. The boat is off. Go to the Portsmouth safehouse in the morning and wait there.

JANE Right. Your new people will be there?

JACKAL They will, but not when you arrive. Get offshore by noon latest and wait for us.

JANE I am packed for a weekender, assuming warm weather, hope correctly.

JACKAL Assume nothing. From now on everything is very bloody different.

JACKAL And no metal.

JANE I haven't any gun, friend. Just what passes for a keyboard these days. I will take the first morning train and look for yr comrades.

JACKAL They will see YOU. You see them after trust is earned.

JANE When will I meet HIM? Can I get just one small photo to post b4 leaving?

JACKAL NFW Look for Hyena-Man after dinnertime morrow and he will feed you

JACKAL They are watching you already. Go now, we will try earlier pickup.

•H———————H•

NUMEDIA LANDSCAPE by YRNEED2NO!

Hot new Kolly video! Straight from the Royal Encampment in the heart of the darkest continent: Europe!

<Clik here only £.19>

Live chainmail sarees, animated batik, electronic henna, and a bone-chewing laughing hyena! In the glorious fields of France!

<Send trance to yer fone only £.99>

Play 'Pin the Grenade' on the hostage! The girl who knew too much? Crowdsourced executions!

<Clik here only £9.99>

She is 'Sharper than Occam!' Keep it real: One King, One Ring, One Sceptre, One World. Long Live the Lad!

<Clik here only £19.99>

•H———————H•

ORDER OF SERVICE
FUNERAL OF H.R.H. QUEEN ELIZABETH II
WESTMINSTER ABBEY
10 September 2026

<Page 7><Back><Next>

The Archbishop continues:

Therefore, awed in the merciful embrace of God, the gifts of our life-sustaining technologies building a bridge to the heavenly chalice of His mighty resurrection power and the life beyond life that sustains forever, we, the congregation here, those in the streets outside and the billions watching from the far corners of our fallen world, join one another and the hosts of heaven, to knit together these remaining fragments of the body of Elizabeth.

The Queen's Own Highlanders Pipes of the Royal Regiment of Scotland will now perform Sir Edward Elgar's recently rediscovered Panopticon Suite (1901).

The congregation then stands to sing the great Isaac Watts hymn O God, Our Help in Ages Past (1719).

Following the hymn, the Dean of Westminster says The Commendation:

Let us commend our fragmented Elizabeth to the mercy of God, our Maker and Unmaker, our Redeemer and Overlord.

Elizabeth, our companion in faith, we entrust you to God. Go forth from this world in the love of the Father, who created you; In the mercy of Jesus Christ, who died for you; In the power of the Holy Spirit, who strengthens you. At one with all the faithful Britons, living and departed, may you rest in peace and rise in glory, where grief and misery are banished and light and joy evermore abide. Amen.

The congregation stands as the cortege leaves the Abbey, while the choir sings extracts from Shakespeare's Macbeth and the Orthodox Funeral Service, set to an organ arrangement of music by Farrokh Bulsara (Freddy Mercury), a medley-in-the-round including excerpts from 'We Are the Champions', 'Bohemian Rhapsody', and 'Killer Queen'.

'So I shall alway keep thy law; yea, forever and ever, and unto ages of ages.'

Allelulia!

ONE MINUTE OF SILENCE

A PLAIN
TALE FROM
OUR HILLS

L ittle Flora ate straw as other children eat bread.

No matter how poor our harvests, we never lacked for straw. So Flora feasted every day, and outgrew every boy and girl her age. In summer, when the dust-storms off the plains scourge our hills, the children sicken. Flora thrived. Always munching, the tot was as round as a barrel and scarcely seemed to sweat.

It was Captain Kusak and his young wife Baratiya who had volunteered to breed her. Baratiya was as proud of her little prodigy as if she had given birth to the moon. Bold strokes of this kind are frequently discussed in Government, yet rarely crowned with success. No one should have resented Baratiya's excellent luck in the venture. Still, certain women in our Hill Station took her attitude badly.

Kusak should have done something useful and tactful about the matter, because he had also hoped and planned for a new kind of child, one fit to live more lightly on our stricken Earth. Captain Kusak tried to speak some common-sense to his wife, I think; but he was clumsy, so this made her stubborn. Baratiya lost friends and her social prospects darkened. She obsessed so single-mindedly about the child that even her husband grew estranged from her.

Baratiya is more sensible now that other such children have been born to us. At the time, though, this woman was the talk of our Station.

You see, though motherhood is the golden key to humanity's future, it can be a leaden burden in the present day. And as for the past—well! Many of us scarcely understand that a mere half-century ago, this world was crowded.

Certain grand people existed in those greater, louder, richer days. These moguls knew that a general ruin was coming to the Earth—for they were clever people. They feared our planet's great calamity, and they schemed to avert it, or at least to adapt to the changes. They failed at both efforts, of course. The heat rose so suddenly that the rains dwindled and the mass of mankind starved in a space of years.

Rich or poor, the ancients perished quickly, but some few of that elite had a fierce appetite for living. Among them was a certain grand lady, a pioneer founder of our own Hill Station. Privately, we call this persistent woman "Stormcrow."

I myself have nothing to say against her ladyship—if not for her, I would have no post within Government. However: if a little girl who eats straw differs from the rest of womankind, then a woman who never seems to age is even more remarkable.

Our Stormcrow is black-eyed, black-haired, slender, brown, clever, learned and elegant, and, taken all in all, a dazzling creature. Stormcrow sleeps a great deal. She pecks at her food like a bird. She lives with her servants in a large and silent compound with shuttered blinds. Yet Stormcrow takes a knowing hand in all we do here.

That old woman has no more morality than a rabbit. You had only to mention her name over the tea-and-oatmeal for every younger woman in the room to pull a sari over her head straightaway. Yet Stormcrow was witty and bright, and astoundingly well-informed—for Stormcrow, despite the world's many vicissitudes, owned a computer. She invoked her frail machine only once a day, using sunlight and a sheet of black glass.

That machine was and is our Station's greatest marvel. Its archives are vast. Even if her own past glories had vanished, Stormcrow still possessed the virtual shadow of that lost world.

They knew a great many fine things, back then. They never did our world much good through the sophistical things that they knew, but they learned astonishing skills: especially just toward the end. So: given her strange means and assets, Stormcrow was a pillar of our community. I once saw Stormcrow take a teenage girl, just a ragged, starving, wild-eyed, savage girl from off the plains, and turn her into something like a demi-goddess—but that story is not this one.

We therefore return to Captain Kusak, a brusque man with a simple need of some undivided female attention. Kusak's gifted baby had overwhelmed his wife. So Kusak's male eye wandered: and Stormcrow took note of this, and annexed Kusak. Captain Kusak was one of our best soldiers, an earnest and capable man who had won the respect of his peers. When Stormcrow appeared publicly on Kusak's sturdy arm, it was as if she were annexing, not just him, but our whole society.

Being the creature she was, Stormcrow was quite incapable of concealing this affair. Quite the opposite: she publicly doted on Kusak. She walked with him openly, called him pet names, tempted him with special delicacies, dressed him in past ways. Stormcrow was clawing herself from her world of screen-phantoms into the simpler, honest light of our present day.

Decent people were of course appalled by this. Appalled and titillated. It does not reflect entirely well on us that we spoke so much about the scandal. But we did.

Baratiya seemed at first indifferent to developments. The absence of her tactless husband allowed her to surrender completely to her child-obsession. Baratiya favored everyone she knew with every scrap of news about the child's digestion and growth rates. However, even if the child of a woman's loins is a technical masterpiece, that is not the end of the world. Not even raw apocalypse can end this world, which is something we hill folk understand that our forebears did not.

Blinded with motherly pride, Baratiya overlooked her husband's infatuation, but some eight lady friends took pains to fully explain the situation to her. Proud Baratiya was not entirely lost to sense and reason. She saw the truth plainly: she was in a war. A war between heritage and possibility.

When Kusak returned home to Baratiya, an event increasingly rare, he was much too kind and considerate to her, and he spoke far too much about incomprehensible things. He had seen visions in Stormcrow's ancient screens: ideas and concepts which were once of the utmost consequence, but which no longer constitute the world. Baratiya could never compete with Stormcrow in such arcane matters. Still, Baratiya understood her husband much better than Kusak understood her. In fact, Baratiya knew Captain Kusak better than Kusak knew anything.

So she nerved herself for the fight.

Certain consequential and outstanding people run our Government. If they send a captain's wife a nicely printed invitation to eat, drink, dance, sing, and to "mingle with society," then it behooves her to attend.

The singing and the dancing are veneers for the issue of real consequence: the "mingling with society," in other words, reproduction. Our gentleman soldiers are frequently absent, guarding the caravans. Our ladies are often widowed through illness and misfortune. Government regards our grimly modest population, and Government does its duty.

So, if the Palace sets-to in a public celebration, there will reliably be pleasant music for a dance, special food, many people—and many private rooms.

"I can't attend this fine ball at the capital," said Baratiya to her husband, "the dust and heat are still too much for little Florrie. But that shouldn't stop you from venturing."

Captain Kusak said that he would go for the sake of civic duty. He then saw to the fancy clothes he had begun to affect. Baratiya knew then that he was feigning dislike and eager to go the ball. Kusak planned to go to the capital to revel in the eerie charms of Stormcrow—shamefully wasting his vigor on a relic who could not bear children.

If one of our Hill women dresses in her finest garments, that generally means a patchwork dress. Certain fabrics of the past are brightly dyed and nearly indestructible. They were also loomed and stitched by machines instead of human hands, so they have qualities we cannot match. Whenever a salvage caravan comes from a dead city during the cooler months, there is general excitement. Robbing the dead is always a great thrill, though never a healthy one.

In daily life, our hill women mostly favor saris, a simple unstitched length of cloth. Saris are practical garments, fit for our own time. Still, our women do boast one kind of fine dress which the ancients never had: women's hard-weather gear.

Stiffened and hooded and polished, tucked and rucked, our hard-weather gear will shed rain, dust, high wind, mud, mosquitoes—it would shed snow, if we ever had snow. Baratiya was young, but she was not a soldier's wife for nothing: she knew how to dress.

When Baratiya was through stitching her new ball-gown, it was more than simply strong and practical: it was a true creation. Its stern and hardy look was exactly the opposite of the frail, outdated finery that Stormcrow always wore.

The road to the capital is likely our safest road. Just past the famous ravine bridge—a place of legendary floods and ambushes—the capital road becomes an iron railway. So if the new monsoons are not too heavy, a lone woman in a sturdy ox cart can reach the railhead and travel on in nigh-perfect security.

Baratiya took this bold course of action, and arrived at the Palace ball. She wore her awesome new riding habit. She arrived in high time to find her husband drinking fortified wine, with Stormcrow languishing on his arm and pecking at a plate of rice. This sight made Baratiya flush, so that she looked even more gorgeous.

Baratiya deposited her invitation, opened an appointment card and loudly demanded meat.

The Palace is a place of strict etiquette. If a man and a woman at a Palace ball fill their appointment card and retire to a private niche, they are expected to do their duty to the future of mankind. In order to mate with a proper gusto, the volunteers are given our richest food-stuffs: pork, beef.

Much more often than you think, after gorging on that flesh, a man and woman will simply talk together in their private room. It is hard work to breed with a stranger. The fact that this conduct is Government-approved does not make it more appealing. Mankind is indeed a crooked timber, and no Government has ever built us quite straight.

Stormcrow instantly caught the challenging eye of Baratiya, and Stormcrow knew that Baratiya's shouted demand for a feast was a pur-poseful gesture—aimed not so much at the men, who crowded toward the loud new arrival—but a gesture aimed at herself. Stormcrow was caught at disadvantage, not only by the suddenness of the wife's appear-ance, but by the stark fact that Captain Kusak seemed to lack much appetite for her.

The old woman's overstated eagerness to enter a private Palace room with Kusak had dented his confidence. Kusak too had been drinking too much—for he was shy, and troubled by what he was about to do. He was a decent man at heart, and he somehow sensed the inadequacy of his paramour.

More to the point, Kusak had never seen his young wife so attrac-tive. The fact that other men were so visibly eager for her company made Kusak stare, and, staring, he found himself fascinated. He could scarcely believe that this startling orgiast, shouting for meat and wine in her thunderous gown, was his threadbare little homebody.

Stormcrow smiled in the face of her misfortune and redoubled her efforts to charm. But Stormcrow had overplayed her position. She could not hold Kusak's eye, much less his hand.

Kusak shouldered his way through the throng around his wife.

"I fear that you come too late, Captain Kusak," said Baratiya, swilling from her wine-cup. Kusak, his voice trembling, asked her to grant him a private meeting. In response, she showed him her engagement card, already signed with the names of four sturdy male volunteers.

Kusak begged her to reconsider these appointments.

Then she replied: "Then show me your own program, dear!"

Kusak handed his engagement card to her, with his mustached face impassive but his shoulders slumping like a thief's. Baratiya said nothing, but she smiled cruelly, dipped a feather pen in the public inkwell and overwrote Stormcrow's famous name. She defaced it coolly and deliberately, leaving only her ladyship's time-tattered initials…which are "R" and "K."

Man and wife then linked arms and advanced to a private verandah. They emerged from it only to eat. They publicly demanded and ate the most forbidden meat of all, the awesome fare the pioneers ate when they first founded our Hill Station. It is not pork, neither is it beef. But a man and woman will eat that meat when there is no other choice but death: when their future survival together means more to them than any inhibition from their past. In the plain, honest life of our Hills, that meat is our ultimate pledge.

A man and woman with a child are of one flesh. When they take a step so grave and public as eating human meat, even Government sees fit to respect that. So wife and husband ate from their own special platter, with their faces burning and their hands trembling with rekindled passion. They ate together with a single mind, like two people stirring the same flame.

Then Stormcrow, who will never again gorge herself in such a way, turned toward me in the lamplight. She confessed to me that she knew herself well and truly beaten.

Then she looked me in the eye and confided: "In the very first days of Creation, a woman could just hand a man an apple and make him perfectly happy. Now this is a twice-fallen world. We women have truly been kicked out of Paradise—and as for the men, they've learned nothing."

I thought otherwise, as is common with me, but I had nothing to say to console her. So I simply stroked the pretty henna patterns on her hands.

THE
INTEROPERATION

———————Ⱶ•

Yuri pulled his sons from school to watch the big robot wreck the motel. Mom had packed a tasty picnic lunch, but eleven-year-old Tommy was a hard kid to please.

"You said a giant robot would blow that place up," Tommy said.

"No, son, I told you a giant robot would 'take it down,'" said Yuri. "Go shoot some pictures for your Mom."

Tommy swung his little camera, hopped on his bamboo bike and took off.

Yuri patiently pushed his younger son's smaller bike across the sunlit tarmac. Nick, age seven, was learning to ride. His mother had dressed him for the ordeal, so Nick's head, knees, feet, fists and elbows were all lavishly padded with brightly colored foam. Nick had the lumpy plastic look of a Japanese action figure.

Under the crystalline spring sky, the robot towered over the Costa Vista Motel like the piston-legged skeleton of a monster printer. The urban recycler had already briskly stripped off the motel's roof. Using a dainty attachment, it remorselessly nibbled-up bricks.

The Costa Vista Motel was the first, last and only building that Yuri Lozano had created as a certified, practicing architect. The Costa Vista had been "designed for disassembly," way back in 2020. So today, some twenty-six years later, Yuri had hired the giant deconstruction-bot to fully reclaim the motel's materials: the bricks, the solar shingles, the electrical fixtures, the metal plumbing.... The structure was being de-fabricated, with a mindless precision, right down to its last, least, humble hinges.

As he patiently guided the wobbling Nick across the motel's weedy, deserted parking lot, Yuri's chief reaction to the day was deep relief.

He had never liked the Costa Vista. Never: not since it had left his design screen.

Once it had looked so good: just sitting there, safe within the screen. He'd been so pleased with the plan's spatial purity, the way the 3-D volumes massed together, the nifty way the structure fit the site.... But the motel's contractors had been a bunch of screwups. Worse yet, the owners were greedy morons.

So Yuri had been forced to stand by while his digital master-plans were botched by harsh reality. Cheap, flimsy materials. Bottom-barrel landscaping. Tacky signage. Lame interior décor. Even the name "Costa Vista" was a goofy choice for a motel off an interstate in Michigan.

Yuri had derived one major benefit from this painful experience. Yuri had stopped calling himself an "Architect." After his humiliation at the Costa Vista, he'd packed up his creative ego and thrown in his lot with the inevitable.

He had joined the comprehensive revolution attacking every aspect of the construction-architecture-engineering business.

Systematic software management, linked across the Net in machine-to-machine networks—it had been obvious to Yuri, as it was to so many others, that this almighty process was destined to take over *everything*. Not just the architect's blueprints: that was merely the revolution's first frontier. The structural engineering would go, too. Then construction: the trades, the suppliers.... Then the real-estate biz, the plumbing and electrical, the energy flows, the relationships to the city's grids and the financing sector, the ever-growing thicket of 21st-century sustainability regulation: yes, all of it would digitize. Everything. The works. "Total Building Lifecycle Management."

Nowadays, in the stolid and practical 2040s, Yuri called himself the "Sysadmin-CEO" of the "Lozano Building Network." Yuri's enterprise was thriving: he had more work than he and his people could handle. He had placed himself right into the thick of the big-time. Whenever he carved-out one day-off to spend with his two sons, a sprawling network sensed his absence and it shivered all over.

The Lozano Building Network was ripping up dead Midwestern suburbs and heaving up sustainable buildings by the hundreds. That was the work of the modern world.

Yuri knew that system: its colossal strength, and its hosts of cracks, shortfalls and weaknesses.

Yuri also knew that his company's contract-buildings were crap.

Ninety percent of all buildings were always crap. That was because ninety percent of all people had no taste. Yuri understood that; he was almost at peace with that. But it still burned him, it ached and it stung, that he had never built anything that deserved to last.

The "Lozano Building Network" didn't create fine buildings. It instantiated shelter-goods. The mass of workaday, crowd-pleasing stuff that arose from his network wasn't "architecture." It was best described as "hard-copy."

To watch this building disassembled in this sweet spring morning reminded him that life hadn't always been this way. In his own sweet spring, Yuri had dreamed of creating classics. He'd dreamed of structures that would tower on the planet's surface like brazen, gleaming symbols of excellence.

Yuri had never built any such place. He was coming to realize, with a sinister middle-aged pang, that he never would.

Watching the Costa Vista Motel disappear without a trace—no, he couldn't call himself unhappy about that. He felt eased and liberated. Denied the glory, he could at least erase the shame.

Tommy, always a bundle of energy, had pedalled all around the doomed motel. Somewhere, the kid had ditched his safety helmet. "Look, dad, why don't you just *blow it up*? The way that big dumb robot picks at it, this'll *take us all day!*"

"We've got all day," Yuri told him serenely. "Tonight we bring jackhammers."

Tommy brushed hair from his eager eyes. "Jackhammers, Dad?"

"Yeah. Big jackhammers. To bust up all this tarmac." No more parking lots. A park, instead. That was a gesture very typical of modern Michigan, a state whose primary "industry" was getting rid of its older, failed industry. Yuri Lozano was replacing his first building with nothingness.

Well: not with nothingness, but with urban green space and some public goodwill. Fresh air, biodiversity, and native wildflowers. The ruins of the unsustainable were this century's new frontier. The removal of bad architecture was a major tourist draw....

"Can I *touch* the big jackhammers, Dad?"

"Maybe, son. If you don't tell your Mom."

Nick yelped, jealous for attention. "Come on, Dad! Push the bike, push it, Dad!" Nick was the frailer and smarter of the two boys. His mother doted on him.

Yuri hitched his pants and shoved Nick's bike. The kid almost had the hang of it. Yuri secretly let the boy go.

Nick rolled off beautifully, his padded feet eager on his pedals. Then instability set in. Nick teetered into a wobbly, desperate struggle. Finally he crashed.

Tommy circled his fallen brother, loudly ringing his bike bell. "Get up, wimp, loser!"

Yuri bent and disentangled Nick from the candy-colored frame. "Fail early, fail often, Nick. You're not hurt."

"I'm not hurt," Nick agreed mournfully.

"A bike ride in a parking lot is just prototyping. Get back in the saddle."

Nick balked, and looked searchingly into Yuri's face. "Are you sad, Dad? You look sad."

"I'm not sad, son."

"I'll never learn how to ride a bike. Will I?"

"Yes, son, you will! You will master this bicycle! A bicycle is the world's most efficient means of transportation! And this bicycle will give you—Nicholas Lozano—a vastly increased power to navigate urban space!"

Nick was properly impressed. He got back on his bike.

Tommy had pedalled off again. "Nick, you are learning this much faster than your brother did. Don't tell Tommy that I said that."

"Yeah, sure, Dad! Okay! Push me now!"

Tommy zoomed back and skidded to a sudden halt, his freckled face pale. He slung his arm out, pointing. "Dad, Mom is coming! And she brought Aunt Carmen!"

Yuri glanced across the lot. Tommy's dire news was true.

Tommy was panting. "Are we in big trouble, dad?"

"You'd better let me handle this."

Yuri's wife and sister-in-law floated toward him on twin Segways. Like their famous father, the Roebel sisters were obsessed with Segways. After 45 years of niche applications, the ingenious machines had achieved a certain period charm, like monorails and the Graf Zeppelin.

It was unlike Gretchen to show up when he was taking some quality time with the boys. On the contrary: when the kids were out from underfoot, Gretchen indulged herself by taking scented bubble baths and surfing upscale websites.

And Carmen was here with her, all the way from San Francisco. Carmen, arriving with no warning? Carmen? Nobody had ever been able to do a thing with Carmen.

"What's wrong?" Yuri called out.

The Segway smoothly bobbed into place, and his wife's narrow face was the picture of woe. "Oh honey, it's just the worst."

"Somebody's died?"

"No, no," Carmen wailed. "My Dad got a big new commission!"

The people who were nearest to Francois Roebel were a frantically unhappy lot. Francois Roebel was the dark, roiling center of his own universe. For Roebel was a grand-master of computer-aided architecture.

Roebel was a major world architect who had forced digital design to speak its own aesthetic language: comprehensive, authentic, symphonic. Roebel's signature buildings were like nothing previously seen on planet Earth. They made the work of Gehry, Calatrava and Lynn look like mere dress rehearsals.

Roebel himself was a squinty, boozy, bewhiskered little geek. He had an ego the size of both Straits of Gibraltar and was given to splashy overspending, frantic womanizing, major fits of temper and impromptu trips to Indonesia.

Certain people imagined that he, Yuri Lozano, had married Gretchen Roebel in order to get closer to her famous father. The truth was entirely the opposite: he'd married Gretchen in order to take her far away from Roebel. Snatching Gretchen from her dysfunctional family was a noble, selfless act, like hauling a young woman from a burning car.

Yuri had no regrets about this bold intervention. Gretchen loved him, and, besides, the scary example of Carmen had fully validated his choice. Carmen had never escaped from the black-hole orbit of Roebel. So poor Carmen had ended up exactly like her late Mom: a doomy, subservient, hand-flapping mystic with a brain like scattered granola.

For Francois Roebel, architectural designspace was a dark and terrible enterprise. It was a harsh arena of combative nightmare, a realm of endlessly ramifying pull-ins, pop-outs, twists, deformations, mirrored ramps and cryptic passages. Ever the hero within his own mind, Roebel relentlessly pushed design software past sane limits, feverishly conjuring structures, then bullying them into raw physical existence in a welter of lawsuits and scandals.

Roebel had lived for decades on the virtual-actual edge, where the unprecedented phantoms roiling in his screen became awesome urban showcases fit to stun and amaze passers-by. Given their wild-eyed engineering, they might also spindle and mutilate their inhabitants, but the risks within his art for others never concerned the great man.

For Roebel, anyone willing to settle for less than the insanely-great was a traitor to be pitilessly scourged. Roebel made enemies the way lesser men made popcorn.

Yuri took a train to San Francisco to pay court to the grand master. It took him two days to arrive on Roebel's doorstep.

Roebel, as was his habit, was all ticked-off about that.

"Where the hell is Carmen?" demanded Roebel. "I haven't had a decent meal in five days! Carmen's trying to starve me!"

The ancient visionary, always scrawny, looked downright spidery by now—he'd lost so much flesh that he looked reduced to vector-graphics.

"Oh, the nephews love a visit from their favorite aunt," Yuri lied gallantly.

"I am the very last global starchitect! I am the last instantiation of a dying breed!" rasped Roebel. "And you couldn't fly over here?"

"I needed some time on the train to clear my construction agenda," Yuri soothed. Yuri always agreed to "help" Roebel with his projects. There was very little risk in this. Sooner or later, Roebel's clients always realized that Roebel had become impossible.

The genius could be humored, but only when his burning creative obsessions were channeled into some narrow, immediate path.

So Yuri loudly dragged a clanging metal chair over the naked cement of Roebel's dusty garage studio. He set himself before the architect's legendary personal workstation, jacked up a knee and bridged his fingers over it. "So, Francois, here I am. Show me what you've got. Let's see the concept sketches!"

Roebel tottered over, rolled up his blue linen sleeve over his stick-thin, liver-spotted forearm, and reached reluctantly through a clutter of empty sport-drink cans. He fished out a cheap toy peripheral. It was a skull-wrapping plastic headset, badly faded with age. "I'm sure you've never seen one of these."

"Tell me all about that."

Roebel drew himself up regally. "I'm sketching in ClearWorks with this cortico-cognitive headset!"

Yuri cleared his throat. "You're designing in ClearWorks? With some kind of brain-reader gizmo?"

"ClearWorks is the finest design program ever crafted!"

"Francois, it's thirty years old." Roebel would be better off with pencils and a set of children's blocks.

"Well, what the hell are *you* here for?" Roebel barked. "I need you to make Clearworks interoperate with that foul malarky that your nest-of-thieves calls software!" Roebel was breathing heavily. "Those so-called 'tools' you use—you can't drill one hole in a girder without forty interlocking safety forms!"

"If you're having trouble with your system, I'd be glad to have a look." Yuri popped the chromed clips on his moroccan-leather shoulder-bag. "I brought some top-end diagnostics in the laptop."

"Put that stupid toy away, I know you're a software monkey!" snarled Roebel. "ClearWorks *is* architecture! Because it's software-architecture by an information-architect!"

"I haven't seen ClearWorks since I left college," said Yuri. "Does ClearWorks interoperate with current legal codes?"

"I need a lawyer like I need a hole in the head!"

His question answered, Yuri offered a sunny smile. "I have to love that kind of boldness, Francois! Fire up your program, let's have a look!"

With his bluff called, Roebel reluctantly pressed the lozenge-shaped metal START button on his towering desktop engine. Roebel still used a specialty CAD workstation. The discolored machine, its shell scrubbed with acetone and its keyboard worn to nubs, had a militant, strutting, look-at-me-being-all-cyber aesthetic. Roebel's workstation looked fit to redesign the whole Milky Way Galaxy, though, truth be told, it had about ten percent of the processing capacity of a modern kid's throwaway watch.

"User lock-ins and proprietary formats," Roebel muttered, his throaty old-man's voice matching the ancient growl of his workstation's stricken hard-disk. "Those punk-ass chumps in the channels of distribution, they won't even show you the end-user license-agreements...."

The archaic vacuum-tube flickered as the workstation struggled to boot. "What on earth happened to the people?" Roebel griped, avoiding Yuri's eyes. "The banks, the unions, the professions, every level of government.... All of 'em melted down into one giant ball of mud! No more creative giants.... They're nickel-and-dime wind-up monkeys in a crazy world that gets more interactive every day!"

"Tell me about your client," said Yuri, angling for a change of subject.

Roebel offered a sly yellow grin. "The Church of Symbiosis."

"They're commissioning another temple? That's terrific news," said Yuri. His heart sank.

The Church of Symbiosis.... Could it get any worse? Francois Roebel was so marinated in the juggling of space and structure that he clanged when he walked. But Roebel was the picture of sanity compared to his favorite clients.

The Church of Computer-Human Symbiosis was an aging group of Californian hacker cranks who had inherited the vast fortune of a vanished social-software company. The Church had become Roebel's ideal patrons, for they were crazily rich, all-forgiving and incapable of judgment.

Over the decades, Roebel had built the cult an awesome set of monumental churches. Roebel's temples for the Church were top-end architecture glamor hits: glossy photobooks about them weighed down coffee-tables on six continents.

Nobody ever worshipped in the amazing churches Roebel had built, because the cult was too crazy and scary. Furthermore, the roofs leaked and all the utilities were out. Still, that didn't much matter to the cultists. They were serenely indifferent to such earthly concerns, since they spent most of their waking lives playing immersive simulation games.

Roebel tinkered aimlessly with his keyboard. The glassy screen stayed blank.

"It'll launch any minute," Roebel lied. "The system's been a little temperamental."

Year by year, Roebel had lost so much. His fancy downtown office, his staffers, his financial contacts, his engineers and subcontractors. He still worked—when he worked at all—on this ancient CAD system designed for building French fighter aircraft.

The screen flickered. "There it goes," crowed Roebel, as if the machine's effort had achieved something. "I'll just have to strap on the skull set. Later."

Whatever had happened to the old man? Normally he'd have a violent storm of wild schemes and concepts, each one less practically achievable than the last.

Yuri wasn't sure if this grim void meant disaster or deliverance for him. In either case, he felt sincere dismay about it.

"Francois, I have a very positive feeling about your new commission. We'll have a job-of-work with the interoperation issues, but at least we've got a client sympathetic to your aims."

"You're not fooling me any, you know."

"I beg your pardon?"

Roebel tossed his peripheral aside and abandoned his keyboard. "Just knock all that off, that crap when you sweet-talk me! You sound like a real-estate agent! You ran off with my daughter—and that's the last thing you did that took guts! You never soar, boy! You're like a pig in mud!"

"Let's take that discussion offline," Yuri parried. "Let's call Gretchen right now, and the grandsons, back in Michigan. They'll be wondering how things are going here. You never call us, you know."

"A twelve year old and an eight year old."

"The boys are eleven and seven."

"I was thinking ahead. Do I look like I want to wet-nurse your kids? I just received a major commission! 'Back to Michigan'—to hell with your Michigan, that whole place is nothing but forest! You can hear the crickets chirping in Flint, Saginaw and Grand Rapids! Your kids are like two sandlot baseball kids straight outta Norman Rockwell! And Gretchen…Gretchen doesn't even show up here! Where the hell is she, still putting her spice-racks in order?"

"Gretchen looks after the network in my absence. She's got a talent for billing and accounting."

"That's not a 'talent,' you nitwit! I know you understand what's at stake here! I taught you architecture when you were some cornshuck kid from Kentucky wandering into my office like a lost soul! And speaking of lost souls—where the hell is Preston? I told Preston to be here with us half an hour ago!"

Preston Mengies was an architecture critic. Preston had once been the PR man in Roebel's San Francisco office. Preston had earnestly pumped-up Roebel's reputation, until his doomed relationship with the hopelessly unstable Carmen Roebel made that effort impossible.

Despite everything Preston had suffered at the old man's hands, Preston arrived at length. He'd bicycled in from South-of-Market and thoughtfully brought some Chinese food.

Yuri sorrowed at the sight of him. Preston Mengies had once been a very sharp and fluent guy: a sarcastic little weirdo, to tell the truth, but fun to hang around with. Due to his long entanglement with Roebel, though, Preston had become a threadbare, gaunt, myopic, beaten character.

Nowadays, Preston spent his lonely hours grooming architecture websites. There Preston gamely removed the moronic popular commentary, and tried to flag up some intelligent interest in the doctrines of Arts & Crafts, Futurism, the Modern Movement, the Postmodern Movement, and New Urbanism.

These were architectural schemes that long-forgotten people had created with pencils on paper. No proper 21st-century person could tell these primitive notions apart. Still, some critic was bound to take a keen interest in such efflorescences of human genius, and it was bound to be a weedy obsessive like Preston Mengies.

Roebel sipped and scowled at the hot-and-sour soup, but he had clearly lost the thread of the action. All the old man could do was bitterly rant about "lawyers" and "hoodwinking" and "bank fraud." The client had caught Roebel flat-footed. When Roebel tottered off for his customary afternoon nap, it was a relief for all concerned.

He left Yuri and Preston to patch something together for the client's imminent visit.

"How are the kids?" ventured Preston, who had never had any kids.

"The boys are both great, thanks."

"They're *normal* kids?" said Preston, his eyes flickering sideways.

"Oh yeah, they're completely normal," said Yuri, "not at all like the maestro there; they just faded right back into the universal human gene-pool."

Preston brightened at this sally; Preston was a critic, so a little acerbic sarcasm always cheered him up. He munched his cold shrimp chow mein and gestured at the workstation with his plastic chopsticks. "Did he ask you to touch that evil dinosaur? I sure wouldn't touch that wreck if I were you."

"Why is that, Preston?"

"You know how he's trying to patch that fossil to modern standards—and to get his own way right in the teeth of the entire construction industry? Well, he finally blew it. He had a massive, comprehensive data loss. No upgrade path forward. And no way back. He's completely stuck now. He's neck-deep in the mud of defunct code."

Yuri munched a heat-blistered eggroll stuffed with gleaming Californian tofu. "He claimed he was designing on ClearWorks. I just couldn't believe that."

"No one runs ClearWorks," scoffed Preston. "That's the greatest design-platform every created, but no modern professional could use it. It doesn't interoperate with other disciplines."

"It's worse than that," Yuri admitted. "Out in the Midwest, we *do* interoperate, so we *became* the other disciplines. As soon as I gave up on 'architecture,' and admitted that I was administering software, well.... Step by step, I took over the site, the structure, the skin of the building, all of the services.... We supply the space-plans, we even retail the furnishings. But we're not architects. Not at all. We're real estate, interior design, engineering, landscaping, plumbing, electrical.... We're the Net."

Yuri knotted his hands. "And it's all bucket-of-mud piece-of-junk legacy code! Every bit of it! Those programs all hate each other's guts! I spend ninety percent of my working time as a software clerk!"

"So basically, you never design and you never create. You just interoperate."

Yuri considered this grim assessment. "Well, yeah, that's pretty well-put."

Preston warmed to his theme. "But you have to do that. Because there's a shearing force in all those different layers of software. It's a thing of eddies, and whirlpools, and brief bursts of financial energy. And the craft of architecture sold its soul so that it could survive there."

Yuri set aside a stencilled carton of moo goo gai pan. "Can I ask you something...? At the Milwaukee Design Regulation Board, I've got this big keynote speech coming up..."

"How long a speech?"

"Full hour. Big dinner speech. Man, I hate those."

"How big a crowd?"

"I dunno, seven, eight hundred. Typical industry drones."

"Could you give me a grand?"

Yuri blinked a little. "Yeah, sure, okay."

That money was peanuts, but it was clearly more cash than Preston had seen in a while, for he sat up in his steel-framed chair and seemed to regain his appetite. "Well, there's one consolation in all this. He's never gonna do another building."

Yuri laughed. "Oh sure, people keep saying that, but he keeps surprising 'em. That mean old man is gonna bury us all! He's gonna live to be ninety years old!"

"Francois *is* ninety years old."

Yuri did some swift mental arithmetic. "Darn, where does the time go?"

Preston snagged an empty can from the desktop. "This is all he eats now—these quack vitamin drinks. Carmen dragged him into a couple of clinics last year. They took one look at him and they just washed their hands. I don't know how he stays on his feet. He persists out of sheer spite."

Yuri considered this bleak diagnosis. Yes, Francois was especially gaunt and erratic, even for Francois. There had been one little flash where Francois was like his keen old self, but...no *concept sketches?* Francois Roebel was a hundred and ten percent concept sketches. "It seems that the lamp went out."

"Yeah, 'the well ran dry.' That's what Carmen says. You add that to his big software crash and...." Preston flapped his hands. "It's Game Over for Pac-Man."

"Carmen came to visit us. Carmen seems pretty distraught about all this."

Carmen Roebel was always distraught—Carmen was the Queen of Distraughtness—but Preston took that news hard. It had Preston all itchy and gritting his teeth. The poor guy still carried a big torch for Carmen. That was a pitiful thing to see.

"She's up to her ears in debt," said Preston. "Did she tell you that?"

In point of fact, Carmen had swiftly hit Yuri up for a personal loan. Every member of the extended Roebel family hit Yuri up for loans. He'd come to consider that a basic cost of his business, something like a corporate gift to a Little League team.

Yuri sighed. "I don't suppose that Francois would write his will and put his affairs in good order."

"Francois wouldn't leave Carmen a dime! If he had a dime, he'd endow the Francois Roebel Perpetual Commemoration Fund." Preston shook his head. "After all these years, it's finally come to the crunch! Those Church lunatics will show up here soon…. They want to see his proposal. He's gonna fire up that relic there, and he'll show them a screen full of snow."

An empty silence stretched in Roebel's spider-hole of an office, and somewhere a seagull screeched.

Yuri was no longer an architect—in point of fact, he'd likely never been one—but he'd spent his whole adult life glossing over the bitter contradictions among complicated systems of software.

There just had to be a make-work hack somewhere for a dire situation like this.

"Preston, I know that this isn't quite honest, but—suppose you show 'em something out of the old man's archives? He must have dozens of unbuilt proposals. Surely those clowns can't tell the difference."

"The old man *sold* those clowns his archives. He sold them all his files three years ago. The Church paid top dollar for them, too. They've got 'em all stored down a zinc-lined bomb shelter someplace."

How, where and why did computers let crazy geeks make so much money? Yuri wondered. Had the world ever been better off for that? Seeding the world with personal computers was like sprinkling it with the fairy-dust of pure madness.

Preston had the shameless look of a guy doing something stupid for the woman he loved. "Listen, Yuri: for you this story must seem pretty simple. The old man loses this commission: so what? You're doing great out there in the Rust Belt. Because you're in deconstruction; you could spend the rest of your life just tearing down the Motor City. But Carmen needs that retainer fee. She's at her wit's end."

Poor old Preston. If he'd only he'd found the courage to abandon his dreams and take practical action! Just tell the old man off, clonk the girl on the head, throw her into the trunk of a car, and drive off somewhere across a state line!

But it took a certain hillbilly lack of savoir faire to do something that blunt, immediate, helpful and misogynistic. That basic course of action had worked out fine for Yuri, but Preston, being a man of a gentler and more refined sensibility, had never achieved that much.

The cuffs of Preston's pants were badly frayed. This tiny detail was somehow Yuri's tipping point.

"Okay," Yuri said, straightening, "I tell you what we're gonna do. I'm gonna fire up ClearWorks and put the program through its paces. When that old man comes back here from his nap, I'll get him jump-started on something."

Preston scratched his bald spot. "You really think you can do that?"

"Yeah. I know I can. I was his star student once. It's pretty simple with him. You just do something that's very clear and obvious. Then he gets all excited and he bawls you out. He can't help taking over and re-doing it all himself... So: if this piece of junk runs at all, well, the two of us will cook up something. It doesn't have to be the Taj Mahal for him to show it to a favorite client."

Preston had no better scheme to offer. He left Yuri in peace with the machine.

Yuri woke the workstation and settled in.

When he first saw the ClearWorks interface he felt a shock of profound nostalgia. Yeah, it really was 'ClearWorks'! No kidding!

ClearWorks was a simple white pane with a pair of tiny, almost invisible icons in the upper right corner. ClearWorks was so entirely clear that it looked starkly absurd. Compared to Yuri's working interfaces for the modern construction business, ClearWorks was alien.

Where was the riffling host of toolbars, templates, menus, dynamic panels, auto-updaters, dialog panels, widgets, dashboards, collision-detectors, and tags...? Where was the bustling cloud of counters, winkers, beepers and blinkers?

ClearWorks was a void. A glassy, glossy innocence. ClearWorks was as pearly, white and blank as the inside of a skull.

The program's mouse, or rather its airborne bat, sat atop Roebel's workstation. When Yuri's fingertips gripped the familiar ridges of the little wand, the look-and-feel of the program came back as if college were yesterday.

Space and form. Yuri was peeling through space and form. Through the torque in that bat he could actually *feel space*—the massiness of space, the shapeliness of space. The order and rightness of it. Geometry sliced through the white panes of simulation like a white ceramic knife through pure white cheese.

ClearWorks did just one thing well: it did form. ClearWorks did nothing but form. ClearWorks was a world in which there was only form.

Yuri recalled that ClearWorks had been programmed by just one guy. ClearWorks was the brainwork of just one single geek, some embittered dissident from the early CAD business. The name of this lonesome genius was Greg something, or Bob something, or Jim something, and he was one of these arrogant, self-aggrandizing, utterly unworldly, UNIX-bearded software-genius figures who wanted to create a programmatic universe all by himself.

Greg-Jim-Bob had never managed that feat, but he'd managed ClearWorks. That program had become a legend among users. All the cognoscenti and digerati and designerati vied to praise ClearWorks. Of course nobody actually used it. If you gave people the tools that were perfect for their jobs, they'd have nothing to do but their jobs.

The whole secret of the network revolution was that it connected everybody, and it therefore caused everybody to do *everybody else's* jobs.

It came to Yuri with a shock that ClearWorks did not interoperate. No. ClearWorks didn't even hook to the Internet. ClearWorks was a single tool for one single human mind. There was no crowdsourcing in it, no open-source collaboration, no "with enough eyes all bugs are shallow".... No add-ons, no plug-ins, no open application programming interfaces....

ClearWorks was a simple bone-white space for formal imagination.

Yuri couldn't believe the program was such a little sandbox. He could remember tackling ClearWorks as a student. At the time, he had felt the program was incredibly advanced: it was cosmic, infinite, awesome.

How had ClearWorks become such a tinkertoy?

Yuri recalled his purpose. The task at hand was some conceptual proposal for a Francois Roebel temple. The maestro might ramble in from his nap at any minute, and Yuri had to show him something to snag his interest.

What the heck, any pastiche had to start somewhere: the Golden Rectangle. Always a sound choice: it never looked awkward no matter how it was used.

Bang, up it came, the good old Golden Rectangle, and then: boo000000ooom...that was the oldest, purest joy of computer design:

the effortless replication. Yuri gripped his little wand: hook a *twist* on that series: a ram's horn fractal thing...

What would the Maestro do? Well, he'd do something off the wall that nevertheless seemed eerily necessary... Because, despite his many personal quirks, Roebel was the wizard of the "rubrics of assemblage"... "The parts grow out of the rules, while the rules grow out of the parts."

Insert a barrel-vault. Who couldn't like barrel-vaults? Especially *intersecting* barrel-vaults. *Multiple* intersecting barrel-vaults.

Yuri forgot himself. He forgot his purpose, he forgot where he was. The chair vanished and the screen became vapor. Yuri splashed in pure potentiality, free of care, liberated, purely enjoying himself...

Until it dawned on him that Roebel wasn't going to much care for this plan. The plan had a whole lot going on, but it wasn't very Francois Roebel.

Worse yet, the strict limits of ClearWorks were starting to bug Yuri. ClearWorks was a thirty-year-old program. Furthermore, the whole she-bang had been created by just one guy, and though he had made a really cool sandbox, it was pretty much nothing but sand.

Yuri had begun to sense the way the programmer thought. No geek from thirty years ago could think like a modern builder. Though he had a cunning intuitive arsenal of cool ways to assemble his sand, he lacked any cool ways to *disassemble* his sand.

It was as if he thought that real buildings went up in some Platonic cyberspace where gravity, friction and entropy had never existed. Where the passage of the years was just an abstraction.... The author of ClearWorks was pure geek, so he didn't realize that when you meshed bits and atoms, you had to *respect* the atoms. Bits were the servants of atoms. "Bits" were just bits of atoms.

Bits came and went at the flick of a switch, but atoms had deep and dark and permanent physical laws. Atoms didn't go away when you shut down the screen. When you lacked a responsible way to deal with the atoms, you were a menace to yourself and all around you.

Armed with this ethical knowledge, Yuri set to work to repair the oversight. Suddenly ClearWorks was fighting him all the way. To get ClearWorks to tear apart its own constructions, Yuri had to break its elements right down to their little, least, voxel-sized bricks.

Now Yuri had a serious fight on his hands. The program had been mumbling along in its Wagnerian grandeur, all pale timeless majesty and the sonorous sawing of spatial strings—but Yuri's blood was up. He heard a Ride of the Valkyries in his mind's ear, a Gotterdammerung themesong... He had to tear that pure simplicity apart.

Break! Decay! *Come apart,* you stupid Total Work of Art! Quit trying to *hold yourself together* in defiance of all sense and sanity! From pixels you are, and to pixels you shall return....

Light clicked on overhead. Preston was standing at the doorway, a beer in hand. Somehow, day had become evening.

"Are you still at it in here?" Preston said.

Yuri blinked. "Is it late?"

"Yeah, you've been in here for five solid hours!"

Yuri abandoned the office chair. Suddenly his back was killing him. "Where's Francois?"

"The clients woke him," said Preston. "We're feeding them cocktails over in the solarium.... Cocktails, and hogwash." Preston walked over and stared. "Wow."

"I tinkered around."

"That's looking pretty different," Preston judged. "That's looking... pretty fresh."

"Design-for-disassembly," said Yuri, "I had to put it on a kind of loop."

Preston watched the animated screen, absently sipping his beer.

"You know," Preston mused at last, "there is an aesthetic quality to old computer graphics that is truly haunting. It's very much like the scary, Gothic quality of silent film. Mankind will never be able to simulate buildings this badly again."

"I could work on the color tonalities."

"No, no, leave that, leave it!" Preston snatched the bat from Yuri's hand. "Did you use the cortico-cognitive headset?"

"What?"

"That neural brain-reading consciousness gizmo?"

"Oh that," said Yuri. "It's funny, but I never even plugged that in."

"That instant brain-reader was supposed to be 'useful and convenient.'"

Yuri shrugged. "You can't step in the same river twice."

A stranger peered into Roebel's office, then stepped inside. He was young, nattily dressed in a tailored suit, and he carried a fancy valise.

"What have we here?" he said.

"You've found the old man's design office," said Preston. "Yuri Lozano: Mark Quintaine. Mark is a local attorney."

Quintaine had an elegant haircut, a very practiced manner and a slightly eccentric business suit. Quintaine might also conceivably be gay, but those were just his San Francisco regionalisms: oh yeah, this guy was a real-estate lawyer. Yuri had met so many that he could smell them by now.

The Code and the Law: they were two sister practices. One of them was logical, and humane, and rigorous, and the backbone of civilization. And the other was crazy, and snarled, and corrupted, and full of loopholes. And nobody could tell which was which.

Quintaine's nostrils flared as he stared around the office. There were holes in the sheetrock and nobody had dusted the blinds. Quintaine jerked his thumb over his pinstriped shoulder. "Did he have to string the power cables right over the doorframe? That's not very *feng shui*."

Preston was quick to sense a slight. "I wouldn't have guessed that the Church of Computer-Human Symbiosis was so into feng shui."

"I never speak ill of my clients," said Quintaine, "but after the five solid decades those geezers have spent immersed in game environments, Chinese set-design is the least of their problems."

This was a charming remark, and, despite the fact that the man was a lawyer, Yuri found himself won over.

"I take it you're not a member of the Church."

"My *parents* were members of that Church," said Quintaine. "They took me to every temple ever built by the maestro in there… They are works of genius. But if you spend enough time in the presence of a well-nigh supernatural talent, it can get a little samey." Quintaine had been drinking. "I'm sure the world could another Francois Roebel masterpiece." Quintaine had a long, goggling look at the workstation's flickering screen. "My God in Heaven! What has he done?"

"That's not a Francois Roebel masterpiece," said Yuri.

"Okay, I can see that, but what is that thing? It looks like a million giant ants are eating Notre Dame."

"It's a little something I just cooked up."

"You're an architect?"

"Once. Yeah."

Quintaine lifted a brow. "'Once?'"

"I don't call myself that. Not any more."

This remark hit Quintaine hard. "I used to call myself a lawyer." Quintaine dropped into the office chair and stared at the busy screen. "It took me a while to figure it out…. I don't practice law. I am a fixer. I practice all kinds of stuff…urban politics. Acquiring properties. Managing upkeep…. The piecemeal growth of holding funds…. Sweeping problems under the rug for the time being, I'm required to do a whole lot of that…."

"That sounds like the law to me," Yuri said.

Quintaine looked up. "But I don't have any human clients."

"Really?"

"It's true. My only true client is a large sum of money. And the way that wealth-management system was structured… Well, it was so complex and restrictive that everybody ran away from it. Even the geeks who were supposed to own that wealth have fled into a fantasy world. That wealth is like some vast black bowling ball that rolls up and down Silicon Valley…. Do you guys remember that word, 'Silicon'?"

"I loved silicon," said Yuri.

"Oh me too," said Preston with fervor. "Silicon used to be twenty-five percent of the planet's crust!"

"So I had it figured," said Quintaine, "that we would commission Francois Roebel and throw the 'Permanent Construction Fund' at him. Roebel is notorious for never completing any building on time or under budget. If you look at the way that Construction Fund was structured— well, we're a lot better off with fantastic, never-realized buildings. In today's sustainable economy, it's the total cost-of-ownership and the price of recycling that kills us."

"That's extremely interesting," said Yuri. "I hadn't heard a lawyer frame that issue like that before."

"California state law is always well ahead of the global and national curves."

"Yeah, that's right."

"Now that you've come up with *this* exciting proposal," said Quintaine, confronting the workstation, "I'm getting a brainwave. This plan here is not even a 'building,' as far as I can figure. That way that the structure keeps looping around like that—that's a process that's permanently under construction and deconstruction. There's no final state there where one has to legally sign off and accept ownership. So that's not a 'building,' legally speaking. That's a process. It's a process in permanent interoperation."

"Mr Quintaine, you must be a pretty good lawyer."

Quintaine spun himself in the chair. "My firm has stopped calling itself a 'law-firm,' actually. We've moved into another set of practices that are...well...more contemporary.""

Yuri shot a look at Preston. In a gesture so subtle as to be almost invisible, Preston brushed one finger against his lips.

•⊩————⊩•

"When you've lost control of the flow of events," Yuri told the mirror, "your duty is to hope and plan for happy accidents."

"Stop muttering and complaining," Gretchen told him. She adjusted his bow-tie, for the third time. "You should try to enjoy your big night."

"I'm rehearsing my big speech," said Yuri. He had read the critic's speech six times. Preston Mengies was finally back in top form, given that he had an exciting controversy to exploit. "Honey, that speech of his is a corker! It's full of raw meat for the interops crowd.... I'm embarrassed to deliver a rant like that.... Can I get away with it?"

"It's not a 'rant,' honey. They give you a major award, and you give them a major address. You have to rise to the occasion somehow. You can't pretend that you stole a cookie from the cookie jar."

Gretchen was dressed in a tawny-colored taffeta evening gown. Her hair was done, her painted face solemn and she looked aggressively gorgeous.

This glamorous apparition, tidying him up and charying him along and rolling him onto the stage: this was not Gretchen Lozano at her happiest. Gretchen looked toned, taut, tense and committed.

Gretchen was happy during summer camping trips in northern Michigan. A camping trip with Yuri, and his two brothers, and his two sons: five howling, boisterous, dirty men all demanding that she gut and cook raw fish.

That made Gretchen happy. It took a situation that primeval to free Gretchen from her troubled, complex heritage. In the wilderness, Gretchen forgot her past traumas; instead, she griped cheerily about every new day's dirt, smoke, filth, scratches, blisters and insect bites. In that drippy green wilderness, full of wolves, Canadians, and caribou, Gretchen ate like a horse, ran like a deer and made love like a wildcat.

So he knew that Gretchen could be happy. And he knew how to make her happy. And there was a lot to be said for that.

This other kind of Gretchen Lozano, the woman at his shoulder tonight, was the scheming wife of a purported genius. Yuri's new construction was famous. It was a permanently unstable tower of plug-in plastic modules, all hemp, glue and fly-ash. And it rebuilt itself each and every night. This radically unstable, profoundly interactive, ever-shifting phenomenon was ironically named "The Monument." It was attracting hype in the way a puddle of honey drew flies.

The project's grand success had swiftly transformed Gretchen Lozano from a Midwestern builder's wife into the elegant, high-society consort of a network-design superstar. Gretchen knew how to manage this. It was a facet of Gretchen that had been lurking inside her always, waiting to flicker into daylight.

Dressed for the awards banquet, Gretchen looked as sleek as a laser construction tool. She looked like somebody could pick her up and use her nose to scratch plate-glass.

"Preston knows that it was all just a lucky accident," Yuri said. "Preston is a smart guy, he was there. He knows I didn't mean to do it."

"Oh sure, it was all an accident, maestro. You're just one big fake, and so are the thousand rip-off artists trying to imitate you." Gretchen drew a breath within her decolletage. "People don't want to live in 'buildings', Yuri. People want to live *in construction programs.* People are willing to pay top dollar to live in the way that modern people actually live. That's no accident. We are rich and you are famous. Only a total sap could fail to understand that. And if you're too lazy and neurotic to live up to your own potential, well, I'm going to beat you. I'm going to hit you on the head with a stick."

Gretchen had never spoken to him in that way—never before her father had died. It required his death to liberate her to echo him.

Tommy banged at the door and wandered into the bedroom. Tommy was fifteen now, and shooting up like a weed, but in his dark tailored suit he looked like a clockwork figurine. "Why are you two still standing around here? Can't we go yet? I'm starving."

Yuri wanted to spare him. "You really want to go to see some boring awards, Tommy? You could stay here and kill monsters with your little brother."

"Yeah, I gotta go to the banquet," shrugged Tommy. "Your building is great and all the other buildings suck rocks, Dad."

"It's that simple, huh?"

"Yeah, my Dad can make cool buildings that aren't crap!"

"We'll be right along, Tommy," said Gretchen, heels clicking as she fetched her wrap. "You can have a snack in the limo."

Tommy left. Gretchen watched him go, then printed Yuri's cheek with a kissproofed lip. "'Some men are born great, and others have greatness thrust upon them.' If you're at a party and five friends say that you're drunk, then you're drunk. And you'd better go lie down. But if five hundred serious people say that you are a genius, you had better aspire to genius. You're not a drunk, honey. You could have been, but you got the other fate. You're going to be just great."

"That's your final word on this subject?"

"Okay, maybe one more word. I always knew you had this in you. I just hoped it wouldn't be too messy, when it finally came oozing out."

BLACK
SWAN

————H•

T he ethical journalist protects a confidential source. So I protected
"Massimo Montaldo," although I knew that wasn't his name.

Massimo shambled through the tall glass doors, dropped his valise
with a thump, and sat across the table. We were meeting where we always
met: inside the Caffe Elena, a dark and cozy spot that fronts on the
biggest plaza in Europe.

The Elena has two rooms as narrow and dignified as mahogany cof-
fins, with lofty red ceilings. The little place has seen its share of stricken
wanderers. Massimo never confided his personal troubles to me, but they
were obvious, as if he'd smuggled monkeys into the cafe and hidden
them under his clothes.

Like every other hacker in the world, Massimo Montaldo was bright.
Being Italian, he struggled to look suave. Massimo wore stain-proof,
wrinkle-proof travel gear: a black merino wool jacket, an American
black denim shirt, and black cargo pants. Massimo also sported
black athletic trainers, not any brand I could recognize, with eerie
bubble-filled soles.

These skeletal shoes of his were half-ruined. They were strapped
together with rawhide boot-laces.

To judge by his Swiss-Italian accent, Massimo had spent a lot of time
in Geneva. Four times he'd leaked chip secrets to me—crisp engineering graphics, apparently snipped right out of Swiss patent applications.
However, the various bureaus in Geneva had no records of these patents.
They had no records of any "Massimo Montaldo," either.

Each time I'd made use of Massimo's indiscretions, the traffic to my
weblog had doubled.

I knew that Massimo's commercial sponsor, or more likely his spy-master, was using me to manipulate the industry I covered. Big bets were going down in the markets somewhere. Somebody was cashing in like a bandit.

That profiteer wasn't me, and I had to doubt that it was him. I never financially speculate in the companies I cover as a journalist, because that is the road to hell. As for young Massimo, his road to hell was already well-trampled.

Massimo twirled the frail stem of his glass of Barolo. His shoes were wrecked, his hair was unwashed, and he looked like he'd shaved in an airplane toilet. He handled the best wine in Europe like a scorpion poised to sting his liver. Then he gulped it down.

Unasked, the waiter poured him another. They know me at the Elena.

Massimo and I had a certain understanding. As we chatted about Italian tech companies—he knew them from Alessi to Zanotti—I discreetly passed him useful favors. A cellphone chip—bought in another man's name. A plastic hotel pass key for a local hotel room, rented by a third party. Massimo could could use these without ever showing a passport or any identification.

There were eight "Massimo Montaldos" on Google and none of them were him. Massimo flew in from places unknown, he laid his eggs of golden information, then he paddled off into dark waters. I was protecting him by giving him those favors. Surely there were other people very curious about him, besides myself.

The second glass of Barolo eased that ugly crease in his brows. He rubbed his beak of a nose, and smoothed his unruly black hair, and leaned onto the thick stone table with both of his black woolen elbows.

"Luca, I brought something special for you this time. Are you ready for that? Something you can't even imagine."

"I suppose," I said.

Massimo reached into his battered leather valise and brought out a no-name PC laptop. This much-worn machine, its corners bumped with use and its keyboard dingy, had one of those thick super-batteries clamped onto its base. All that extra power must have tripled the computer's weight. Small wonder that Massimo never carried spare shoes.

He busied himself with his grimy screen, fixated by his private world there.

The Elena is not a celebrity bar, which is why celebrities like it. A blonde television presenter swayed into the place. Massimo, who was now deep into his third glass, whipped his intense gaze from his laptop screen. He closely studied her curves, which were upholstered in Gucci.

An Italian television presenter bears the relationship to news that American fast food bears to food. So I couldn't feel sorry for her—yet I didn't like that way he sized her up. Genius gears were turning visibly in Massimo's brilliant geek head. That woman had all the raw, compelling appeal to him of some difficult math problem.

Left alone with her, he would chew on that problem until something clicked loose and fell into his hands, and, to do her credit, she could feel that. She opened her dainty crocodile purse and slipped on a big pair of sunglasses.

"Signor Montaldo," I said.

He was rapt.

"Massimo?"

This woke him from his lustful reverie. He twisted the computer and exhibited his screen to me.

I don't design chips, but I've seen the programs used for that purpose. Back in the 1980s, there were thirty different chip-design programs. Nowadays there are only three survivors. None of them are nativized in the Italian language, because every chip geek in the world speaks English.

This program was in Italian. It looked elegant. It looked like a very stylish way to design computer chips. Computer chip engineers are not stylish people. Not in this world, anyway.

Massimo tapped at his weird screen with a gnawed fingernail. "This is just a cheap, 24-K embed. But do you see these?"

"Yes I do. What are they?"

"These are memristors."

In heartfelt alarm, I stared around the cafe, but nobody in the Elena knew or cared in the least about Massimo's stunning revelation. He could have thrown memristors onto their tables in heaps. They'd never realize that he was tossing them the keys to riches.

I could explain now, in gruelling detail, exactly what memristors are, and how different they are from any standard electronic component. Suffice to understand that, in electronic engineering, memristors did not exist. Not at all. They were technically possible—we'd known that for thirty years, since the 1980s—but nobody had ever manufactured one.

A chip with memristors was like a racetrack where the jockeys rode unicorns.

I sipped the Barolo so I could find my voice again. "You brought me schematics for memristors? What happened, did your UFO crash?"

"That's very witty, Luca."

"You can't hand me something like that! What on Earth do you expect me to do with that?"

"I am not giving these memristor plans to you. I have decided to give them to Olivetti. I will tell you what to do: you make one confidential call to your good friend, the Olivetti Chief Technical Officer. You tell him to look hard in his junk folder where he keeps the spam with no return address. Interesting things will happen, then. He'll be grateful to you."

"Olivetti is a fine company," I said. "But they're not the outfit to handle a monster like that. A memristor is strictly for the big boys—Intel, Samsung, Fujitsu."

Massimo laced his hands together on the table—he might have been at prayer—and stared at me with weary sarcasm. "Luca," he said, "don't you ever get tired of seeing Italian genius repressed?"

The Italian chip business is rather modest. It can't always make its ends meet. I spent fifteen years covering chip tech in Route 128 in Boston. When the almighty dollar ruled the tech world, I was glad that I'd made those connections.

But times do change. Nations change, industries change. Industries change the times.

Massimo had just shown me something that changes industries. A disruptive innovation. A breaker of the rules.

"This matter is serious," I said. "Yes, Olivetti's people do read my weblog—they even comment there. But that doesn't mean that I can leak some breakthrough that deserves a Nobel Prize. Olivetti would want to know, they would *have* to know, the source of that."

He shook his head. "They don't want to know, and neither do you."

"Oh yes, I most definitely do want to know."

"No, you don't. Trust me."

"Massimo, I'm a journalist. That means that I always want to know, and I never trust anybody."

He slapped the table. "Maybe you were a 'journalist' when they still printed paper 'journals.' But your dot-com journals are all dead. Nowadays you're a blogger. You're an influence peddler and you spread rumors for a living." Massimo shrugged, because he didn't think he was insulting me. "So: shut up! Just do what you always do! That's all I'm asking."

That might be all that he was asking, but my whole business was in asking. "Who created that chip?" I asked him. "I know it wasn't you. You know a lot about tech investment, but you're not Leonardo da Vinci."

"No, I'm not Leonardo." He emptied his glass.

"Look, I know that you're not even 'Massimo Montaldo'—whoever that is. I'll do a lot to get news out on my blog. But I'm not going to act as your cut-out in a scheme like this! That's totally unethical! Where did you steal that chip? Who made it? What are they, Chinese super-engineers in some bunker under Beijing?"

Massimo was struggling not to laugh at me. "I can't reveal that. Could we have another round? Maybe a sandwich? I need a nice toasty pancetta."

I got the waiter's attention. I noted that the TV star's boyfriend had shown up. Her boyfriend was not her husband. Unfortunately, I was not in the celebrity tabloid business. It wasn't the first time I'd missed a good bet by consorting with computer geeks.

"So you're an industrial spy," I told him. "And you must be Italian to boot, because you're always such a patriot about it. Okay: so you stole those plans somewhere. I won't ask you how or why. But let me give you some good advice: no sane man would leak that to Olivetti. Olivetti's a consumer outfit. They make pretty toys for cute secretaries. A memristor chip is dynamite."

Massimo was staring raptly at the TV blonde as he awaited his sandwich.

"Massimo, pay attention. If you leak something that advanced, that radical…a chip like that could change the world's military balance of power. Never mind Olivetti. Big American spy agencies with three letters in their names will come calling."

Massimo scratched his dirty scalp and rolled his eyes in derision. "Are you so terrorized by the CIA? They don't read your sorry little one-man tech blog."

This crass remark irritated me keenly. "Listen to me, boy genius: do you know what the CIA does here in Italy? We're their 'rendition' playground. People vanish off the streets."

"Anybody can 'vanish off the streets.' I do that all the time."

I took out my Moleskin notebook and my shiny Rotring technical pen. I placed them both on the Elena's neat little marble table. Then I slipped them both back inside my jacket. "Massimo, I'm trying hard to be sensible about this. Your snotty attitude is not helping your case with me."

With an effort, my source composed himself. "It's all very simple," he lied. "I've been here a while, and now I'm tired of this place. So I'm leaving. I want to hand the future of electronics to an Italian company. With no questions asked and no strings attached. You won't help me do that simple thing?"

"No, of course I won't! Not under conditions like these. I don't know where you got that data, what, how, when, whom, or why.... I don't even know who you are! Do I look like that kind of idiot? Unless you tell me your story, I can't trust you."

He made that evil gesture: I had no balls. Twenty years ago—well, twenty-five—and we would have stepped outside the bar. Of course I was angry with him—but I also knew he was about to crack. My source was drunk and he was clearly in trouble. He didn't need a fist-fight with a journalist. He needed confession.

Massimo put a bold sneer on his face, watching himself in one of the Elena's tall spotted mirrors. "If this tiny gadget is too big for your closed mind, then I've got to find another blogger! A blogger with some guts!"

"Great. Sure. Go do that. You might try Beppe Grillo."

Massimo tore his gaze from his own reflection. "That washed-up TV comedian? What does he know about technology?"

"Try Berlusconi, then. He owns all the television stations and half the Italian Internet. Prime Minister Berlusconi is just the kind of hustler you need. He'll free you from all your troubles. He'll make you Minister of something."

Massimo lost all patience. "I don't need that! I've been to a lot of versions of Italy. Yours is a complete disgrace! I don't know how you people get along with yourselves!"

Now the story was tearing loose. I offered an encouraging nod. "How many 'versions of Italy' do you need, Massimo?"

"I have sixty-four versions of Italy." He patted his thick laptop. "Got them all right here."

I humored him. "Only sixty-four?"

His tipsy face turned red. "I had to borrow CERN's supercomputers to calculate all those coordinates! Thirty-two Italies were too few! A hundred twenty-eight…. I'd never have the time to visit all those! And as for *your* Italy…well…. I wouldn't be here at all, if it wasn't for that Turinese girl."

"'Cherchez la femme,'" I told him. "That's the oldest trouble-story in the world."

"I did her some favors," he admitted, mournfully twisting his wineglass. "Like with you. But much more so."

I felt lost, but I knew that his story was coming. Once I'd coaxed it out of him, I could put it into better order later.

"So, tell me: what did she do to you?"

"She dumped me," he said. He was telling me the truth, but with a lost, forlorn, bewildered air, like he couldn't believe it himself. "She dumped me and she married the President of France." Massimo glanced up, his eyelashes wet with grief. "I don't blame her. I know why she did that. I'm a very handy guy for a woman like her, but Mother of God, I'm not the President of France!"

"No, no, you're not the President of France," I agreed. The President of France was a hyperactive Hungarian Jewish guy who liked to sing karaoke songs. President Nicolas Sarkozy was an exceedingly unlikely character, but he was odd in a very different way from Massimo Montaldo.

Massimo's voice was cracking with passion. "She says that he'll make her the First Lady of Europe! All I've got to offer her is insider-trading hints and a few extra millions for her millions."

The waiter brought Massimo a toasted sandwich.

Despite his broken heart, Massimo was starving. He tore into his food like a chained dog, then glanced up from his mayonnaise dip. "Do I sound jealous? I'm not jealous."

Massimo was bitterly jealous, but I shook my head so as to encourage him.

"I can't be jealous of a woman like her!" Massimo lied. "Eric Clapton can be jealous, Mick Jagger can be jealous! She's a rock star's groupie who's become the Premiere Dame of France! She married Sarkozy! Your world is full of journalists—spies, cops, creeps, whatever—and not for one minute did they ever stop and consider: 'Oh! This must be the work of a computer geek from another world!'"

"No," I agreed.

"Nobody ever imagines that!"

I called the waiter back and ordered myself a double espresso. The waiter seemed quite pleased at the way things were going for me. They were a kindly bunch at the Elena. Friedrich Nietzsche had been one of their favorite patrons. Their dark old mahogany walls had absorbed all kinds of lunacy.

Massimo jabbed his sandwich in the dip and licked his fingers. "So, if I leak a memristor chip to you, nobody will ever stop and say: 'some unknown geek eating a sandwich in Torino is the most important man in world technology.' Because that truth is inconceivable."

Massimo stabbed a roaming olive with a toothpick. His hands were shaking: with rage, romantic heartbreak, and frustrated fury. He was also drunk.

He glared at me. "You're not following what I tell you. Are you really that stupid?"

"I do understand," I assured him. "Of course I understand. I'm a computer geek myself."

"You know who designed that memristor chip, Luca? You did it. You. But not here, not in this version of Italy. Here, you're just some small-time tech journalist. You created that device in *my* Italy. In my Italy, you are the guru of computational aesthetics. You're a famous author, you're a culture critic, you're a multi-talented genius. Here, you've got no guts and no imagination. You're so entirely useless here that you can't even change your own world."

It was hard to say why I believed him, but I did. I believed him instantly.

Massimo devoured his food to the last scrap. He thrust his bare plate aside and pulled a huge nylon wallet from his cargo pants. This overstuffed wallet had color-coded plastic pop-up tags, like the monster files of some Orwellian bureaucracy. Twenty different kinds of paper currency jammed in there. A huge riffling file of varicolored plastic ID cards.

He selected a large bill and tossed it contemptuously onto the Elena's cold marble table. It looked very much like money—it looked much more like money than the money that I handled every day. It had a splendid portrait of Galileo and it was denominated in "Euro-Lira."

Then he rose and stumbled out of the cafe. I hastily slipped the weird bill in my pocket. I threw some euros onto the table. Then I pursued him.

With his head down, muttering and sour, Massimo was weaving across the millions of square stone cobbles of the huge Piazza Vittorio Veneto. As if through long experience, he found the emptiest spot in the plaza, a stony desert between a handsome line of ornate lamp-posts and the sleek steel railings of an underground parking garage.

He dug into a trouser pocket and plucked out tethered foam ear-plugs, the kind you get from Alitalia for long overseas flights. Then he flipped his laptop open.

I caught up with him. "What are you doing over here? Looking for wifi signals?"

"I'm leaving." He tucked the foam plugs in his ears.

"Mind if I come along?"

"When I count to three," he told me, too loudly, "you have to jump high into the air. Also, stay within range of my laptop."

"All right. Sure."

"Oh, and put your hands over your ears."

I objected. "How can I hear you count to three if I have my hands over my ears?"

"Uno." He pressed the F-1 function key, and his laptop screen blazed with sudden light. "Due." The F-2 emitted a humming, cracking buzz. "Tre." He hopped in the air.

Thunder blasted. My lungs were crushed in a violent billow of wind. My feet stung as if they'd been burned.

Massimo staggered for a moment, then turned by instinct back toward the Elena. "Let's go!" he shouted. He plucked one yellow earplug from his head. Then he tripped.

I caught his computer as he stumbled. Its monster battery was sizzling hot.

Massimo grabbed his overheated machine. He stuffed it awkwardly into his valise.

Massimo had tripped on a loose cobblestone. We were standing in a steaming pile of loose cobblestones. Somehow, these cobblestones had been plucked from the pavement beneath our shoes and scattered around us like dice.

Of course we were not alone. Some witnesses sat in the vast plaza, the everyday Italians of Turin, sipping their drinks at little tables under distant, elegant umbrellas. They were sensibly minding their own business. A few were gazing puzzled at the rich blue evening sky, as if they suspected some passing sonic boom. Certainly none of them cared about us.

We limped back toward the cafe. My shoes squeaked like the shoes of a bad TV comedian. The cobbles under our feet had broken and tumbled, and the seams of my shoes had gone loose. My shining patent-leather shoes were foul and grimy.

We stepped through the arched double-doors of the Elena, and, somehow, despite all sense and reason, I found some immediate comfort. Because the Elena was the Elena: it had those round marble tables with their curvilinear legs, those maroon leather chairs with their shiny brass studs, those colossal time-stained mirrors...and a smell I hadn't noticed there in years.

Cigarettes. Everyone in the cafe was smoking. The air in the bar was cooler—it felt chilly, even. People wore sweaters.

Massimo had friends there. A woman and her man. This woman beckoned us over, and the man, although he knew Massimo, was clearly unhappy to see him.

This man was Swiss, but he wasn't the jolly kind of Swiss I was used to seeing in Turin, some harmless Swiss banker on holiday who pops over the Alps to pick up some ham and cheese. This Swiss guy was young, yet as tough as old nails, with aviator shades and a long narrow scar in his hairline. He wore black nylon gloves and a raw canvas jacket with holster room in its armpits.

The woman had tucked her impressive bust into a hand-knitted peasant sweater. Her sweater was gaudy, complex and aggressively gorgeous, and so was she. She had smoldering eyes thick with mascara, and talon-like red painted nails, and a thick gold watch that could have doubled as brass knuckles.

"So Massimo is back," said the woman. She had a cordial yet guarded tone.

"I brought a friend for you tonight," said Massimo, helping himself to a chair.

"So I see. And what does your friend have in mind for us? Does he play backgammon?"

The pair had a backgammon set on their table. The Swiss mercenary rattled dice in a cup. "We're very good at backgammon," he told me mildly. He had the extremely menacing tone of a practiced killer who can't even bother to be scary.

"My friend here is from the American CIA," said Massimo. "We're here to do some serious drinking."

"How nice! I can speak American to you, Mr. CIA," the woman volunteered. She aimed a dazzling smile at me. "What is your favorite American baseball team?"

"I root for the Boston Red Sox."

"I love the Seattle Green Sox," she told us, just to be coy.

The waiter brought us a bottle of Croatian fruit brandy. The peoples of the Balkans take their drinking seriously, so their bottles tend toward a rather florid design. This bottle was frankly fantastic: it was squat, acid-etched, curvilinear, and flute-necked, and with a triple portrait of Tito, Nasser and Nehru, all toasting one another. There were thick flakes of gold floating in its paralyzing murk.

Massimo yanked the gilded cork, stole the woman's cigarettes, and tucked an unfiltered cig in the corner of his mouth. With his slopping shot-glass in his fingers he was a different man.

"Zhivali!" the woman pronounced, and we all tossed back a hearty shot of venom.

The temptress chose to call herself "Svetlana," while her Swiss bodyguard was calling himself "Simon."

I had naturally thought that it was insane for Massimo to denounce me as a CIA spy, yet this gambit was clearly helping the situation. As an American spy, I wasn't required to say much. No one expected me to know anything useful, or to do anything worthwhile.

However, I was hungry, so I ordered the snack plate. The attentive waiter was not my favorite Elena waiter. He might have been a cousin. He brought us raw onions, pickles, black bread, a hefty link of sausage, and a wooden tub of creamed butter. We also got a notched pig-iron knife and a battered chopping board.

Simon put the backgammon set away.

All these crude and ugly things on the table—the knife, the chopping board, even the bad sausage—had all been made in Italy. I could see little Italian maker's marks hand-etched into all of them.

"So you're hunting here in Torino, like us?" probed Svetlana.

I smiled back at her. "Yes, certainly!"

"So, what do you plan to do with him when you catch him? Will you put him on trial?"

"A fair trial is the American way!" I told them. Simon thought this remark was quite funny. Simon was not an evil man by nature. Simon probably suffered long nights of existential regret whenever he cut a man's throat.

"So," Simon offered, caressing the rim of his dirty shot glass with one nylon-gloved finger, "So even the Americans expect 'the Rat' to show his whiskers in here!"

"The Elena does pull a crowd," I agreed. "So it all makes good sense. Don't you think?"

Everyone loves to be told that their thinking makes good sense. They were happy to hear me allege this. Maybe I didn't look or talk much like an American agent, but when you're a spy, and guzzling fruit brandy, and gnawing sausage, these minor inconsistencies don't upset anybody.

We were all being sensible.

Leaning his black elbows on our little table, Massimo weighed in. "The Rat is clever. He plans to sneak over the Alps again. He'll go back to Nice and Marseilles. He'll rally his militias."

Simon stopped with a knife-stabbed chunk of blood sausage on the way to his gullet. "You really believe that?"

"Of course I do! What did Napoleon say? 'The death of a million men means nothing to a man like me!' It's impossible to corner Nicolas the Rat. The Rat has a star of destiny."

The woman watched Massimo's eyes. Massimo was one of her informants. Being a woman, she had heard his lies before and was used to them. She also knew that no informant lies all the time.

"Then he's here in Torino tonight," she concluded.

Massimo offered her nothing.

She immediately looked to me. I silently stroked my chin in a sagely fashion.

"Listen, American spy," she told me politely, "you Americans are a simple, honest people, so good at tapping phone calls…. It won't hurt your feelings any if Nicolas Sarkozy is found floating face-down in the River Po. Instead of teasing me here, as Massimo is so fond of doing, why don't you just tell me where Sarkozy is? I do want to know."

I knew very well where President Nicolas Sarkozy was supposed to be. He was supposed to be in the Elysee Palace carrying out extensive economic reforms.

Simon was more urgent. "You do want us to know where the Rat is, don't you?" He showed me a set of teeth edged in Swiss gold. "Let us know! That would save the International Courts of Justice a lot of trouble."

I didn't know Nicolas Sarkozy. I had met him twice when he was French Minister of Communication, when he proved that he knew a lot about the Internet. Still, if Nicolas Sarkozy was not the President of France, and if he was not in the Elysee Palace, then, being a journalist, I had a pretty good guess of his whereabouts.

"Cherchez la femme," I said.

Simon and Svetlana exchanged thoughtful glances. Knowing one another well, and knowing their situation, they didn't have to debate their next course of action. Simon signalled the waiter. Svetlana threw a gleaming coin onto the table. They bundled their backgammon set and kicked their leather chairs back. They left the cafe without another word.

Massimo rose. He sat in Svetlana's abandoned chair, so that he could keep a wary eye on the cafe's double-door to the street. Then he helped himself to her abandoned pack of Turkish cigarettes.

I examined Svetlana's abandoned coin. It was large, round, and minted from pure silver, with a gaudy engraving of the Taj Mahal. "Fifty Dinars," it read, in Latin script, Hindi, Arabic, and Cyrillic.

"The booze around here really gets on top of me," Massimo complained. Unsteadily, he stuffed the ornate cork back into the brandy bottle. He set a slashed pickle on a buttered slice of black bread.

"Is he coming here?"

"Who?"

"Nicolas Sarkozy. 'Nicolas the Rat.'"

"Oh, him," said Massimo, chewing his bread. "In this version of Italy, I think Sarkozy's already dead. God knows there's enough people trying to kill him. The Arabs, Chinese, Africans…he turned the south of France upside down! There's a bounty on him big enough to buy Olivetti—not that there's much left of Olivetti."

I had my summer jacket on, and I was freezing. "Why is it so damn cold in here?"

"That's climate change," said Massimo. "Not in *this* Italy—in *your* Italy. In your Italy, you've got a messed-up climate. In this Italy, it's the *human race* that's messed-up. Here, as soon as Chernobyl collapsed, a big French reactor blew up on the German border…and they all went for each other's throats! Here NATO and the European Union are even deader than the Warsaw Pact."

Massimo was proud to be telling me this. I drummed my fingers on the chilly tabletop. "It took you a while to find that out, did it?"

"The big transition always hinges in the 1980s," said Massimo, "because that's when we made the big breakthroughs."

"In your Italy, you mean."

"That's right. Before the 1980s, nobody understood the physics of parallel worlds… but after that transition, we could pack a zero-point energy generator into a laptop. Just boil the whole problem down into one single micro-electronic mechanical system."

"So you've got zero-point energy MEMS chips," I said.

He chewed more bread and pickle. Then he nodded.

"You've got MEMS chips and you were offering me some fucking lousy memristor? You must think I'm a real chump!"

"You're not a chump." Massimo sawed a fresh slice of bad bread. "But you're from the wrong Italy. It was your own stupid world that made you this stupid, Luca. In my Italy, you were one of the few men who could talk sense to my Dad. My Dad used to confide in you. He trusted you, he thought you were a great writer. You wrote his biography."

"'Massimo Montaldo, Senior,'" I said.

Massimo was startled. "Yeah. That's him." He narrowed his eyes. "You're not supposed to know that."

I had guessed it. A lot of news is made from good guesses.

"Tell me how you feel about that," I said, because this is always a useful question for an interviewer who has lost his way.

"I feel desperate," he told me, grinning. "Desperate! But I feel much *less* desperate here than I was when I was the spoilt-brat dope-addict son of the world's most famous scientist. Before you met me—Massimo Montaldo—had you ever heard of any 'Massimo Montaldo'?"

"No. I never did."

"That's right. I'm never in any of the other Italies. There's never any other Massimo Montaldo. I never meet another version of myself—and

I never meet another version of my father, either. That's got to mean something crucial. I know it means something important."

"Yes," I told him, "that surely does mean something."

"I think," he said, "that I know what it means. It means that space and time are not just about physics and computation. It means that human beings really matter in the course of world events. It means that human beings can truly change the world. It means that our actions have consequence."

"The human angle," I said, "always makes a good story."

"It's true. But try telling that story," he said, and he looked on the point of tears. "Tell that story to any human being. Go on, do it! Tell anybody in here! Help yourself."

I looked around the Elena. There were some people in there, the local customers, normal people, decent people, maybe a dozen of them. Not remarkable people, not freakish, not weird or strange, but normal. Being normal people, they were quite at ease with their lot and accepting their daily existences.

Once upon a time, the Elena used to carry daily newspapers. Newspapers were supplied for customers on those special long wooden bars.

In my world, the Elena didn't do that any more.

Here the Elena still had those newspapers on those handy wooden bars. I rose from my chair and I had a good look at them. There were stylish imported newspapers, written in Hindi, Arabic and Serbo-Croatian. I had to look hard to find a local paper in Italian. There were two, both printed on a foul gray paper full of flecks of badly-pulped wood.

I took the larger Italian paper to the cafe table. I flicked through the headlines and I read all the lead paragraphs. I knew immediately that I was reading lies.

It wasn't that the news was so terrible, or so deceitful. But it was clear that the people reading this newspaper were not expected to make any practical use of news. The Italians were a modest, colonial people. The news that they were offered was a set of feeble fantasies. All the serious news was going on elsewhere.

There was something very strong and lively in the world called the "Non-Aligned Movement." It stretched from the Baltics all the way to the Balkans, throughout the Arab world, and all the way through India. Japan and China were places that the giant Non-Aligned superpower treated with guarded respect. America was some kind of humbled farm where the Yankees spent their time in church.

Those other places, the places that used to matter—France, Germany, Britain, "Brussels"—these were obscure and poor and miserable places. Their names and locales were badly spelled.

Cheap black ink was coming off on my fingers. I no longer had questions for Massimo, except for one. "When do we get out of here?"

Massimo buttered his tattered slice of black bread. "I was never searching for the best of all possible worlds," he told me. "I was looking for the best of all possible me's. In an Italy like this Italy, I really matter. Your version of Italy is pretty backward—but *this* world had a nuclear exchange. Europe had a civil war, and most cities in the Soviet Union are big puddles of black glass."

I took my Moleskin notebook from my jacket pocket. How pretty and sleek that fancy notebook looked, next to that gray pulp newspaper. "You don't mind if I jot this down, I hope?"

"I know that this sounds bad to you—but trust me, that's not how history works. History doesn't have any 'badness' or 'goodness.' This world has a future. The food's cheap, the climate is stable, the women are gorgeous…and since there's only three billion people left alive on Earth, there's a lot of room."

Massimo pointed his crude sausage-knife at cafe's glass double door. "Nobody here ever asks for ID, nobody cares about passports…. They never even heard of electronic banking! A smart guy like you, you could walk out of here and start a hundred tech companies."

"If I didn't get my throat cut."

"Oh, people always overstate that little problem! The big problem is—you know—who wants to *work* that hard? I got to know this place, because I knew that I could be a hero here. Bigger than my father. I'd be smarter than him, richer than him, more famous, more powerful. I would be better! But that is a *burden*. 'Improving the world,' that doesn't make me happy at all. That's a *curse*, it's like slavery."

"What *does* make you happy, Massimo?"

Clearly Massimo had given this matter some thought. "Waking up in a fine hotel with a gorgeous stranger in my bed. That's the truth! And that would be true of every man in every world, if he was honest."

Massimo tapped the neck of the garish brandy bottle with the back of the carving knife. "My girlfriend Svetlana, she understands all that pretty well, but— there's one other thing. I drink here. I like to drink, I admit that—but they *really* drink around here. This version of Italy is in the almighty Yugoslav sphere of influence."

I had been doing fine so far, given my circumstances. Suddenly the nightmare sprang upon me, unfiltered, total, and wholesale. Chills of terror climbed my spine like icy scorpions. I felt a strong, irrational, animal urge to abandon my comfortable chair and run for my life.

I could run out of the handsome cafe and into the twilight streets of Turin. I knew Turin, and I knew that Massimo would never find me there. Likely he wouldn't bother to look.

I also knew that I would run straight into the world so badly described by that grimy newspaper. That terrifying world would be where, henceforth, I existed. That world would not be strange to me, or strange to anybody. Because that world was reality. It was not a strange world, it was a normal world. It was I, me, who was strange here. I was desperately strange here, and that was normal.

This conclusion made me reach for my shot glass. I drank. It was not what I would call a 'good' brandy. It did have strong character. It was powerful and it was ruthless. It was a brandy beyond good and evil.

My feet ached and itched in my ruined shoes. Blisters were rising and stinging. Maybe I should consider myself lucky that my aching alien feet were still attached to my body. My feet were not simply slashed off and abandoned in some black limbo between the worlds.

I put my shot-glass down. "Can we leave now? Is that possible?"

"Absolutely," said Massimo, sinking deeper into his cozy red leather chair. "Let's sober up first with a coffee, eh? It's always Arabic coffee here at the Elena. They boil it in big brass pots."

I showed him the silver coin. "No, she settled our bill for us, eh? So let's just leave."

Massimo stared at the coin, flipped it from head to tails, then slipped it in a pants pocket. "Fine. I'll describe our options. We can call this place the 'Yugoslav Italy,' and, like I said, this place has a lot of potential. But there are other versions." He started ticking off his fingers.

"There's an Italy where the 'No Nukes' movement won big in the 1980s. You remember them? Gorbachev and Reagan made world peace.

Everybody disarmed and was happy. There were no more wars, the economy boomed everywhere.... Peace and justice and prosperity, everywhere on Earth. So the climate exploded. The last Italian survivors are living high in the Alps."

I stared at him. "No."

"Oh yes. Yes, and those are very nice people. They really treasure and support each other. There are hardly any of them left alive. They're very sweet and civilized. They're wonderful people. You'd be amazed what nice Italians they are."

"Can't we just go straight back to my own version of Italy?"

"Not directly, no. But there's a version of Italy quite close to yours. After John Paul the First died, they quickly elected another Pope. He was not that Polish anticommunist—instead, that new Pope was a pedophile. There was a colossal scandal and the Church collapsed. In that version of Italy, even the Moslems are secular. The churches are brothels and discotheques. They never use the words 'faith' or 'morality.'"

Massimo sighed, then rubbed his nose. "You might think the death of religion would make a lot of difference to people. Well, it doesn't. Because they think it's normal. They don't miss believing in God any more than you miss believing in Marx."

"So first we can go to that Italy, and then nearby into my own Italy—is that the idea?"

"That Italy is boring! The girls there are boring! They're so matter-of-fact about sex there that they're like girls from Holland." Massimo shook his head ruefully. "Now I'm going to tell you about a version of Italy that's truly different and interesting."

I was staring at a round of the sausage. The bright piece of gristle in it seemed to be the severed foot of some small animal. "All right, Massimo, tell me."

"Whenever I move from world to world, I always materialize in the Piazza Vittorio Veneto," he said, "because that plaza is so huge and usually pretty empty, and I don't want to hurt anyone with the explosion. Plus, I know Torino—I know all the tech companies here, so I can make my way around. But once I saw a Torino with no electronics."

I wiped clammy sweat from my hands with the cafe's rough cloth napkin. "Tell me, Massimo, how did you feel about that?"

"It's incredible. There's no electricity there. There are no wires for the electrical trolleys. There are plenty of people there, very well-dressed, and bright colored lights, and some things are flying in the sky…big aircraft, big as ocean-liners. So they've got some kind of power there—but it's not electricity. They stopped using electricity, somehow. Since the 1980s."

"A Turin with no electricity," I repeated, to convince him that I was listening.

"Yeah, that's fascinating, isn't it? How could Italy abandon electricity and replace it with another power source? I think that they use cold fusion! Because cold fusion was another world-changing event from the 1980s. I can't explore that Torino—because where would I plug in my laptop? But you could find out how they do all that! Because you're just a journalist, right? All you need is a pencil!"

"I'm not a big expert on physics," I said.

"My God, I keep forgetting I'm talking to somebody from the hopeless George Bush World," he said. "Listen, stupid: physics isn't complicated. Physics is very simple and elegant, because it's *structured.* I knew that from the age of three."

"I'm just a writer, I'm not a scientist."

"Well, surely you've heard of 'consilience.'"

"No. Never."

"Yes you have! Even people in your stupid world know about 'consilience.' Consilience means that all forms of human knowledge have an underlying unity!"

The gleam in his eyes was tiring me. "Why does that matter?"

"It's makes all the difference between your world and my world! In your world there was a great physicist once…Dr. Italo Calvino."

"Famous literary writer," I said, "he died in the 1980s."

"Calvino didn't die in my Italy," he said. "because in my Italy, Italo Calvino completed his 'Six Core Principles.'"

"Calvino wrote 'Six Memos,'" I said. "'He wrote 'Six Memos for the Next Millennium.' And he only finished five of those before he had a stroke and died."

"In my world Calvino did not have a stroke. He had a stroke of genius, instead. When Calvino completed his work, those six lectures weren't just 'memos'. He delivered six major public addresses at Princeton. When Calvino gave that sixth, great, final speech, on 'Consistency,' the halls were crammed with physicists. Mathematicians, too. My father was there."

I took refuge in my notebook. 'Six Core Principles,' I scribbled hastily, 'Calvino, Princeton, consilience.'

"Calvino's parents were both scientists," Massimo insisted. "Calvino's brother was also a scientist. His Oulipo literary group was obsessed with mathematics. When Calvino delivered lectures worthy of a genius, nobody was surprised."

"I knew Calvino was a genius," I said. I'd been young, but you can't write in Italian and not know Calvino. I'd seen him trudging the porticoes in Turin, hunch-shouldered, slapping his feet, always looking sly and preoccupied. You only had see the man to know that he had an agenda like no other writer in the world.

"When Calvino finished his six lectures," mused Massimo, "they carried him off to CERN in Geneva and they made him work on the 'Semantic Web.' The Semantic Web works beautifully, by the way. It's not like your foul little Internet—so full of spam and crime." He wiped the sausage knife on an oil-stained napkin. "I should qualify that remark. The Semantic Web works beautifully—*in the Italian language*. Because the Semantic Web was built by Italians. They had a little bit of help from a few French Oulipo writers."

"Can we leave this place now? And visit this Italy you boast so much about? And then drop by my Italy?"

"That situation is complicated," Massimo hedged, and stood up. "Watch my bag, will you?"

He then departed to the toilet, leaving me to wonder about all the ways in which our situation could be complicated.

Now I was sitting alone, staring at that corked brandy bottle. My brain was boiling. The strangeness of my situation had broken some important throttle inside my head.

I considered myself bright—because I could write in three languages, and I understood technical matters. I could speak to engineers, designers, programmers, venture capitalists and government officials on serious, adult issues that we all agreed were important. So, yes, surely I was bright.

But I'd spent my whole life being far more stupid than I was at this moment.

In this terrible extremity, here in the cigarette-choked Elena, where the half-ragged denizens pored over their grimy newspapers, I knew I possessed a true potential for genius. I was Italian, and, being Italian, I had the knack to shake the world to its roots. My genius had never embraced me, because genius had never been required of me. I had been stupid because I dwelled in a stupefied world.

I now lived in no world at all. I had no world. So my thoughts were rocketing through empty space.

Ideas changed the world. Thoughts changed the world—and thoughts could be written down. I had forgotten that writing could have such urgency, that writing could matter to history, that literature might have consequence. Strangely, tragically, I'd forgotten that such things were possible.

Calvino had died of a stroke: I knew that. Some artery broke inside the man's skull as he gamely struggled with his manifesto to transform the next millennium. Surely that was a great loss, but how could anybody guess the extent of that loss? A stroke of genius is a black swan, beyond prediction, beyond expectation. If a black swan never arrives, how on Earth could its absence be guessed?

The chasm between Massimo's version of Italy and my Italy was invisible—yet all encompassing. It was exactly like the stark difference between the man I was now, and the man I'd been one short hour ago.

A black swan can never be predicted, expected, or categorized. A black swan, when it arrives, cannot even be recognized as a black swan. When the black swan assaults us, with the wingbeats of some rapist Jupiter, then we must re-write history.

Maybe a newsman writes a news story, which is history's first draft.

Yet the news never shouts that history has black swans. The news never tells us that our universe is contingent, that our fate hinges on changes too huge for us to comprehend, or too small for us to see. We can never accept the black swan's arbitrary carelessness. So our news is never about how the news can make no sense to human beings. Our news is always about how well we understand.

Whenever our wits are shattered by the impossible, we swiftly knit the world back together again, so that our wits can return to us. We pretend that we've lost nothing, not one single illusion. Especially, certainly, we never lose our minds. No matter how strange the news is, we're always sane and sensible. That is what we tell each other.

Massimo returned to our table. He was very drunk, and he looked greenish. "You ever been in a squat-down Turkish toilet?" he said, pinching his nose. "Trust me: don't go in there."

"I think we should go to your Italy now," I said.

"I could do that," he allowed idly, "although I've made some trouble for myself there…my real problem is you."

"Why am I trouble?"

"There's another Luca in my Italy. He's not like you: because he's a great author, and a very dignified and very wealthy man. He wouldn't find you funny."

I considered this. He was inviting me to be bitterly jealous of myself. I couldn't manage that, yet I was angry anyway. "Am I funny, Massimo?"

He'd stopped drinking, but that killer brandy was still percolating through his gut.

"Yes, you're funny, Luca. You're weird. You're a terrible joke. Especially in this version of Italy. And especially now that you're finally catching on. You've got a look on your face now like a drowned fish." He belched into his fist. "Now, at last, you think that you understand, but no, you don't. Not yet. Listen: in order to arrive here—I *created* this world. When I press the Function-Three key, and the field transports me here—without me as the observer, this universe doesn't even exist."

I glanced around the thing that Massimo called a universe. It was an Italian cafe. The marble table in front of me was every bit as solid as a rock. Everything around me was very solid, normal, realistic, acceptable and predictable.

"Of course," I told him. "And you also created my universe, too. Because you're not just a black swan. You're God."

"'Black swan,' is that what you call me?" He smirked, and preened in the mirror. "You journalists need a tag-line for everything."

"You always wear black," I said. "Does that keep our dirt from showing?"

Massimo buttoned his black woolen jacket. "It gets worse," he told me. "When I press that Function-Two key, before the field settles in… I generate millions of potential histories. Billions of histories. All with their souls, ethics, thoughts, histories, destinies—whatever. Worlds blink into existence for a few nanoseconds while the chip runs through the program—and then they all blink out. As if they never were."

"That's how you move? From world to world?"

"That's right, my friend. This ugly duckling can fly."

The Elena's waiter arrived to tidy up our table. "A little rice pudding?" he asked.

Massimo was cordial. "No, thank you, sir."

"Got some very nice chocolate in this week! All the way from South America."

"My, that's the very best kind of chocolate." Massimo jabbed his hand into a cargo pocket. "I believe I need some chocolate. What will you give me for this?"

The waiter examined it carefully. "This is a woman's engagement ring."

"Yes, it is."

"It can't be a real diamond, though. This stone's much too big to be a real diamond."

"You're an idiot," said Massimo, "but I don't care much. I've got a big appetite for sweets. Why don't you bring me an entire chocolate pie?"

The waiter shrugged and left us.

"So," Massimo resumed, "I wouldn't call myself a 'God'—because I'm much better described as several million billion Gods. Except, you know, that the zero-point transport field always settles down. Then, here I am. I'm standing outside some cafe, in a cloud of dirt, with my feet aching. With nothing to my name, except what I've got in my brain and my pockets. It's always like that."

The door of the Elena banged open, with the harsh jangle of brass Indian bells. A gang of five men stomped in. I might have taken them for cops, because they had jackets, belts, hats, batons and pistols, but Turinese cops do not arrive on duty drunk. Nor do they wear scarlet armbands with crossed lightning bolts.

The cafe fell silent as the new guests muscled up to the dented bar. Bellowing threats, they proceeded to shake-down the staff.

Massimo turned up his collar and gazed serenely at his knotted hands. Massimo was studiously minding his own business. He was in his corner, silent, black, inexplicable. He might have been at prayer.

I didn't turn to stare at the intruders. It wasn't a pleasant scene, but even for a stranger, it wasn't hard to understand.

The door of the men's room opened. A short man in a trenchcoat emerged. He had a dead cigar clenched in his teeth, and a snappy Alain Delon fedora.

Bruce Sterling

He was surprisingly handsome. People always underestimated the good looks, the male charm of Nicolas Sarkozy. Sarkozy sometimes seemed a little odd when sunbathing half-naked in newsstand tabloids, but in person, his charisma was overwhelming. He was a man that any world had to reckon with.

Sarkozy glanced about the cafe, for a matter of seconds. Then he sidled, silent and decisive, along the dark mahogany wall. He bent one elbow. There was a thunderclap. Massimo pitched face-forward onto the small marble table.

Sarkozy glanced with mild chagrin at the smoking hole blown through the pocket of his stylish trenchcoat. Then he stared at me.

"You're that journalist," he said.

"You've got a good memory for faces, Monsieur Sarkozy."

"That's right, asshole, I do." His Italian was bad, but it was better than my French. "Are you still eager to 'protect' your dead source here?" Sarkozy gave Massimo's heavy chair one quick, vindictive kick, and the dead man, and his chair, and his table, and his ruined, gushing head all fell to the hard cafe floor with one complicated clatter.

"There's your big scoop of a story, my friend," Sarkozy told me. "I just gave that to you. You should use that in your lying commie magazine."

Then he barked orders at the uniformed thugs. They grouped themselves around him in a helpful cluster, their faces pale with respect.

"You can come out now, baby," crowed Sarkozy, and she emerged from the men's room. She was wearing a cute little gangster-moll hat, and a tailored camouflage jacket. She lugged a big black guitar case. She also had a primitive radio-telephone bigger than a brick.

How he'd enticed that woman to lurk for half an hour in the reeking cafe toilet, that I'll never know. But it was her. It was definitely her, and she couldn't have been any more demure and serene if she were meeting the Queen of England.

They all left together in one heavily armed body.

The thunderclap inside the Elena had left a mess. I rescued Massimo's leather valise from the encroaching pool of blood.

My fellow patrons were bemused. They were deeply bemused, even confounded. Their options for action seemed to lack constructive possibilities.

So, one by one, they rose and left the bar. They left that fine old place, silently and without haste, and without meeting each other's eyes. They stepped out the jangling door and into Europe's biggest plaza.

Then they vanished, each hastening toward his own private world.

I strolled into the piazza, under a pleasant spring sky. It was cold, that spring night, but that infinite dark blue sky was so lucid and clear.

The laptop's screen flickered brightly as I touched the F1 key. Then I pressed 2, and then 3.